1/8/02

 KEEPERS

JANET LAPIERRE

KEEPERS

A PORT SILVA MYSTERY

with Patience and Verity Mackellar

PERSEVERANCE PRESS
JOHN DANIEL & COMPANY
SANTA BARBARA, CALIFORNIA · 2001

A Perseverance Press Book
Published by John Daniel & Company
A division of Daniel & Daniel, Publishers, Inc.
Post Office Box 21922
Santa Barbara, California 93121
www.danielpublishing.com/perseverance

10 9 8 7 6 5 4 3 2 1

Book design by Studio E Books, Santa Barbara
Cover photo by Morgan Daniel

LIBRARY OF CONGRESS CATALOGING-IN-PUBLICATION DATA
LaPierre, Janet.
    Keepers : a Port Silva mystery with Patience and Verity Mackellar / by Janet LaPierre.
    p.   cm.
    ISBN 1-880284-44-8
    1. Port Silva (Calif. : Imaginary place)—Fiction. 2. California—Fiction.   I. Title
    PS3562.A624 K44 2001
    813'.54—dc21   00-011037

Since this story turned out to be mostly about mothers and daughters, I dedicate it with love and gratitude to my own daughters, Jacqueline and Adrienne. They taught me all I know.

AUTHOR'S NOTE

Port Silva, California, is a fictitious town. Stretch the Mendocino coast some twenty miles longer, scoop up Mendocino village and Fort Bragg, toss in a bit of Santa Cruz. Set this concoction on a dramatic headland over a small harbor and add a university. Established 1885. Elevation 100 feet. Population 24,020, a mix of old families, urban escapers, students, academics, and tourists in season.

 KEEPERS

1

The examining room was clean but small. The usual gear—sink, small desk, metal counter and cupboard, plastic chair, padded examining table—filled the space to the bursting point, and made her feel like a giant. Perched on the edge of the table to await the doctor, she tucked her blue cotton workshirt around her thighs and her cotton underpants and stared down at her long, thin legs, the left bare and dusty and the right wrapped from instep to halfway up the calf in a grubby elastic bandage.

The doctor had stopped to answer the telephone; she could hear his voice but could not make out the words. No one else was in the building, because his nurse-receptionist worked only on the clinic's regularly scheduled days, Monday through Wednesday. On Thursdays, like today, or Fridays, Dr. Sundermann would come in upon request to deal with welfare or work-related injuries. The kind of stuff that paid practically nothing, he'd told her when he unlocked his door to admit her; so his nurse was on call, but unless the patient objected, he'd usually just handle things himself.

The voice stopped, and almost at once footsteps sounded, shoes squeaking on the floor out there. She hunched her shoulders and swallowed against tension, pulling the dirty billed cap more tightly into place on her head. She knew that her face was dirty, too, and tear-streaked; skinny and hollow-cheeked as she presently was, she must look like a helpless waif.

"Well, young lady, let's have a look at that leg now." He stepped inside, closed the door behind him, and peered at her through thick, round glasses. Dr. Sundermann was somewhere in his sixties, a

spindly, sharp-featured man of less than medium height with a long neck, sloping shoulders, and unusually long arms. Now he put his hands on his hips in irritated-housewife fashion and frowned.

"Jane Jensen, isn't it? From Bernillo Paving and Construction? Miss Jensen, I thought I told you to undress."

She ducked her head still further, and laid a grimy, broken-nailed hand on her left thigh. "Sir, I figured you meant I should take my jeans off. It's just my leg that's hurt." She paused to swallow again and clear her throat.

"See, what happened, yesterday we'd put fresh asphalt on half of the road, it's kind of high, and there's a ditch besides, and this morning I accidentally stepped off into that. I guess I wasn't really looking, sun was in my eyes," she added apologetically. "I thought maybe I might of felt something snap, and it hurt pretty bad, so the foreman sent me right here."

"Young lady, I can't examine you without checking your heart and lungs, and blood pressure." He pulled open a drawer in the metal cupboard, fished out a folded blue something, and tossed it at her. "Here. Opens down the front," he added as he turned to the sink and began to wash his hands.

She unbuttoned her shirt quickly, shed it and her bra, and pulled on the vestlike plastic and paper garment, holding its buttonless front closed with one hand.

"Mm." Sundermann dried his hands slowly and carefully, then came to stand very close to her and cradle her leg between his arm and hip as he unwrapped the elastic bandage.

"Ouch."

"Mm," he said again, palpating her lower leg with long, thick fingers. "Nothing obvious. Isn't even swollen." The eyes peering through the glasses were narrowed now with suspicion.

"Nossir, it wasn't the last time, either, couple years ago. But the doctor x-rayed it and said it was, uh, a hairline fracture. Down by the heel."

"Well, it might be that again. Or a bad sprain; people always feel relieved to hear that because they don't know a bad sprain can be more trouble than a break. What we'll do, we'll send you over to my lab for X rays. Local girl, are you?"

"Nossir. I come from this little town in Iowa."

"Ah, a big, healthy farm girl. Family come out here with you?"

"Not my folks, nossir," she said. "Just me and my two boys, they're real little. And I really need this job, 'cause it's sure hard to find work here in California if you quit school after tenth grade. Uh, Doctor, my ankle's what I hurt, not way up my leg there."

"Hush, girlie."

She scrooched back on the table, closer to the wall. "I guess I'll probably need a cast. I had one last time."

"I'm the doctor here, young lady. You do as I say now, if you want me to sign off on this."

"Yessir. Oh, that's cold!" she exclaimed, as he pulled the vest open and laid a stethescope disk against her chest.

"Cough now, that's good. And again. And one more time. Nice clear lungs, sounds like. Now you just lie down there," he said, and in a surprisingly quick move he swung her legs up onto the table, then took hold of her shoulders and pushed her flat.

"Ow! What are you doing?"

"Be a mistake not to perform a breast check, long as you're here." He was bending over her now, breathing noisily. "Even young women can't be too careful about breast cancer." He pushed the vest wide and curled those long fingers around her breasts.

"I don't need it!" she said in a voice that shook. "I just had one of those last month, and I check myself, too."

"With big breasts like these…" he squeezed with both hands, and she yelped "…it's extremely difficult for the woman herself to be sure there are no abnormalities. Takes experienced hands."

"Doctor Sundermann, I don't think you should be messin' with my boobs that way. I'm askin' you to stop."

"Hush," he said urgently, and squeezed again with his left hand as he slid his right under his tunic and moved against it with a groan of pleasure. "Just you hush for a minute, I'm not hurting you we're both having a good time here. *Ooof!*"

"Get away!" she said, and nearly floored him with a second push as she swung herself upright on the table.

He caught himself just before crashing into the door, then stood

shaking his head as if to clear it. "Look here. Look here, young woman, I could have you arrested for assault!"

She shrank herself smaller, shoulders tight and head low, and pulled the edges of the paper vest together with both hands. Said, in a very small voice, "Please. Just leave me alone. Go away and let me get dressed before my ride comes."

"I want you out of here quick!" he snapped, turning to the door. "Or I'm calling the police."

As the door slammed, she slid from the table, stripped off the vest and threw it to the floor. Scrambled into her jeans, her bra, pulled on her shirt. Thrust her feet sockless into the boots she'd left in the corner of the room; crouched beside the open backpack resting in the same corner and spoke a few words before reaching inside.

With a grimace, she yanked the zipper shut and stood up to sling the pack over her shoulder. At the door, she said, "Shit!" and turned to grab her nearly forgotten crutch. If that slimy-fingered son of a bitch so much as looked at her on the way out, she'd wrap it around his neck.

Outside, Verity Mackellar moved several steps away from the one-story stucco building before stopping to lean on her crutch and scan the not-very-busy street. And draw deep draughts of air into a chest tight with rage, which she'd expected, and fear, which she hadn't. A horn brought her head up and around; she waved at the white Toyota pickup just down the street and set off in that direction, making use of her crutch just in case the doctor or anyone else should be watching. Stay in character.

"Hey! You're okay." Harley Apodaca put aside a fat paperback with a winged, ray-headed goddess on the cover and reached over to open the passenger door of his truck. "I was getting worried, about ready to go knock on the door and say the kids needed you at home or something."

"I'm fine," Verity snapped. She set her backpack carefully on the floor and maneuvered herself and her supposedly injured leg into the vehicle. "And actually, Harley, I appreciate your restraint. Your appearance at the door would have turned that old prick permanently limp." She took a deep breath, blew it out hard, and managed a grin

for her chauffeur. Harley Apodaca's mother, an artist, had conceived her only child during what she called her "biker period." Harley, who proclaimed himself grateful his long-gone father hadn't favored a Kawasaki, was now nineteen years old, six-feet-four in height, and nearly as wide as your average door. Harley wasn't quite as tough as he looked, but he didn't really need to be.

"I was timing it," he assured her, flourishing his wristwatch before sticking that arm out to signal his intended entry into the sporadic stream of traffic. "You had ten minutes to go. What's the story with this doctor, anyhow? Is he selling drugs or something?"

"Sorry, sweetie, but that's confidential."

Harley received the answer he'd expected with a shrug and a grin. "Okay. So, where now?"

"Back to my car. And then you'll have plenty of time to get to the university and sign up for pre-freshman English. Isn't this the last day for registration?"

"Right," he said glumly. Underneath Harley's wild thatch of rough black hair lurked a mind full of *1*s and *0*s, hot keys and electronic pathways. He much preferred messing with his Mac, or anyone's, to getting himself up to college level in ordinary boring subjects. "Didn't Patience say something about a new software package she wanted me to install?" he asked now as he turned onto a residential street.

"Call tomorrow and ask her. Okay, there's the Alfa," Verity said. "Still intact, like me."

"Huh?"

"Nothing. Never mind." Harley pulled to the curb just behind her little cream-colored ragtop, and she collected the backpack carefully before opening the truck's door. "Oops, and my prop," she muttered, picking up the crutch. "Thanks, Harley. Be sure to record your time."

"Right. I'll log it in from home. So long, babe. Have a good one," he called as he pulled away.

"Right," she echoed. She settled her gear in the little car, then climbed in and lowered both windows. About to turn on the ignition, Verity looked at her own hands gripping the steering wheel,

knuckles white through the grime. Her forehead was damp, she noted, and her heart was still beating fast. She was inches taller than that pathetic old man, broader of shoulder, and she'd bet, stronger. So why...?

Because today, there in his office, she was Jane Jensen—poor and not very bright and trained to be a victim. Clearly there was such a thing as getting too far into your adopted character. Painful and possibly even dangerous, that was. But instructive.

She looked at her watch, then laid two fingers on the inside of her right wrist to check her pulse as she did after running. Still a little fast, and she was still simmering and probably not safe to drive the winding roads to the coast. She started the engine and pulled into a driveway, to reverse and get back to a main street and thus the highway. Just a few miles south of here, in the hamlet of Hopland, was a nice little brew pub. There she could find a quiet corner table for her laptop computer, and have a beer while she transcribed the material on the recorder in her backpack and added her own notes.

It was the redwoods that ultimately soothed her spirit, the redwoods and her sweet little Alfa that she'd been thinking of trading for something less exotic, more ordinary. Dumb idea, dreadful to think of driving the fifty-some-mile stretch of Highway 128 in a truck or an ordinary boring car. She negotiated the narrow, winding part, up and down and around blind curves on watch for lumber trucks and fat-backed motor homes, then sailed through the sun-washed vineyards of the Anderson Valley. And after the vineyards came the redwoods, their towering majesty shrinking human nastiness to its proper size: puny.

As the sheltering redwoods released her to the open sky, she reached for the sunglasses draped over the visor; the Pacific Ocean, just coming into view, glittered brightly blue on this late-spring day. Maybe she was getting the hang of this business, and could expect to be a credit to Patience Smith, Investigations. And in fact, getting groped was relatively painless compared to the way the rest of the week had gone. Tall and athletic, a runner, she'd been astonished to find herself completely wiped out by doing a full day's work on a

highway crew. Several days, in fact, and the next person who talked to her about the moral worth of honest labor could eat it.

Highway 128 ended at Coast Highway One, which snaked its way north through cooler, salt-tinged air past vacation cottages and mini-mansions, bed-and-breakfast farmhouses, sheep pastures and broken-edged bluffs. Verity crossed bridges over half a dozen creeks or rivers, slowed as instructed by highway signs for several spiffy tourist enclaves. Gave a little mock bow out her window as she passed Mendocino village, picture-perfect in its carefully preserved Victorian charm. Slowed and drove carefully past a road crew that reminded her of her week's work and the other women on her crew, less articulate and well educated than she was and much more dependent on their jobs. She fervently hoped that her report would erase Dr. Asshole Sundermann as a nasty possibility in their lives. One small battle, didn't count much in the whole war but what the hell.

Before long she'd crossed a larger bridge over a real river mouth and was in Port Silva. Highway One was called Main Street here, which was pretty silly since nearly all the town lay off to the right on streets running inland and over a ridge, so that the eastern two-thirds of the place was always warmer than its coastal edge by a good ten degrees. Port Silva was an ordinary-looking town on a spectacular site, worn and raggedy-edged rather than charming; as she drove through, Verity remembered how much she'd loved coming here all through her childhood. For her the chilly California north coast was a haven, then and now.

The north end of the town was the high-rent district, where big old houses originally built by lumber barons shared pride of place with less ostentatious but probably no less expensive newer structures. Main Street at this end was lined with the kinds of bright little shops kept in business by the Port Silva branch of the University of California, up the road a piece.

She drove past the university, past the occasional house tucked into the hillside above the road, across another creek that flowed out to a sandy beach. As she swung the Alfa right at the massive old cedar marking Raccoon Lake Road, she discovered that she was ravenously

hungry. Maybe she could talk Patience into going into town for some fish and chips.

Half a mile down the narrow road was the mailbox on its post: P. MACKELLAR. She'd get some black paint, she told herself as she pulled into the graveled drive; change that to P. & V. MACKELLAR. Or maybe P. MACKELLAR and under that, V. MACKELLAR. She drove down the tunnel of tall bushes into an open expanse of patchy grass and scattered wildflowers, where a 1920s Colonial-style cottage, raised over a half basement, was framed by leggy old rhododendron bushes and shaded by a pair of enormous Monterey pines. The house, white paint gleaming under a green-shingled roof, looked...quiet, she thought. No windows open, no Bach or Vivaldi pouring out into the sunshine. And the rustic structure to the right of the house, built by a former owner as a studio, was also closed tight. Hadn't Patience said something about opening it up today, to air it out?

Damn, Patience had company. In the graveled area between house and studio, behind the dark gray Ford pickup with a shell over its bed, sat an elderly, open-topped red sports coupe, an MG. Whoever the driver was, Verity selfishly hoped he, or she, wasn't here for long; besides being starved, she was eager to report to Patience on her morning's work.

She tucked the Alfa behind the truck, opened her door and stepped out, to stretch in the sun. As a poor injured female visiting the doctor-god, she'd harked back to college drama training and had adopted a stance and body attitude that made her look smaller and non-threatening. In reality, she was nearly six feet tall, with a bearing that some, her soon-to-be-ex husband for example, had called agressive...although she herself preferred the term "assertive."

She stretched again, then linked her hands behind her, lifted them and leaned back, eyes closed against the sunshine. If she went around to the kitchen door, she could probably avoid whoever Patience was entertaining. Verity tossed aside the cap she'd been wearing, meant like her tight braids to conceal the flamboyance of strawberry blond hair; she retrieved her crutch, a prop today and the relic of an earlier ski accident. The backpack and the laptop computer could stay in the Alfa's trunk until she'd tended to her first need, a nice hot shower.

Skirting the front of the house, she paused, and cocked her ears. Voices, and they were too close to be coming from the living area. On this side of the house, a short flight of shallow steps led down to Patience's basement office; and the single door there was slightly ajar. Whoever was talking—quite loudly—was in there.

And there was another sound, in the background. From the upper house, she thought: Ralph, the terrier-mix Patience had rescued, was barking in short bursts. *Yap yap yap.* Silence and then *yap yap yap* again. Clearly something was upsetting Ralph.

Okay. With pigtails, no lipstick, and naked eyes, she was not going to be a wonderful advertisement for Patience Smith, Investigations. Nevertheless, she would investigate.

She moved across the gravel and down the steps. About to call out, Verity instead stood still and listened, and for the first time in more than an hour gave serious attention to someone other than herself. He, whoever he was, had a really nasty edge to his voice. And she was not at all happy about what he was saying, presumably to Patience.

She crept closer, reached out a long arm and pushed the door gently; it moved wider on mercifully well-oiled hinges, and she was looking at the back of a tall, broad-shouldered man wearing a blue checked shirt and off-white Levi's. His graying dark head was thrust forward, and she could see that he had one hand wrapped around the upraised forearm of the small woman he was crowding against the oak table that served as desk.

"You fat interfering old bitch!" He jerked his hand, and Patience staggered and then regained her balance.

"Let go of me." Her eyes were wider and bluer than usual in her round face, but her voice was even. The short gray curls were rumpled, Verity noticed with further alarm; had this bastard already roughed her up? She had her own mouth open to yell when the blue gaze touched hers like electricity for just a moment before concealing itself behind lowered lids: be careful.

"Who the fuck do you think you are, messing around in other people's lives?" Another yank.

"Nancy Henderson hired me to make sure that you were what

you told her you were," said Patience. "Single, educated, and financially secure."

"Listen, you—"

"And you are none of those things."

"And *you're* going to wish you'd kept your mouth shut," he said through his teeth, yanking her captive arm forward and down as he cocked his free fist for a blow.

Measuring the distance with her eyes, Verity took two silent steps forward, planted her feet wide, slid her hand down the crutch and tipped it sideways to get a double grip on its shaft. "Excuse me?"

Her soft words jerked him upright and around, face a mask of astonishment, hands empty. "Who the goddamned—?"

Verity put both shoulders into her swing, like a power-hitter going after a low outside pitch. The heavy upper section of the crutch caught him mid-shin with a dreadful crack of bone or wood or both; he hit the floor howling, then thrashed about trying to disentangle himself from the crutch and claw his way toward Verity.

"Stop!"

Verity, about to try to regain her wooden weapon, looked up at Patience and stepped quickly aside. The older woman stood behind the table, beside its open drawer; in her steady, two-handed grip was a large revolver.

"Out," Patience ordered.

"You're crazy," the man breathed, hitching himself backwards toward the door. "Shit, I think my leg's broke. Listen, I'm gonna sue somebody's ass for this."

There was a small but definite click as Patience thumbed the revolver's hammer back. "Out. Now."

He pulled himself to his feet with the help of the big wooden chair beside the door. "I think it's broke," he said again, and gave a little whimper of real or imagined pain as he tried his weight on his left leg. "Lady, I can't walk on this."

"Take the crutch," said Verity, giving it a kick in his direction.

"Take it," agreed Patience. "And you'd better move fast with it, because in two minutes I'm calling the police."

Red-faced with fury, he made a laborious production of picking

up the crutch and getting it into position. As he finally hobbled out, muttering invective, Verity moved to the door and stood watching until the little open car roared to life, shot out backwards and swung wide, and fled down the drive, scattering gravel as it went.

"So much for the broken leg," she muttered, and let her shoulders slump as she turned a look of weary inquiry into the room behind her. Patience was at the desk, closing the drawer. She held up empty hands in demonstration, gave a slow, catlike blink, and curved her lips in a smile of such pure satisfaction that Verity found herself grinning back.

"Well, shit," she said, and sank into the wooden chair with her legs stretched out before her. "Okay, Mom, one thing: was that gun loaded?"

"Verity, I'm surprised at you. As your father would have said or maybe did, an empty gun is about as much protection as a leaky condom."

"Right. Sorry."

"Nothing to be sorry about. You did very well," said Patience. "And I'm grateful."

"Actually, I enjoyed bashing that guy; I'd have to say it rounded my day out nicely. But the sight of my little gray-haired mother, in her pink shirt and denim jumper and sneakers, with a big old revolver in her hand...that's just about more than I can handle. On an empty stomach, anyway."

"I'm hungry, too. Why don't you shower and change, and we'll go for some fish and chips."

2

"Mackellar?" called the blond teenager as she set their order on Sea Cook's high counter.

"Here," said Patience, handing her the receipt. And then, to Verity: "Let's eat outside." The two of them could talk more or less privately outdoors; and besides, sitting for a sunny, breezy half hour above a busy harbor would make them both feel better. Patience Smith Mackellar had held a private investigator's license for twenty years, but she couldn't think of half a dozen times during those years that she'd actually pointed a gun at anyone.

Verity picked up the twin cardboard baskets of deep-fried snapper, French fries, and coleslaw and set them on a tray; Patience added salt, catsup, and tartar sauce, and the two bottles of beer. Then she led the way out the door and around to the rear deck of the little waterfront restaurant, shooing squawking seagulls out of her way.

"Yum," said Verity. She set the tray on a redwood picnic table, sat down on the attached bench, and swung her long legs under the table. "I may have to go back for seconds."

"Why not?" Patience dipped a piece of fish in tartar sauce and took a bite, covertly eyeing her daughter. Three months earlier, when Verity suddenly turned up on her mother's doorstep in flight from a failed marriage, she'd been not lean but gaunt, with a harried, hangdog look that nearly broke Patience's heart. Wherever the fault lay (and Patience had her own opinion about that, which, like her opinion of Ted Blake, Esquire, she mostly kept to herself) Verity took failure very, very hard. Now she had some color, she'd put on a few

softening pounds, and there were occasional glimpses of her old high-headed, free-striding self.

(Hardheaded and pushy, even, Patience added to herself with an inner sigh. Not comfortable. But that was authentic Verity, the soul and temperament she was born with.)

She might even turn out to be fairly good at the family business. Patience had come to it involuntarily, after the gunshot wound that put her tall policeman husband permanently in a wheelchair. When Mike decided to become a private investigator, he'd needed her help and she'd given it willingly. Probably she'd have been a poor school-teacher, anyway; institutions and schedules made her cranky.

"It's very strange, Mom." Verity wiped her fingers with a paper napkin, then used both hands to push back and spread out her mop of still-damp hair. Red-gold, straight, and reaching nearly to her waist, it shone in the sun like a beacon.

"What is?"

"After Dad died, when you sold the Berkeley place and moved up here to the summer house, I expected you to—be retired. To read a lot, maybe garden, join the church and the choir."

"Verity, I was fifty years old when Mike died. Everything still very much in working order. I do go to church occasionally, and I belong to the Choral Society; but planting a garden on Raccoon Lake would merely provide a more interesting diet for the local deer."

"Well, you could have returned to the university for an advanced degree, or traveled, or… See, what's strange is that I didn't know you really got off on this stuff. I mean," she amended, in response to Patience's raised eyebrows, "I always thought you did this work just to help Dad out."

"I thought so, too, at first." Patience looked at the thick country-style chips, thought fleetingly of her disappearing waistline, and reached for the basket. "His friends in the department helped him get a license, but he needed an assistant with legs. Preferably someone who was curious, stubborn, inconspicuous, not easily intimidated or embarrassed. And fairly smart, but willing to work cheap. Turned out I just fit the job description."

"But when you had to manipulate people, involve yourself with

bastards like this Dr. Sundermann—didn't it make you feel grubby?"

"Oh, yes. Those were the days you'd come home from school and find your mother soaking in a bubble bath with a glass of wine on the tub rim." Verity unconsciously stroked her own clean, shining hair, and Patience grinned at her.

Verity grinned back, and shrugged. "For the moment at least, it feels like an improvement on wearing a suit and pantyhose and carrying a briefcase. Do you think Claude Bernillo will go to the police about Dr. Sundermann?"

"More likely to Dr. Sundermann's family, and perhaps the county medical association—to try to get the old man to give up practicing. Claude hired us because neither of the mistreated women he knew of was willing to file an official complaint."

"They can't afford to," said Verity with a grimace. "Dolores Ruiz, the Mexican woman from the road crew, has a work permit; but I think her husband and her little girl are here illegally. The other woman—the one who burned herself at the restaurant where she and Claude's daughter work—has a sick kid and is clearly on the run from something, or someone, she won't talk about. And here's what I've been reminded of over the past week, Mother: a fairly shitty world is even shittier if you're poor, uneducated, and female. Spend all your time with bankers and lawyers, you tend to forget basics like that."

Verity got to her feet, picked up her beer bottle, and began to pace the deck, disturbing the seagulls anew. "So now you've heard all about my work day, what about yours? I remember very clearly your telling me, soon after I got here, that you always saw clients at your office in town, never *ever* at the house. So who was that dickhead I almost broke my crutch on?"

Patience sighed and reached for the last piece of fish in her basket. "His name is Walker Tolliver—originally Walter Tully. Nancy Henderson, the woman who hired me to investigate him, apparently told him my full name." One of the specialties of Patience Smith, Investigations, was doing a thorough background check for the woman —usually older, educated, and either well-off or well-employed—who

feared being conned or robbed or worse by a man she was interested in. "You'd think a woman with a Ph.D. would have more sense. And I'll certainly tell her so," Patience added.

Verity propped her rump on the deck rail and crossed her arms. "What would you have done if I hadn't come in?"

"Taken a punch or two, probably—not for the first time. I should never have let him in. Maybe old age or country living is turning my brain to mush," she said with a grimace. "One thing I've decided, though: I need a new gun. That old revolver of your father's is too big and heavy for my hands."

"Certainly looked that way to me," said Verity. "What did you have in mind?"

"Um. Maybe a nine-millimeter automatic. I'll talk to Hank Svoboda about it." Patience popped the final bit of snapper into her mouth and found a last few fries in the bottom of her basket, then wiped her hands on a paper napkin. "So, love, what are your plans for the weekend? Are you going to the City?"

Verity froze for a moment, shoulders tight and face blank. Then she sighed, bent her head and gathered her hair in one hand, twisting it into a rope at the back of her neck. "One of the things Ted wanted me to do was cut my hair short, maybe even dye it. Too flashy, he said. Can you imagine?"

"I can." Patience thought there were some pieces she'd happily cut off Ted Blake—with a rusty knife. "But you didn't do it."

"Nope. And I am going to the City. Cory Benitez, my attorney, called this morning to tell me she's back in town and can see me at one on Saturday. I'll drive down, spend an hour or so with her. After that I'll go by the house, to set aside some pieces I plan to have brought here, along with my books and the rest of my clothes. I'll stay the night with a friend, a colleague from the bank, and head back here Sunday morning."

Pieces? What kind of pieces and how *many?* wondered Patience as she made a mind's-eye survey of her small, comfortably cluttered house. She pushed such selfish issues aside and got to the real point. "Are you going to see Ted?"

"Mom, I can't pretend the poor jerk doesn't exist. I was married to

him for three years, after all." She straightened and blew out a long breath. "Yes, I'm having dinner with him Saturday night. But please don't worry; nothing, including a long night of fantastic sex, would make me change my mind about the divorce."

"I wasn't worrying."

"Absolutely not. That's why your eyes squinch shut and your lips curl back from your teeth whenever you say his name." Verity reached out and rumpled her mother's hair, not a gesture Patience really appreciated.

"But that's all Saturday. I am still your humble, hardworking employee for this afternoon and all of Friday."

"Good." Patience picked up her beer bottle and found that she had several swallows remaining. "Let's go to the office. We can print your report on Sundermann; I'll look it over and then call Claude Bernillo."

"That's it? No missing poodles or beagles today?"

"Locating lost pets is a perfectly respectable way to earn a few dollars," snapped Patience, who could never resist rising to this bait. "Besides, it gets me out of doors.

"But something has come up for tomorrow morning, a possible new client," she added. "It sounds interesting. A man wants help finding his young daughter. Apparently she has disappeared, along with his ex-wife, who has custody. He thinks they may be in trouble. And he believes they might have come here to the north coast."

"Mother," said Verity quickly, "watch out. This sounds like one of those parental child-snatch things. Too nasty to mess with."

"I haven't yet agreed to take the case," said Patience. "I'm seeing the father—a David Simonov—tomorrow morning. We'll see how it goes."

3

H ands braced against the rutted trunk of an old Monterey pine, Verity bent and stretched, then reached back to take hold of her right ankle and pull it up. Then the left. This morning, instead of driving to a beach to run, she'd pounded out her five-mile minimum right here on Raccoon Lake Road, east to road's end and back to the highway and then home. She had things to do today; she was also, she suspected, still edgy about yesterday's invasion of what she'd come to think of as their safe haven here. She meant to remind Patience about getting another gun, and to inquire about the possibility of a permit for herself; she was an official employee of a licensed private investigator, after all. And she was a good shot, taught early by her father.

Fog that lay thick along the highway was the thinnest of misty veils here. The Mackellar property lay just beyond the edge of the real fog belt, and was nearly always sunny well before the coast was. Verity pulled off her headband, threw her head back and sniffed the air; didn't smell at all like San Francisco, thank God. She'd seen only four cars this morning, and was sure her lungs were growing pinker and healthier by the moment, away from the permanent haze of auto exhaust.

She walked swiftly down the driveway to its end, then back, loosening her legs. Several women she had worked with in San Francisco had left there recently—not in the old back-to-the-land mode, more in search of a smaller, quieter, safer place to live and work. One friend had even developed a theory: while the *percentage* of crazies in a town of fifty thousand might be the same as that in a city of a million, the raw numbers were much more tolerable.

Port Silva was no fifty thousand—more like twenty-five—and she doubted that any of her old colleagues would be interested in the kind of work she was now doing. But for the moment, at least, the situation seemed a good fit for her. Perhaps without knowing it she had run not away from something, but toward something.

Startled out of self-analysis by engine-sound close behind her, she swung around so quickly that her loose hair flared out around her head. It was a black and white car, with the words PORT SILVA POLICE DEPARTMENT lettered in black and silver around a seven-pointed star. She stared for a moment, then smiled in welcome.

The man who got out of the car was big, several inches taller than she was and a lot wider. He stood in a kind of easy slouch, surveying her from heavy-lidded eyes of a very bright blue; his thick curly hair, and his equally curly beard, were densely black. Johnny Hebert— pronounced *he-bear*, which suited him—was a detective, one of Patience's many friends on the Port Silva force. Sloppy-looking for a cop, almost pudgy, he had a sweet smile and a nice deep voice with precise enunciation. "Good morning, Verity. You're looking good."

"Thank you. I'm feeling good."

"I heard from Captain Svoboda about the trouble you and Patience had here yesterday. Everything still quiet?"

"Very quiet, but thank you for checking."

"My pleasure," he said, with a grin that crinkled his eyes. Verity thought Johnny Hebert, somewhere near her own age and single, was politely exploring possibilities here. Problem was, she'd been out of the social-sexual routine for so long that she didn't know what the signals were anymore. Or even what she wanted to signal. Could she simply say something like "closed for repairs"?

"Well, I'd better get to work. Maybe I'll see you at The Spot tomorrow night? I've been working on my darts game."

The Spot was the favorite bar of Port Silva's police force, and Saturday night was everybody's favorite night there. "Sure," she said, and then remembered her carefully worked-out schedule. "I'm sorry," she told him, and meant it. "I have business in San Francisco tomorrow, and I don't plan to drive back until the next day."

"Another time, then." He settled back into his car, gave a half salute and a half smile, and drove off.

An empty coffee mug in one hand, Patience Mackellar pulled the door of the basement office shut behind her, gathered up the skirts of her long robe and headed for the front steps. Halfway up, she heard a car and turned to look down the driveway, where Verity stood with bright head tilted as the familiar figure of Johnny Hebert unfolded from a police car.

The picture of the two of them chatting amicably in the sunshine remained in Patience's mind's eye as she finished her climb, and cheered her considerably. Johnny Hebert was an engaging young man; bright but not abrasive, good-tempered without being lazy, he should be a telling contrast to Theodore Lloyd Blake, Esquire, spoiled rich kid and wife abuser.

"It's all right, Ralph, I'm back," she said to the dog waiting just inside the door. Ralph was a small tan animal, terrier type. Square body balanced neatly on short legs, brief straight tail wagging politely, pointed ears upright above a foxy, alert face: overall he had a rough-coated, slightly whiskery, and very cheerful look.

"And who'd have thought it?" said Patience, who had found him six months earlier in a roadside rest, battered by a car or some large animal and barely able to walk. "You cost a fortune in vet bills," she added, as she bent to rub his head, "but you were worth every penny." Ralph wagged more vigorously and trailed her to the kitchen, where he settled onto his blanket in the corner.

She turned on the fire under the still-hot kettle and scooped some dark beans into the little machine that would noisily grind them—as instructed by her daughter, the coffee purist. Verity would contest the "abuser" label; she had insisted that the abrasion reddening her jaw the night she came home was her own fault, the result of a fall. But Patience knew, as Verity did, that from the beginning of their marriage Ted had been belittling his wife, undermining her self-confidence and trying to break her spirit. That kind of behavior was as bad as fists, maybe worse.

She took a deep breath, restorative to her habitual calm, as she

went on with her task. Verity's arrival three months ago had caused Patience's heart to lift at exactly the same moment as her stomach tightened. Although she loved her daughter deeply, she had learned in the five years since Mike Mackellar's death to treasure her own semi-solitude, to enjoy a life that was, if not exactly simple, at least well-ordered and of her own choosing. She and Ralph had managed quite nicely out here, just the two of them.

About to take her coffee to her bedroom, she heard footsteps on the back stairs, and sat down at the kitchen table instead.

"Good morning, Mother!" Verity came into the room—bounded in, rather, looking as if she might fling those long, lithe arms and legs into cartwheels right there in the kitchen. In brief running shorts and a tank top, she was a picture to send a plump middle-aged woman into depression or a serious snit. Unless, of course, the vision of love-liness was your own daughter, so you could bask in reflected glory. Claim some responsibility, even.

"Good morning, Verity."

"Have you had breakfast?" asked Verity from the depths of the fridge. "Want a tangerine? Some grapefruit? An onion bagel? God, it's a beautiful morning, and I had a great run. You ought to come with me sometime, Mom. It's hard work, but you feel terrific after."

Patience, enjoying her coffee and wishing as she did every morn-ing for a cigarette, had a sudden vivid image: a willowy golden Af-ghan hound loping effortlessly along, trailed way back by a round gray poodle with knees that creaked and ankles that popped. She giggled.

Verity turned with a questioning look that became a rueful grin. "Well, I guess running might not be your thing."

"The day I turned fifty, Verity, I made a promise to myself. From that time on, so far as possible, I would do only the things I felt good *during*."

"I bet all your Baptist ancestors are stirring up the dirt in their graveyards over that one," Verity said. She sliced a bagel, put it in the toaster, and set about peeling a grapefruit, sectioning and eating it as if it were an orange. "So. Any chores for your humble employee this morning?"

The smell of twice-burnt onions that wafted from the toaster would not have been Patience's first-thing-in-the-morning choice of perfumes. She picked up her coffee mug and got to her feet. "Just don't make any big plans until I've talked to Mr. Simonov. The man about the missing child," she added. "I'm seeing him at the office at nine-thirty."

Patience's office was on Adams Street, which ran parallel to Main three blocks inland. Midway along a block once residential, now mostly commercial, the building was pink stucco, a pink echoed in the climbing rose twining around a doorside post to the sign at the top: MARILYN'S PROFESSIONAL WORD PROCESSING— MANUSCRIPTS, REPORTS, RÉSUMÉS. Lower on the post was a much smaller sign: PATIENCE SMITH, INVESTIGATIONS. Even at this early hour people were out and about on Adams Street, several of them with business at Marilyn's.

Patience tucked her truck into its slot in the small lot behind the building and climbed out, pausing to smooth her neat dark blue denim skirt and twitch its matching jacket into place. She had on stockings as well, and real shoes in place of sneakers. Businesswoman, small-town variety, likely to inspire confidence and trust.

The sun was bright and warm today, in a continuation of sweet-tempered weather not totally out of character for early June but not likely to last much longer, either. Patience moved along the narrow sidewalk on the north side of the building to the white wooden door where a metal frame displayed her business card. She unlocked the door and left it open to morning air and the perfume of the nearby bakery. She opened the single window as well, paused to unlock her filing cabinet, then sat down behind her desk to deal with the blinking answering machine. There was a second door in the wall behind her desk, its pebbled-glass top panel admitting light and faint sounds of activity from the interior of the building.

Messages noted and two quick calls made, she got up to retrieve several file folders from the cabinet, sat down with them and a notepad, and was reaching for the telephone as it rang.

"Smith Investigations. Ah, Carol." Patience stretched her mouth

tight and held the receiver away from her ear as an angry female voice announced displeasure.

"Yes, I know. I'm working on it, and I believe I'm making progress." A pause, for more complaint.

"Carol, I will not harass his aunt further; and I don't think you should, either. I believe she's told us all she knows." Pause. "If she has warned him somehow, there's nothing we can do about it." Pause. "I won't return your retainer; I've worked many more hours already than you paid for. But if you'd like to hire a different investigator, I'd be happy to cooperate and turn over my results so far."

This bought a fresh rush of words, in a tone just on the edge of weeping. "No, no, I understand. I won't abandon you. Please just go to work and try to live your daily life, and let me concentrate on finding your ex-husband."

She hung up the phone with a grimace, and resolved to tie this case up as soon as possible, perhaps today. She had a very good line on Carol Heffernan's missing husband, Duane; but she wanted to make absolutely sure she'd located the right man before turning Carol loose on him. Feeling a twinge of sympathy for any man who'd abandoned this particular wife and hulking, sullen son, Patience reminded herself that she'd never make a living working only for nice people.

She sighed and glanced at her watch. If she went to the doughnut shop for another cup of coffee, she might miss her new potential client. But there was a tantalizing aroma from here in this very building....

The door between her office and Marilyn's quarters was locked with a small turn-bolt. Patience turned it, pulled the door open, and put her head inside. Yes, there was the coffee urn, on the table against the wall. And next to it a plate of...oh, dear, Danish. She stiffened her spine and was about to retreat when she was seized in a perfumed embrace.

"Patience! You get your fanny in here, I haven't seen you for *ages*! Are you coming to the Friends of the Library tonight? And what about the Bed-and-Breakfast Faire next weekend? Here, you need a cup of coffee and a Danish."

Marilyn Ritter, an unmarried but definitely not maiden lady of

about Patience's age, had straight dandelion-white hair and pale gray eyes; a bit taller than Patience, she was lath-thin, with an energy level so high that she could probably eat pastries all day long without gaining an ounce.

Patience accepted the coffee and a pineapple Danish, dividing guilt neatly between her forbidden fruit or at least fat, and her recent social/civic dereliction. She hadn't talked with Marilyn in days, had in fact missed the last Friends meeting as well as many of the practice sessions of the Choral Society.

"I've been busy," she said now, weakly.

"I know, dear, I know. But I miss you. If you need some help organizing your life, I'd be just thrilled to help."

"I bet," said Patience with a shudder only partly mock. "I'll try to make the Friends meeting tonight."

"How about a teensy bite of supper before?"

"No such thing exists, Marilyn. I'll call you later. But I think I'll pass on the B&B Faire. It's a promotion meant for tourists, not locals; and I'd eat too many of the goodies they'll have out for sampling. Anyway, I am busy; I just came in to say hello and scavenge some coffee before my next client arrives."

"Well, you're quite welcome, dear, any time; the pot's always on. You take care, now."

"Ms. Smith?"

She'd seen his shadow as he approached, and was facing the door, telephone at her ear, as he appeared in the doorway. Tall and sturdy, was her first thought as she set the receiver back on the machine. "Mr. Simonov? Come in, please," she said, tucking her sheet of notes into the open folder she then set aside.

Not really tall, she decided as she stood to greet him; five-ten, perhaps. His hair was somewhere between dark blond and light brown, in the currently popular shaved-near-the-skull cut; his round face was weary or worried or both, flesh puffy under blue eyes. In plaid flannel shirt, baggy corduroy trousers, and battered hiking boots, he looked like a mildly depressed version of the community college biology teacher he'd claimed to be.

He tossed a look over his shoulder as he stepped in, then closed the door—not an unusual action in someone with investigative business. Patience gestured to the chair across from her, and he sat down.

"Ms. Smith," he said, leaning forward, "like I told you when we spoke yesterday, I'm eager to find my daughter. I hope you can help me."

Patience clasped her hands on the blotter before her. "Perhaps I can. But the first thing I should tell you is that the police are much better equipped to look for missing persons than any private investigator."

He sat back in his chair—slouched, really. "I know. But they wouldn't be interested in me, because I've got no legal connection to the daughter—well, daughter and former wife—I'm looking for."

Patience simply raised her eyebrows, and he spread his hands. "Lily, my wife, left me for another man five years ago, when our daughter Sylvie was not quite two. Lily said she was going to divorce me and marry Dev, Devlin Costello, and she did, as soon as possible."

He sighed and squared his shoulders. "I knew they wouldn't stay in Susanville, where Lily and I were living; she hated the place. In fact, I was pretty sure they'd be moving around a lot, the way Dev always did. There wasn't any way I could continue to be a real father, and Lily wasn't asking for support, so I relinquished all claims. Lily has full custody."

"Did her new husband adopt Sylvie?"

"I doubt it," he said with a shrug. "Even at two she was a skinny, scowling, demanding little kid, and I think he'd have happily left her with me. But Lily was totally in thrall to Sylvie, and Dev wanted Lily."

Lily, whom the man across the desk had apparently given up without a qualm. "Mr. Simonov, five years is a long time in a child's life. Why are you looking for Sylvie now?"

He blinked hard, as if her blunt question had startled him. He blinked again, sniffed and pulled a handkerchief from a pocket to touch it to his eyes. "Sorry. I'm allergic to a lot of spring pollens."

She waited, and he shifted position in the chair, crossing his legs. "Could I give you some background, please?"

Patience was a sucker for a story. Sometimes she counted this a failing, sometimes she thought it was the quality that had made her an investigator in the first place: *what happened*? She moved her yellow notepad into place on the blotter, picked up a pencil, and said, "Of course."

"The three of us—Dev Costello, Lily Medina, and I—all grew up in Red Bluff."

Patience nodded. A town with a population in the ten-to-fifteen thousand range, Red Bluff was located north of and well inland from Port Silva, on Interstate Highway Five. Beyond that, Patience knew only that it lay along the Sacramento River and was hell-hot in summer, which was the only time of year she'd been there.

"Dev and I were buddies from kindergarten—Dev-and-Dave, like one word. Lily was younger by almost four years; a neighborhood couple, the Mangrums, took her in as a foster child when she was ten, and we were her, oh, friends and big brothers for a long time. Then we went away to college, me to Humboldt State and Dev to UCLA. And Lily grew up."

"And married you?" asked Patience when it seemed he wouldn't go on.

"Yeah. I finished school and came home to ask her. Dev had dropped out in the middle of his sophomore year and just kind of gone off to see the world, I guess. He liked doing things his own way and school always either irritated or bored him. Anyway, it was a fairly bad time for Lily, so she married me."

And later married Dev. Lily sounded like a woman who had trouble making up her mind. But she must have been fairly young the first time around, if she was four years younger than this—what, thirtyish?—fellow.

"How long were you married?"

"Almost five years. Lily worked while I finished my master's. Then I landed a teaching job at this community college over in the eastern part of the state, in Lassen County, and Lily got pregnant. I was working hard trying to establish myself, and she was staying home with the baby, maybe a little depressed and bored, when Dev showed up, the way he did every now and then." He made a palms-up,

what-can-you-do? gesture. "See, when we were kids, except that I was the better student, Dev was always the leader. He was good-looking, he had energy, ideas—charm, I guess. People always took to him right away. Lily probably wouldn't have married me in the first place if Dev had been around then."

Patience thought David Simonov seemed surprisingly unabashed by this admission of his own second-class status. "Mr. Simonov, what I still don't understand is why you are looking, now, for your daughter—and for Lily as well, I believe you said?"

He blew out a long breath and slumped lower in his chair. "Lily kept in touch, sort of. She'd send me a card from Phoenix, months later maybe a card from San Diego. Now and then a picture of Sylvie; Sylvie is turning out to look just like her."

Another huge sigh, and a harried look. "Last Christmas I got a card from her, as usual, but the note on it said Dev was making her crazy and she was thinking about leaving him."

"From where?"

"Uh, I think they were in San Francisco by then. Look, Lily was always like that, very dramatic and everything life-or-death; I didn't pay a lot of attention. Anyway, it—the note—said she'd call me, but she didn't. Then in early March I got this birthday card; she always remembered my birthday. Inside with the card was a letter that said she was taking Sylvie and running away from Dev. She might come to see me, but she'd have to be careful so he couldn't follow her. Mostly she was writing to say that if anything happened to her, she wanted me to be responsible for Sylvie."

"She didn't arrive?"

"Not while I was there; I was off on trips with the biology students for a week here, a week there. I mean, I had my own life to live, after all," he said in defensive tones. "And like I said, Lily always over-dramatized everything; I think regular daily life was sometimes just too ordinary for her.

"Anyway," he went on with a shrug, "she obviously *had* taken off, because Dev turned up at my place two or three weeks later. He'd expected her to come back to him in a few days, like she'd apparently done before, and when she didn't, he figured I might have taken her

in. She didn't have anyone else to go to, after all. So we cried on each others' shoulders and drank a lot of Scotch and said a lot of dumb things about women, and then he went home."

"Has he seen her, since then?"

Simonov shook his head. "He hadn't, up to a couple of weeks ago. But I haven't been able to get hold of him recently. I called this pub in San Francisco that he'd been managing, and they said he didn't work there anymore."

"Mr. Simonov, this is all…" Too distant, too far-fetched, too not quite believable, she was going to say, but he interrupted.

"Here are pictures," he said, and reached across the desk to lay two photos before her. In one, two skinny young men, one fair-haired and the other carroty, stood like sentinels on either side of a slim girl with long black hair and a narrow, intense face. The second was a head shot of the same young woman, three-quarter face: hollow cheeks, heavy dark brows over deep-set dark eyes, sharply cut nose with the hint of an arch. The only softness in that face was in the full, drooping mouth.

"See?" he said in a near-whisper. "Lily has always had this… compelling, I guess is the word…quality. Something that made any-body, any guy at least, believe she had wonderful secrets to tell just to you, if you could only find the right way to ask her. Men can't leave her alone." He sighed, looked at the photo still in his hand as if surprised to find it there, and then set it in front of Patience. "This came with the birthday card. That's Sylvie with her."

In this picture Lily stood beside a child whose head reached almost to her shoulder. Looking at the straight, dark hair and long limbs, Patience caught her breath audibly, and Simonov straightened and said, "What?"

"Oh. Sorry," she said quickly. "A young girl with a superficial resemblance to your daughter, with this kind of long dark hair, was killed near here recently—hit by a car that didn't stop." This child, this Sylvie, was not really like the dead Melody Harker except in being thin and dark. This was indeed Lily's daughter, with features that echoed her mother's; but while the woman's face now seemed spiritless, Sylvie's was full of light and energy.

"I saw that little girl's picture in the paper," he said with a grimace. "It's what gave me an extra push. I thought, something like that could happen to my daughter, and I'd never know it. So I came here to the north coast, the place Lily loves most of all. Her foster father had lived in Port Silva as a kid, and I think the only pleasant memories she had of her childhood were the camping and fishing trips she took with him in Mendocino and Humboldt Counties. If Lily was looking for safe haven for herself and Sylvie, I know this is where she'd head."

He leaned forward, intent as a bird dog on point. "But it turns out nobody will talk to me; I'm a man and a stranger and they see domestic violence or something and won't get involved. I was trying to think what to do, and then by accident, or luck, I came across your Yellow Pages ad. 'Patience Smith, Investigations. Licensed. Experienced. Quiet.' It sounded, you sounded, just perfect." He sighed, and sank back into his chair. "And now that I've met you, I see how right I was."

"Mr. Simonov…"

"Another thing is, I have a job I like, and I hope to be head of the department next year. Even though the regular school year has ended, I shouldn't be here now; I'm supposed to be making some ecological surveys of wildlife refuges up in Modoc County."

"Mr.…."

"Besides that, I'm planning to get married again soon, really looking forward to making a home and having a family and all that. But there's this old responsibility I've basically dodged for five years and now I need to take care of it."

"Have you considered the possibility that Lily is back with her husband and they've simply moved on?" asked Patience.

"I—don't think that's likely. From what she said in her letters, I got the feeling that her trouble with Dev was about Sylvie. I mean, she may still love Dev, but she's always been completely out of her mind over her kid."

Patience came to stiff-backed attention. "Mr. Simonov, if you believe Lily's second husband has been abusing your daughter, you must go to the police with your suspicions and her letters."

"Look, she didn't accuse Dev of anything specific, and he's not the kind of guy to hurt a kid. What he told me was, she was spoiling Sylvie rotten, turning her into an aggressive brat. No control, no discipline, and if he tried to set any rules, Lily would go wild." He paused for breath, tears brightening his eyes once again. "Ms. Smith, Lily is basically an unstable woman. She had a rotten childhood and a pretty weird adolescence, and she has never, ever lived on her own. Whatever the truth is, she and that little girl should not be out there at the mercy of who knows what. They need help."

Patience Mackellar, you're out of your mind. This is a messy circumstance and anyway beyond your resources. Patience reached out to push the photos back to their owner, but her hand disobeyed her and picked up the picture of the child. "Mr. Simonov, are you intending to seek custody of your daughter?" She lifted her gaze from the dark, intense face to the mild countenance across her desk.

"Oh no, ma'am! My fiancée, well…" He tipped his head and gave her a rueful grin. "She's a kind woman, but she wants to have a family of her own instead of walking into what they call a 'blended' one. Not that I—we—won't help the two of them financially, if it's needed. No, I just need to know that they're okay. What it is, I'm a selfish guy trying to get this niggling little worry cleared up so I can get on with my life."

Niggling little worry? Patience looked from the child's face to that of the father, her own eyes chilly. He caught the glance and smoothed all humor from his countenance. "Please. Help us."

She picked up her pencil and pulled the yellow pad closer. "I'll need some specifics. And an advance payment."

4

"I didn't know you'd located the guy, what's his name, Heffernan." Verity snapped the camera's case shut, then stowed it and two bottles of mineral water in a canvas tote bag. When there was no reply, Verity turned to look at her mother's face, and surprised a look of distaste.

"Duane Heffernan, and I almost wish I hadn't," muttered Patience. "Anyway, I'm not absolutely sure about it, which is why we're going to Garberville. Did you check the batteries in the Pentax?"

"Yes, ma'am. And the film." Garberville was a dusty little highway town with two minor claims to fame: it was the gateway to the big redwood parks, and something of a center for California's three-county "Green Triangle" of marijuana farming. Focal point of lots of edgy law-enforcement activity during the harvest months of September and October, it would no doubt be boringly peaceful in June. "Should I bring my other crutch? Or your revolver?"

"Oh, I don't think so—just the camera with the zoom lens."

"You're the boss. I certainly hope ol' Duane is a small guy and not likely to be seriously pissed off when a strange woman points a camera at him." Verity slung the tote over her shoulder and followed Patience to the door. "You stay here and repel invaders," she told Ralph, and pulled the door shut behind her.

"Okay, so what are you so upset about?" Verity asked a few minutes later as the Ford truck headed north on the coast highway at a tooth-rattling clip.

"I'm not sure." Patience kept her eyes on the road, but tightened her mouth as if she were swallowing something unpleasant. "Carol

42

Heffernan's second marriage broke up, her salary at the university is frozen, her son demands new hundred-dollar sneakers every six weeks."

"I don't think you call those sneakers, Mom."

"Oh, good. So when she got word that her first ex-husband had returned to northern California, she decided to pursue back child support. Carol has an education, a house, and a job. Duane is an itinerant plumber with a drinking problem."

"But he's legally responsible for supporting his son."

"True, if simplistic. Sorry. Mustn't take irritation out on the help," she said, slowing to edge right and let a small sedan slip past. The driver honked his thanks, and Patience waved at him. Highway One was a very narrow two lanes along its northern end, snaking now between a green and treeless upslope and a direct drop to the ocean. The big Ford could manage a good turn of speed on the freeway, but was at a disadvantage here.

"Should have driven the Alfa," suggested Verity.

"Not if we want to be inconspicuous."

"True," said Verity as they entered Westport; a moment later the muddy streets and leaning wooden buildings were receding in the rearview mirror. "How did you find the guy? Did you call your cop buddies?" Her mother, she'd learned, had friends on seemingly every police force and sheriff's department in northern California.

"Yes, but they couldn't help. So I just plugged along," Patience said, and told of checking telephone books from Willits northward with no success, of calling listed plumbers in all the little towns.

"Nobody would admit knowing him. But finally a man in Laytonville told me that sometimes plumbers and mechanics and roofers and such, working for cash, could be found by word of mouth." Patience sat straighter and concentrated on the road through a series of spectacular hairpin switchbacks that had the truck tires squealing. "So that's how I spent Monday and Tuesday—going into grocery stores and variety stores and even a bar or two, all upset over not being able to find a good plumber I could afford. And in a grocery check-out line in Garberville, a nice woman told me about this Duane, no last name that she knew and he wasn't listed in the

phone book but some woman would take a message for him at this phone number she happened to have in her purse and would gladly share with me."

"Aha! Plugging pays off!" Verity said gleefully. "And you called him?"

Patience shook her head. "I found the number in the cross-reference directory and got the name, P. Johnson; and the regular listing under that name gave the address. Now we'll go by and have a look."

"But if you know...?"

"I *suspect* someone at that address is taking calls for a plumber named Duane. I need to find out whether this is Carol's Duane, and something about his circumstances, before I report to Carol."

"And we'll get this guy's picture."

"If we can do that without risking our necks."

Verity considered this, as they moved along on a small connector highway and quickly reached Highway 101. At the bend of the intersection, a row of large, chainsawed redwood bears grouped beneath a sign reading CARVING FOR CHRIST reminded her how high the level of weirdness could be in rural northern California. Poking into people's private lives might be quite a risky business up here, maybe bring somebody after you with a chain saw or worse. But Patience was both smart and subtle, Verity had recently learned; and she, Verity, was quick and strong. This thought cheered her, as did the next: it was some days since she'd been bored.

Twenty-five miles later Patience pulled off into Garberville, slowed to a sedate pace and peered at signs, and finally turned off into a neighborhood of small, one-story houses with cluttered, scrubby yards, many of which were enclosed by chain-link fences. Verity assumed those fences were necessary to contain the Rottweilers that were clearly the dog of choice up here. When had this black-and-tan behemoth replaced the pit bull as the symbol of machismo?

"I don't think much of this town," she muttered.

"I prefer Port Silva myself," said Patience. "Now, we'll need to watch for number 1127." She turned right and drove even more slowly. There were pickups in many driveways, Verity noted; and in

theirs, with the shell over the back, she and Patience were not particularly visible.

Moments later, in the next block, Patience said, "There, your side. The blue cinderblock with the picket fence. See what you can as I drive by."

"Um. Old car in the driveway, with a baby seat in it. There's other baby stuff in the yard, a little plastic pool and a swing. Nobody outside, curtains pulled." Verity straightened in her seat as the truck's shell cut off her view. "Looks pretty shabby, Mom; plumbers must not make much up here. And wouldn't a plumber have a truck?"

"We can hope that he has, and is out in it somewhere." Patience circled the block and came back to the street of the blue house; she stopped before reaching it, pulling to the curb in front of a weedy vacant lot. "I may be on the wrong track, Verity; or possibly the nice lady gave me the wrong number. You stay here, and I'll go see what I can find out."

Verity found herself leaning forward to watch her mother pause on the sidewalk, then push open the gate and move up the path toward the low-roofed open porch along the front of the house. With just that little picket fence, presumably the residents had no nasty big dog. Patience wore pants today, lightweight denim in a loose, unstylish cut; her tails-out shirt was a ginghamy check, and she had a faded cotton sweater over her shoulders. She looked like somebody's not very prosperous grandmother. She looked, Verity noted, very small.

The door opened, and a blond woman stood in the doorway to talk to Patience. Over jeans, a man's T-shirt hung loose from her shoulders but clung to her bulging belly. She had a child astride her right hip; it was white-haired, clad in only a diaper, and to Verity at least, indistinguishable as to either sex or age.

Patience and the woman moved inside, and the door closed. Verity freed the camera from its case, removed the lens cap, and checked the zoom by focusing on the door through which Patience had disappeared. Then she sat back and nibbled at a hangnail, her teeth worrying the edge of her thumb until she realized, shocked, that she'd drawn blood. Come on, Patience. This is making me crazy.

A car passed by, a nondescript American sedan; its driver, male

and middle-aged, paid no attention to the dusty gray Ford nor the person slouched low in its cab. Verity gritted her teeth and stared at the door of the house, then jumped as the Ford's side mirror showed a rust-marked black pickup with a utility body turning the corner at the end of the block. Was that the kind of truck a plumber drove?

Oh, shit. It was slowing, and the man behind the wheel looked big. And the door to the blue house stayed dumbly closed. Verity thumbed the Pentax on; point-and-shoot was what it was supposed to do, but there was sun glare on the windshield. Could she get the window down without attracting attention? Would she be more visible if it were down? What are you, a wuss? she asked herself silently, and turned the ignition key and lowered the window. Silently.

The truck pulled past and into the driveway, the driver taking no notice of her. Scrunched back in her seat as far as possible, Verity pointed and shot at the truck with most of her attention on the door of the house. Should she create a distraction to permit Patience to get out of there? Or would that only make a tricky situation worse?

The truck's driver climbed out and came around the back of his vehicle in a shambling gait that probably bespoke weariness but looked apelike. He was a big man, with one of those overbalanced bodies that are all chest and gut, no ass. Verity pointed and shot and then, as he turned toward the house, leaned out the window and took a real shot.

He reached the door, opened it, and stepped through into darkness. Verity put her hand on the latch of her door; she'd count to ten, and if Patience had not appeared by then…

No movement, no noise. She started the count again, and at eight the door swung wide and Patience stepped partway out. Smiling, nodding, but moving rather fast? Verity unlatched her door and eased it open. Still talking, Patience stepped across the porch and down its single step. Rapidly. The figure framed now in the doorway was the big man, head thrust forward from between hunched shoulders.

Looks like a mean son of a bitch, was Verity's grim thought as she lifted the camera and got one last good shot before shoving the truck door fully open with her foot. Then she flung herself over the gear

console into the driver's seat and started the engine just as Patience reached the truck and climbed neatly but quickly in. Verity thrust the camera at her and pulled away from the curb without waiting until the door was shut.

"Oh, my," said Patience as they reached the corner. She thrust her lower lip out and blew a stream of air toward her flushed forehead as she set the camera down and fastened her seat belt.

"So what happened?" demanded Verity, taking the truck around the next corner so fast that she caught part of the curb with a back wheel. "Sorry. What did you say, to get her to let you in? That you were from the welfare department or something?"

"Oh, no. You never go in under color of authority," Patience said. "It's illegal, for one thing. But mainly, with people on the edges like this, it would be counterproductive; they want no part of anything bureaucratic, anything connected with government. No, I told them my son and daughter-in-law were moving here from Eureka, to get away from the cold foggy coast, and someone had said the blue house might be for sale."

"Oh. Live and learn. But ol' Duane looked pretty pissed there at the end; did he figure out what you were after?"

"I don't think so. I think he's just the kind of man who doesn't want any strangers in his house, and doesn't want his wife to have anything to do with anyone at all except him."

"Wife?"

"Well, so she says."

"But that was Duane Heffernan?"

"Yes indeed. That baby, Trish's little boy, is named Duane, Junior. And the man looks like the picture Carol gave me, except a lot heavier."

"So you did it!" Verity slapped the steering wheel with her right hand as she turned onto the main street and then angled across to follow the freeway sign.

"Yes, I did. But I'm not sure I should have."

"Mother! That man is avoiding his legal—and moral—responsibilities."

"Yes, he is. And if Carol sets the law on him, he'll probably take

off and avoid several more—if he doesn't blow up and do something dreadful first."

Verity remembered the skinny, big-bellied woman in the doorway. And the weary walk and hunched shoulders of the man who seemed to be successful at little but making babies.

"So what are you going to do?"

"Tell Carol what I've found. I really don't have a choice. But I'm going to remind her that she, at least, has a good job and some education. Unlike that dim little waif I just met...or Duane, either. I can't see how any good could come of putting pressure on that man."

"What do you think she'll do?"

"Carol?" Patience shook her head and leaned back in her seat. "I don't know. I hope she'll be sensible. I hope she'll pay the rest of our bill."

"Hey, Mom? It does not appear to me that you've got a very dependable way of making a living."

"I know," said Patience. "But isn't it interesting?"

"Well, it's not boring." A look into the rearview mirror revealed no black pickup—no one at all close behind. Verity relaxed a bit and settled into the slow lane. "So what about the new job, this missing kid. Are we taking it?"

"We are." Patience fished a bottle of mineral water from the tote bag, opened it, and took several long swallows. Then she handed the bottle to Verity and told her the tale of David Simonov and his wife and daughter.

The recital ended at about the time the Highway One junction came up. Verity made the transition before speaking. "So basically, you bought the guy's story."

"Its major elements, at least. And I verified that a David Simonov, whose description matches nicely, does teach biology at Northeast Community College in Susanville. His colleagues like him, his students respect him. The department secretary says Professor Simonov usually teaches summer school, but this summer he's out surveying wildlife refuges, a project that's to be part of his doctoral dissertation. His neighbor says that he keeps his lawn mowed and his house painted and never makes loud noise late at night."

"Now he sounds boring," said Verity. "But the woman doesn't. Neither does this Dev character; what a name, Devlin Costello."

"He's been an actor, among other things. David says he's a very attractive person, full of energy and charm."

"Charm. God spare me charm." Verity spoke in a deep, bitter drawl, her jaw tight. "And a man who finds his charm isn't working any longer can turn quite—unpleasant."

"David Simonov says Dev has a quick temper but gets over it quickly; in his opinion, Dev has picked up and gone off on some new deal or adventure, the way he has all his life. David's interest is in seeing that Lily and Sylvie, particularly Sylvie, are safe and know he will help them if they need help."

Verity tossed a look at her mother, who had perked up noticeably. All full of enthusiasm, Patience was; Verity felt like the mother here, ready to caution an eager daughter against taking chances out there in the big bad world. This was not a reversal she liked; she herself had some need yet of being mothered, after all.

"Mother, perhaps the reason David Simonov hasn't heard anything from Lily recently is that she's out there doing just fine on her own, thank you very much, and wants to avoid her present husband and the old one, too. Maybe she's even found a new guy, if she's as sexy as Simonov says."

Patience shot her an irritated look. "Oddly enough, that possibility had occurred to me. My agreement was that if I find Lily, I will simply tell her David is worried about her and would like her to get in touch with him. The decision is hers."

"Um." Verity thought this over as she settled into a noisy slot between two lumber trucks—a position she was unable to escape until they reached their turnoff at Raccoon Lake Road. That road was quiet, the driveway free of the hanging dust that would have signaled recent use; the house looked bright and welcoming in the late-afternoon sun.

And Ralph was sleepily happy to see them, Verity noted as she let him out and then, moments later, back in. "Funny thing," she remarked to Patience, who was warming a teapot with hot tap water. "A couple of days ago, I took Ralph along when I went to the store in

town. And when I came back to the car, he was growling—apparently at some woman he'd spotted clear across the parking lot. First time I ever heard him growl."

"Probably his former owner," said Patience. "When I found him, she denied he was the dog she'd lost and hired me to find. Hundreds of dollars' worth of vet bills later, she changed her mind. Silly woman. Would you prefer Earl Grey, Darjeeling, or Orange Pekoe?"

"About tea, I have no opinions," said Verity. She sat down at the kitchen table, opened the folder labeled SIMONOV and began to sift through Patience's notes.

"Thanks," she said absently when Patience set a mug before her. "So, okay. No credit cards, no checking or savings accounts with her name on them—so my banking connections won't be of any use. What the hell kind of life did this woman live? And how did she plan to finance…? Ah."

"Isn't that interesting? It seems her husband gave her access to the pub's account, so she could get cash for the till and bank the receipts when he was busy. David Simonov says Costello thought she was too moral to take someone else's money."

"I hope the bastard had to pay it all right back," said Verity. "But she was obviously too moral to take very much. How could she possibly have stretched fifteen hundred dollars into food and lodging for two people over, what, almost three months?"

"She's driving a Toyota minivan." Patience leaned over Verity's shoulder to point out the description and license number. "Sleep in that, cook over a camp stove or fire—I could do that on ten dollars a day, plus whatever it cost to park wherever."

Verity rolled her eyes, took a sip of tea, and flipped to the next page. "So she loved this part of the country and did a lot of camping around here as a kid. But Simonov didn't know just where. Mom, in addition to all the parks and campgrounds, there's zillions of acres of plain old woods and backcountry out there."

"I know." Patience sat down across the table from Verity, cradling a mug of tea in both hands. "But with a child along, presumably she wouldn't get too far out."

"Well, I guess that makes sense. Besides, it says here she's a serious

Christian and would definitely look for a church. Born Catholic, raised Baptist, 'messed around with' fundamentalist groups, he says. No wonder she's confused."

"Mm," said Patience, who had strayed from but never entirely forsaken her own Baptist upbringing.

Verity scanned the last page of notes, then put the little sheaf neatly back in its folder. "Here's a woman so concerned with the well-being of her kid that she leaves her husband. At least, that's what I read as her reason. Wouldn't such a good mother have her kid in school?"

Patience shook her head. "Not necessarily. Dev Costello told David that since they moved around so much, Lily often taught Sylvie at home."

"Moved around, so no friends, probably. And no family."

"Just her former foster mother—her name and ten-years-ago address are there—but David says the two had a bad relationship and he doubts Lily would have tried to connect. The foster father hasn't been around for some time, possibly has died."

Once again Verity had a quick sense of her own good fortune and the insignificance of her personal problems. Maybe she was slated for transformation from whiny overeducated yuppie to Good Person. Vowing to avoid self-satisfaction should that happen, she pulled the three photos from under the clip on the front of the folder, and spread them out on the table.

"Ah. Okay, Mom. I know why you took this case, and it wasn't David Simonov's *beaux yeux* or even the thousand-dollar advance. You fell for this kid."

"Oh, well," said Patience and buried her face in her mug of tea for a moment. "She looks like a tough, smart little kid—my favorite kind."

"Like me."

"Absolutely. You always had scabbier knees than any boy on the block, and you hardly ever cried when you got hurt."

Verity examined the picture, her own face expressionless. "The mom doesn't look tough. More like very, very tired."

"So she needs help."

"I'd say so," said Verity with a grimace. "You know what's truly

weird about this, Mom? You just spent most of a week tracking down a guy who totally abandoned his own kid and risked jail rather than pay support. Now here's this one spending big bucks to find and probably pay support for a kid he isn't even much interested in. Sad fact is, I find the second guy the odder of the two."

"That's an interesting point, Verity. One I'll keep in mind." Patience set the empty mug aside and got to her feet, to fetch a bottle of sauvignon blanc from the fridge and a pair of glasses from the cupboard. "A little glass of calm, before I go off to a Friends of the Library meeting," she said, applying a foil-cutter and then the two-pronged cork puller. She didn't look at Verity, nor invite her along; without an effort to maintain separate interests, the two of them could turn quickly into some sort of odd couple.

"Cheers," she said. "Now. You're going to the City tomorrow."

Verity reached for the proffered glass of wine and took a healthy swallow. "Right. To set my life in order. Sounds like making a last will and testament, huh?"

"Verity…"

"You never liked Ted, did you?"

"I didn't dislike him," said Patience carefully. "It's just that he never struck me as a keeper."

"Patience Mackellar, you have an unerring talent for finding the simple but precisely appropriate word." Verity gave a sad little giggle and shook her head. "Should have unhooked the poor guy and tossed him back years ago; Dad always made me do that with the fish that were too little and I always threw a fit. Don't look at me like that, I'm not losing it."

"Good. Because I have a chore for you." Patience opened the Simonov folder and pulled out a sheet of paper. "Somebody should go to this San Francisco pub Devlin Costello was managing before he disappeared or left town or whatever it was. And find out what they have to say about him and his wife and maybe her child."

Verity's face cleared, and her eyes brightened. "You mean, just drop in and chat people up?"

"Just that. And you can charge your mileage to the business."

"You've got a deal."

5

The sun was finally warming her, as she'd figured it would once she got rid of that wet dress. Wet dumb ugly dress. Sylvie had made herself a kind of nest in a patch of long grass and flowers—poppies and little four-petaled white or pink things on long necks and the stiff purple and white ones that Lily had told her were lupine.

None of them had a smell that she could catch, but the dry air was full of dust anyway, and maybe she was smelling the goat. Stretched full-length on her belly, chin resting on her elbow-propped hands, she gazed down the slight slope into the crazy eyes of the long-eared brown lady goat named Gertrude. Dumb name for anything that looked so smart, thought Sylvie. So witchy.

The goat made this *enh-enh-enh* sound like a laugh and went back to pulling up and munching whatever green stuff was within the length of the rope tying her to her stake. The goat was the most interesting animal around here, in Sylvie's opinion. The two cows were dumb and ugly, with bulgy wet eyes and those drippy big nose-holes; and the two half-grown calves were just as yucky only smaller. The chickens were mean, the old hens especially.

And the pigs—she didn't like to think about them, because they scared her and she tried to not be scared of anything. But the little ones moved so fast, and the mother was so big. And made this sound like she was going to snort up everything in her way and swallow it whole.

A fly lit on Sylvie's bare shoulder, and she shook her head to sweep her hair across, like a horse's tail. That's what she wished they had

here, a horse. She'd get on it and ride and ride until she found the end of this place and a way out. Except, she admitted to herself with a sigh, she couldn't do that, because then Lily wouldn't know where she was. Maybe what she should wish for was a dog, to protect her and be her friend.

Somebody was calling her. She put her head down and scrooched as flat as she could, but without much hope. The voice came closer, and then was right here; she turned her head and through the green stems she saw high-top black shoes and jeans with their dirty bottoms folded up. Ugh.

"I knew you'd be out here talking to the goat," said fat Eddie like he'd just won a prize. "Mama says you have to come do your chores. Hey, what're you doing laying around naked?"

"I'm not naked, stupid." She sighed and pushed herself up to her knees, pausing there to brush grass and dust from her skin and her cotton underpants.

"And look at this, your dress is all dirty." He pulled the blue cotton dress from the bush where she'd spread it to dry. "You're a constant burden, that's all," he told her, his voice low and hollow like Brother Daniel's on Sunday morning talking to God. "A burden and a sinner, just like your mother."

Sylvie launched herself silently from her hands and knees and whammed the top of her head right into his soft belly. He screeched and fell backwards, fat white Eddie rolling and choking in the dirt while she picked up her dress, draped it over her shoulders and set off for the house. Eddie was almost two years older than her, and a lot bigger, but he was a slug.

In spite of herself, she slowed her steps as she approached the tall old house. Remembering that she'd left her wet shoes back there in the weeds, she paused and would have turned, but a voice stiffened her spine and brought her chin up.

"Sylvie Simonov! You get yourself in here right now, young lady!"

Eddie's mother, Mrs. Ives—Sister Catherine here in the Community—stood on the back porch with a hand shading her eyes. Wild yellow eyes, Sylvie knew they were, in a long bony face; Sister Catherine looked and sometimes acted a lot like Gertrude the goat.

"What on earth is wrong with you, girl, walking around with no clothes on? Eddie?" she called, her voice sharpening into a sound like a hen's squawk, "what have you been doing?"

"She butted me!" whined Eddie from behind Sylvie as she trudged up the steps. "She's worse than that dumb goat!"

"You shut up, you…!"

"Sylvie, stop that. Come inside." This was not Sister Catherine, but the woman Sylvie was supposed to call Aunt Marsha. Her round, flat face, already red from the heat of the kitchen, grew redder still as she looked at Sylvie. "Shame on you. You're an embarrassment to me and an insult to Community, displaying yourself like that."

The kitchen floor was smoother under her feet than the splintery porch. Pulling the dress closer around her shoulders, Sylvie looked down and realized that she was making big dirty footprints. "Eddie called my mother a sinner, is why I hit him. I'm sorry about the floor."

Sister Catherine sighed and shook her head. "We're all sinners before God, Sylvie. But Eddie knows it's not a word to use in meanness. Don't you, Eddie?"

"Yes, ma'am," he muttered. His mother took him by the arm and led him out of the room, saying something about cleaning up.

"Sylvie, why did you take your dress off?" Aunt Marsha turned down the fire under a big pot of something on the stove.

"It got wet." When the woman just kept looking at her without saying anything, Sylvie added, "I fell in the creek."

"Young lady, you've been told not to go near the creek. What if one of the babies had followed you?"

"I know how to swim, I'd have saved her. And I bet I wouldn't have fallen in," she added quickly, "if I'd had on jeans instead of that dumb dress."

Aunt Marsha's lips disappeared as she made her mouth a hard, ugly line. "Pants are for men and boys. Women and girls wear skirts. And you know that children who disobey have to be punished. Bring me a switch."

Sylvie set her jaw, let the dress fall to the floor, and walked straight to the corner where an old bucket held a bunch of skinny green

branches. She pulled one free, turned, and marched back to hand it to the waiting woman.

Aunt Marsha took hold of Sylvie's shoulder and turned her around. "You are such a bad girl." With a whistling *swish* the switch slapped smartly across the backs of her bare legs, but Sylvie stood like a stone.

"You disobey." *Swish.* "And you lie." *Swish.* "And you hit people." *Swish.* "God loves all his children but he hates disobedience." *Swish swish SWISH.*

"There." She tossed the switch onto the table and brushed her hands against each other, making a smaller *swish swish.* "Go clean up now. Then come right back here; there are vegetables to peel. And after your chores, you'll sit in the corner in the meeting room for an hour and pray, that God will forgive you and let you love Him."

Sylvie bent to pick up her dress. When she straightened, her eyes were dry. "I do not lie, not ever. And who says it's okay for *you* to hit people, but I can't?" she flung over her shoulder as she ran out of the room.

"My!" Catherine Ives, who had moved out of the doorway to let Sylvie pass, now shook her head in sorrow. "Isn't she something! She just runs circles around Eddie, drives him absolutely crazy."

"I could almost believe she was sent here to provoke us to unchristian behavior," said Marsha Simms. "She pushes me to the point where I'm afraid I'll lose control and really harm her. I have a hard time remembering she's only seven years old."

"That little girl is a very old soul." Catherine, who had strayed down several side roads on her journey to Jesus, picked up the switch and broke it in two. "When she looks at me I could swear I see the devil himself in those black eyes. Your sister laid a sorrowful burden on us."

"Lily isn't my sister." Marsha grimaced as she brushed wispy pale hair back from her face.

"Well, your foster sister. You still felt compelled to take her in, her and her brat. God forgive me. Her *child.*"

"It was my Christian duty." With two pots steaming on the six-burner stove and the oven on as well, the big high-ceilinged kitchen

was almost unbearably hot. Marsha moved to the sink and pushed the open window there higher. "Shall I make some tea?"

Without waiting for an answer, she set a kettle on the stove and lit the burner. "When the Mangrums decided to take in a second foster child, I thought she'd be like my real little sister; she was only ten and I was twelve."

She took a teapot from a shelf and a canister from another. "But it was Lily, twice as smart as me and ten times prettier. It didn't make any difference with Edna; she treated us both like poor relations she'd brought in as household help. But Max was crazy about Lily from the start. Took her along in his truck to work sometimes, took her fishing and camping."

She spooned tea into a metal tea ball, dropped it into the pot, and turned to watch the kettle, which was beginning to steam slightly. "It wasn't Lily's fault, I knew that even then. It was wrong of me to hate her and to…make trouble for her. So I'm trying to earn her forgiveness, and God's. But it's hard."

"Listen, you're a good woman. And whatever trouble you made for her…" Catherine let her voice trail off in a gently questioning tone as she put two mugs on the table and then added a sugar bowl. "Well, anyway. Some women are just born to cause grief. Even here at Community the men just got all big-chested and stiff-legged whenever Lily came by. Probably stiff somewheres else, too. Maybe she *is* a witch, and her kid, too! I mean, there *are* witches in the Bible, isn't that so?"

"I believe so," said Marsha cautiously.

"Well then," said Catherine as she settled into a chair at the table. "Whatever they are, Community will be better off with the pair of them out of here for good."

Marsha set the teapot on the table and pulled out a chair for herself, wiping her sweating face with the edge of her apron as she sat down. "It's strange. It's almost two weeks since Lily left, and there's been no word at all."

Catherine snickered. "I bet she found a new man. Her kind doesn't sleep alone for long."

Marsha shook her head. "She may be a slut, and self-centered as a

cat, but she seemed real devoted to Sylvie. It doesn't seem to me that she'd just…abandon her."

"Hey, who's abandoned? This isn't the dog pound here. No joke, I bet she got out and got a taste of life without a kid dragging at her and thought, Wow! Real stuff! Maybe she even went back to her husband. Didn't you tell me he was real good-looking and totally crazy about her?"

The two women stared at each other for a moment; then Catherine pushed her chair back and reached across the table to pour the tea. The screech of chair legs on linoleum covered the soft gasp made by Sylvie, who was hunched outside the door, listening.

She stuffed the sleeve of her dress in her mouth and squeezed her eyes tight shut to keep herself from crying, from making noise. Against the black she could see Lily's face that last time: still as a stone or the trunk of the giant tree behind her, eyebrows and mouth straight and quiet, big dark eyes unblinking. Sylvie had begged her mother not to go, had promised to try to be good here at Community and get along better with people, had finally begged to be taken along. But Lily went anyway, to say good-bye or something to Dev, who was *no way* Sylvie's father. They knelt in the soft stuff under the tree and prayed, God bless Sylvie and watch over her God bless Lily and forgive her Amen. And Lily left.

"So what happens if she *never* comes back?" Sister Catherine's voice, sharp, made Sylvie's eyes snap open.

"I don't know." Aunt Marsha, softly. "I think she made some arrangements with Brother Daniel."

"Do you know who Sylvie's father is?"

"I don't suppose even Lily knows for sure," said Marsha. There was a moment of silence, and then a sigh. "I'm sorry, that was a sinful thing to say. I know she was still *married* to David Simonov when Sylvie was born. He was the quieter of this pair of boys that started sniffing after Lily while she was hardly more than a child. Then later she married the good-looking one, Dev Costello."

"Holy sh—" Sister Catherine turned the second word into a long hiss; Sylvie knew she meant to say "shit," had heard her say it when nobody else was around. "Well, whatever. But the guy her mother

was married to when she was born is her *legal* father. Maybe Brother Daniel could get in touch with him and point out his moral responsibility here."

"Well…" There was a clink and a scraping noise, as of spoon against cup. "Dev Costello comes from a family of trashy, mean people, and he's still Lily's husband. If he's mad about her leaving him, I don't think David Simonov would want to mess with him. And Brother Daniel probably shouldn't, either."

Feeling as if she might throw up, Sylvie spit out the soggy cloth and got to her feet, to creep quietly toward the stairs. No matter what those stupid women thought, she knew Lily wouldn't have stayed away from her this long if she could help it. Something had happened to her, that was the only answer and Sylvie had been trying not to see it. Maybe she was sick. Maybe she'd got hit by a car. Maybe Dev had tied her up or locked her in a closet and wasn't letting her go.

Sylvie wasn't going to peel any vegetables now, or pray to be forgiven, either. She was going to get some clothes on and go outside on her own, she knew plenty of places where nobody would find her. She'd be alone and think and pray her own prayer: Please dear Lord God in heaven bless Lily and protect her bless Sylvie and help her and please please please kill the Devil. Amen.

6

After a satisfactory meeting with her lawyer, a light lunch, and a touristy cruise of San Francisco's Union Square shops, Verity Ann Mackellar not-for-long-Blake was easy with herself and the world as she pulled to the curb in the spot usually occupied by Ted's BMW. She'd called him yesterday to adjust the timing of their date; but she was at least an hour early. An hour she could use well.

She climbed out of her Alfa and stood there on the sidewalk for a moment looking at the house. Her house, where she'd mended·and painted the old plaster walls and refinished the long staircase banister, where she'd supervised installation of a red oak floor in the kitchen and new wooden windows to replace some earlier owner's aluminum mistakes. Not quite a Victorian but almost, the house was tall and slightly prim in its white-trimmed gray paint; she waited a moment for her heart to sink, but it marched stoutly on.

So, up the dozen steps and onto the small porch, where she was pleased to find that her key still worked. The high-ceilinged foyer was warmed by long shafts of sunlight; the Oriental runner carpet on the staircase looked pristine. Ted must have kept the cleaning service.

Verity hung her shoulder bag on the newel post, draped her linen jacket over it, and set about her task. Most of her books and clothes were in boxes already, packed months earlier and stowed in the spare bedroom. She tucked in a few missed items, closed the boxes, and sealed them. Then she moved from room to room through the house, to put yellow Post-it stickers on an antique nursing rocker with a cane seat and back, a delicate cherry-wood tea cart, a pair of

mismatched wicker armchairs. A worn chaise longue she'd kept in the bedroom. A cedar-lined blanket chest, an old rolltop desk. Some framed posters, a garden watercolor done by a friend.

By the time she reached the kitchen Verity was feeling a bit weepy. The sound of a key in the front door, and then Ted's "Very?" were welcome distractions. "Out here," she called in reply. "Teddy, do you mind if I raid your wine cellar?"

"You're welcome to anything there. Or there's an open bottle of chard in the fridge." He came through from the hall, running a smoothing hand over his already smooth fair hair, neatly turned out as always in polished Bally loafers, gray slacks, maroon paisley tie, and pale blue shirt. As he moved into sunlight flooding in from the west-facing windows, she saw the eager warmth in his face, and guilt flicked her with its barbed edge; he looked so happy to see her.

"Verity. You look terrific." He reached for her; she presented her cheek and stepped back as soon as he had brushed it with his lips.

His face cooled and his eyes narrowed; then he shrugged and produced a grin. "Sorry. Reflexes. Have a useful session with Cory?" he asked, as he pulled a bottle from the fridge and uncorked it. As a partnership-track attorney in his father's firm, Ted knew nearly every other attorney in San Francisco.

"She just confirmed what we both know: that our affairs are not tangled enough to be much trouble. I've always used my maiden name professionally, we've both had well-paying jobs and kept separate bank accounts, there are no children or even pets to fight over. Thanks," she added and took a grateful sip from the glass of wine he'd handed her.

"What about the house?"

Verity shrugged. The house, a wedding present from her father-in-law, Amos Blake, belonged to both of them. "My preference would be to sell it. But if you'd like to keep it and buy me out, I'll give you a reasonable amount of time—maybe even a mortgage. I've been marking the few pieces of furniture I'd like to take; shall I show you?"

He shook his head. "Take whatever you want."

"Thanks. Anyway, I got this far and decided I didn't really care about the kitchen stuff."

"The pots and pans aren't going anywhere; if you change your mind, we can sort them out later."

"Right. Okay." She took another sip of wine. "Good chardonnay. Ted, I've tentatively arranged to have movers come Monday morning; could you be here to let them in?"

He quickly controlled an involuntary grimace. "If I can't, I'll send one of the secretaries over. Where are you planning to live?"

"In Port Silva. With my mother."

"Really?" This time the frown clung to his face. Ted's feelings for Patience were much like hers for him. "And how is Patience?"

"Fine. I'm working for her, which is why we need to go for a pre-dinner drink at this pub out on Folsom Steet."

"Working... My God, Verity! An M.B.A. from Stanford and you're running errands for a two-bit 'investigation' outfit?"

Verity hadn't come to fight. "It's a small, respectable agency. Patience has been licensed by the state for twenty years. After working a given amount of time for her, I can get a license myself."

"Jesus."

"And you, sweetie, can enjoy looking down on me from the pinnacle of Amos A. Blake *et al.* Come on, I'll buy you a pint at the Bull and Bear."

The Bull and Grizzly, that was the name of the place. No doubt there was a reason. She spotted the garish sign from a block away, turned onto the first side street and found a place to park right there. Magic, she thought. Sign of good stuff to come. And about time.

"Who on earth told you about this place?" Ted, unwilling to take two cars anywhere in this crowded town, had reluctantly settled for being a passenger in hers. Now he uncoiled himself from his seat and paused to brush a scatter of tan dog hairs from his blue blazer before following Verity around the corner and up the sidewalk. "Doesn't look like much."

"Mm," said Verity, and reached for the door just as it was pushed open. The man coming out, slim and curly-haired with eyes crinkled

from recent laughter, collided with her and said, "Oops, sorry, love," as he took hold of her shoulders for a moment to steady her.

"That's okay," she said, but Ted grabbed her arm and swung her behind him. "Keep your hands off my wife, you bastard!" he said through his teeth.

"Ted, stop it." She did some pulling of her own, to get him out of the other man's way. "Sorry. Little family fight here. Have a nice evening."

The man shrugged and departed without looking back, and Ted took her arm again, more gently. "Verity, I was just trying to—"

"You were about to make fools of both of us. If you want to spend an evening with me, you'd better cool down." She pulled the door open and led the way into a tall room with slowly moving ceiling fans, wooden tables and chairs, a long bar with a few stools. Clearly the place didn't serve prepared food but settled for chips and jerky and such, and popcorn in big bowls on the bar.

"Why Bull and Grizzly?" she asked the bartender, a tall man with a graying ponytail and a dangling, delicate gold earring that seemed at odds with the tattoos on his slightly stringy biceps.

"Bullterrier for Britain," he said, relieving her mind as to the nature of the odd white beast whose long face was next to that of the bear on the sign, "and grizzly for California. We serve good British ales and good California brews here. Or Bud and Coors if you prefer cat piss to the real stuff."

"Not usually," said Verity. She propped an arm on the bar, asked for a half pint of Whitbread pale ale, and surveyed the room. Two guys and one woman at the bar, half a dozen tables occupied mostly by couples, one by two elderly women. No yuppie scum in here; looked like a working-neighborhood kind of clientele. There was a sad-looking potted tree of some kind in one corner, and some dusty twisted stuff probably left over from Christmas strung over the bar mirror. Gleaming glasses, though, and the bar top was shiny clean.

"What do most of your people like, British or Californian?" she asked the bartender. Ted, not much of a beer drinker, took her advice and asked for a light wheat beer from a small northcoast brewery.

"The older group—my age group—prefers the product of the old

country. Youngsters like Californian. Have some popcorn," he suggested and pushed a bowl closer. "You folks not from the neighborhood, I guess," he said in half question, eying Verity with obvious approval. In well-cut black linen pants and an ink-blue silk shirt, she was the most noticeable woman in the place.

Ted snorted, and Verity shook her head. "But somebody told me that a guy I used to know in L.A.—Devlin Costello—was working here. I was in town, so I came by to say hello."

Ted was regarding her with astonishment; she stepped back as if unsure of her footing, and gripped his arm for a warning squeeze, spilling a few drops of beer on his blazer in the process. "Oh, dear. I'm sorry."

The bartender ignored Ted. "Now that's too bad. See, Dev quit recently, after managing this place for close to a year, I think it was. I was real sorry to see him go, don't need the grief of being in charge. Part-time at heart, that's me."

"I can identify with that," said Verity with a grin. "Do you think he's still in town?"

The man shook his head, and the earring danced. "Bart Willoughby," he said by way of introduction, reaching a long chilly hand over the bar for a shake.

"Annie. Annie Mack," she replied, and set her foot down hard on Ted's instep.

"I kind of doubt Dev's in town," Bart went on. "See, this was where he lived, there's three nice little apartments upstairs and one of 'em goes with the manager's job. Did you know his wife?"

"Not really. I saw her once, from a distance. Very striking-looking woman."

"Lily was that, all right. And kind of quiet, but nice. Dev was just crazy about her. What happened, she run out on him, sometime in March that was. He got real depressed but stayed on and kept working, guess the poor guy thought she'd maybe come back." Another head-shake sent the earring aglint again; Bart picked up a glass, pulled a half pint, and took several swallows.

"Anyhow, Dev kept getting lower and lower, took to holing up in his room and drinking for a day here, day there. Fact is, I was worried

he might, you know, off himself, from despair. Toward the last I was running up and checking on him every now and then, even if it did piss him off some."

"That was nice of you, Bart."

"Well, shit, I kind of liked the guy. And we sure didn't need the hassle," he added with a shrug. "Anyway, two, three weeks ago we were real busy and I hadn't seen Dev for a couple days; so I went steaming up there looking for a little help for a change, and turns out he's cleared out completely. Took just his personal stuff, left a fifty to pay for clean-up and a note said we should give the furniture to the Salvation Army, he was heading out to start a new life."

"What a shame," said Verity.

"Yeah, it was. Ol' Dev was real popular with our regulars. 'Scuse me," he said, and then "Coming," more loudly, in response to a loud "Hey, Bart!" from the other end of the bar. "If I should hear from him, I'll sure tell him you stopped by."

"Verity," said Ted in low, irritated tones, "what the hell is going on here? What are you up to?"

"Hush. Let's find a place to sit." She picked up her mug and headed for an empty table. "Good beer," she added as she pulled a chair out and sat down. "How's yours?"

"Maybe I should pour it on your head," he snapped.

"I don't think this would be a good place to do that," she said with a grin. "Most of the guys in here are older than you, but I bet they're tougher."

"Verity," he said through clenched teeth.

"Look, I told you I'm working for Patience. She needed some information, and I was going to be in town anyway. And while we're here, call me Ann, okay? You always said you thought Verity was a pretentious name," she added. "I'm going to the john; would you order me another, please?"

The rest rooms were a pair of unisex closets. She washed her hands, refreshed her lipstick, touched up her eye makeup just a bit. Reknotted her hair, to soften the effect around her face. On her way back to the table, she peered into a long alcove at the end of the room and made a happy discovery.

"Ted!" she said, as she reached the table and picked up her fresh drink. "There's a dartboard. Come on, let's have a game."

"I came out for a pleasant evening," he snapped, "not a public humiliation."

Poor sport. About to reply that she'd repay him by playing bridge the next time he asked, Verity remembered that she wouldn't have to. "I'm going to toss a few. Just enjoy your beer; I won't be long."

It was a regulation board, well used but in fair condition. Verity flipped the switch for the overhead light, took three brass darts from a mug on a shelf beside the scoreboard, and stepped back of the throwing line. She balanced a dart, made a couple of practice moves, and threw. And a second dart, and a third. Twelve, double twenty, eighteen.

"Like a game of three-o-one?" He was somewhere in his fifties, with meaty, workingman's shoulders and a bit of a gut. And thinning gray hair and nice blue eyes.

"The old lady won't play these days—says she's stood up enough in life already," he said. He waved a hand in the direction of a nearby table, and the woman seated there raised her beer glass in salute. "Name's Frank; that's Sally."

"Annie," said Verity. "Sure, why not." She picked up her bag and fished out the flip-top darts case. Although she might not use them for months at a time, she regarded her darts as somehow talismanic and kept them in her favorite bag, a big leather shoulder number that could be modified for carrying as a backpack.

"Nice," said Frank when he saw the Freeflight tungsten darts with their silvery-iridescent flights. "You a tournament player?"

Verity shook her head. "And I'm out of practice."

"Well, ladies first," he said, and winced as she put her first toss into the outer bull.

"Well, I damn near won the second leg," Frank said twenty minutes later to his wife. "Then she went out with a triple twenty and a double nine. This little lady is some shooter. Can I buy you a brew, Annie?"

"I think winner ought to buy. Let me get Ted," she said, and hurried to the table where he sat grimly reading a newspaper. If she could simply get him across the room, things would be fine; Ted had

beautiful manners and could, if he chose, make conversation with anyone. "Come and be sociable," she said softly into his ear, "and I'll buy dinner tonight."

While Ted put on his social face and took beer orders, Verity explained her darts prowess to Frank and Sally. "It was our family game. My dad was in a wheelchair; he was a cop and he got shot in the spine. But darts was something we could all three do."

"Do you live near here, dear?" asked Sally, a solidly built woman with crinkled, bright blond hair and mascara-fringed brown eyes. She and Frank, it turned out, were regulars at the Bull and Grizzly, neighborhood people.

Verity shook her head and repeated her earlier tale, about seeking out her old friend Devlin Costello.

"Oh, that's too bad. You just missed him by about two weeks," said Sally. "Were you in TV, too, in L.A.?"

"No, I was working in a bank," Verity told her. Not really a lie.

"I bet that Dev was a good actor," said Frank. "He could just charm anybody that walked by, including the old lady here. 'Course, green eyes and curly red hair and all them muscles probably helped. Dev was a guy that worked out regular."

Sally sighed loudly. "I liked him because he was…attentive, is that the word? He listened when you talked, which is pretty rare in a man. And he was never, you know, overfamiliar with women, even young pretty ones. He was a one-woman man, poor Dev. I guess you heard his wife left him."

"He did have the knack of making people feel at home," said Frank. "Profitable quality in a barman; business here looks to be down since he left."

"I never met his wife," said Verity. "Did she work here in the pub?"

"Oh, no!" Sally looked shocked. "Dev was real particular about her, real careful. She came from a well-off background, you know, and her family cut her off without a penny when she took up with an actor. Dev always thought the guys in here were too rough for Lily. And they do sometimes get a little careless, in language anyway." She directed a playfully stern look at her husband.

"Lily was a pretty little thing," said Frank. "Had a little girl looked just like her; I only saw her once, the girl."

"What happened? I mean, why did this Lily person leave her handsome, charming husband?" Ted's voice was tight, and Verity avoided his glance.

"Dev said she made it up with her family. She wanted the little girl to know her grandparents. And probably be in line for their money," added Sally. "Dev tried to put a good face on it, but he was real broken up."

But not truthful, Verity noted to herself. Frank's face wore a hint of skepticism; clearly he'd been less personally affected by Dev's charm. But Verity couldn't see any way to pursue the matter without offending Sally.

"Ver—Ann, we should get on our way or we'll miss our reservation," Ted said with a pointed glance at his watch.

"Oh, right. We have to drive clear across town. But first I need to spend a few moments in the rest room," she said delicately. "Sally, Frank—it was nice meeting you."

"Sure was," said Frank. "Drop in again some time and give me a chance to try those darts of yours."

Verity collected her bag and headed for the corridor. Instead of entering one of the rest rooms, however, she sprinted two steps at a time up the staircase she'd noticed earlier. With three apartments, presumably there were other tenants besides the Costellos. Probably even tenants who'd known the Costellos.

The first door was closed tight. Her knock drew no response, and she could hear no sound of movement inside. She knocked once more before moving across the hall to a similar door. Sounds of television came from that apartment; and after her knock she was rewarded by a young voice saying, "Go away. My mother isn't home yet and I don't let people in."

A girl, Verity thought. Definitely preteen. "Good for you," she said softly, and crouched before the door. "I don't need you to open the door. I'm just looking for your neighbors, Lily and Sylvie."

"Ooh." There was movement inside, and the next words were closer. "I knew them, but they went away a long time ago. Lily was

a nice lady, and Sylvie was my friend. We used to play sometimes, after school."

"You must miss them," said Verity. "Do you know where they went?"

"No. My mama told me not to bother Mr. Costello about it. I don't think he likes kids. I was going to ask Lily for her address, that day she came back, but she didn't stay long enough." She heaved a gusty sigh. "My name is Amanda. What's your name?"

"Uh, Annie." Verity dropped to her knees and sat back on her heels. "Amanda, can you remember when it was that Lily and Sylvie came back?"

"It wasn't Sylvie," Amanda said. "Just Lily."

"But you saw her?"

"Oh yes. From our back window, when she got out of her van in that parking lot back there. I could see in the van when its light came on, and Sylvie wasn't there.

"Did Lily come in?

"Sure, she came up the back stairs. Everybody does."

Verity turned to look toward the end of the hall, where there was a doorway with a small light above it. "Did you talk to her? Or did your mother?"

"I couldn't, I was really sick," Amanda said in tones of importance. "With this extremely high fever and I was supposed to stay in bed. Then the van was gone next day, and I said something to my mom about it but she thought I'd just had a dream. Because of being sick."

"I'm sorry you were sick, Amanda. Can you remember what day that was?"

"It was the last Friday."

"You mean yesterday?" Verity found herself breathing quickly. Success so soon?

"No. The last Friday in a month. My dad comes to visit me on the last Friday, but that time he couldn't because I was sick. He's coming this month, though. He promised."

Verity thought she could feel waves of impatience wafting up to her from Ted in the pub below. "Amanda, was this anywhere near the time Mr. Costello went away?"

"Oh, just before. I think. Annie, do you want to come in and have a Coke with me?"

"No, no! Amanda, you must never open the door, even to somebody who sounds nice. In fact, you probably shouldn't be talking to me. You be a good girl now and go back to your television program."

"Okay. Good-bye," said Amanda rather sadly, and Verity got to her feet feeling like a corruptor of children. Amanda's mother shouldn't be leaving her alone. But probably, with a once-a-month husband/father, she had limited choice in the matter.

Just before Dev's departure. If Amanda was correct, if her sighting of Lily had not been merely a feverish dream, then Lily had been here without her daughter not much more than two weeks ago. Where was she now? And where was Sylvie then and now?

Be patient, Ted, she said silently as she crossed the hall again to the third door. She tapped, waited, tapped again, and the door opened to the length of a sturdy chain. A bad-tempered, elderly female face peered out at about the level of Verity's breastbone, then tipped back. "What do you want here? This floor is private, nothing to do with that place downstairs."

"My name is Annie Mack. I'm looking for your former neighbors, the Costellos, and I thought perhaps…"

"I don't know anything about them." The old woman worked her wrinkled mouth as though she might spit, then slid back behind the door, out of sight. "Go away," she muttered. "I don't talk to floozies." The door slammed, and a lock clicked.

Floozies? Verity had never heard that word spoken by anyone but her grandmother. She headed for the stairs, unhappily aware that there was more to be learned here but it didn't seem to be within her reach. Probably she was just too tall, too young, eyes too made-up, and hair too bright. Probably Patience would have been admitted and offered tea. And possibly it didn't matter, anyway. Whatever Simonov's opinion, or that of Bart the bartender, Verity herself knew how stickily tenacious the fact of marriage could be. Lily had been married to Devlin Costello for years and it was possible, even likely, that the two had reconciled and gone away together.

"I'm really sorry," she said to Ted moments later. "My stomach

was suddenly upset. Probably something I had for lunch." With a good-bye wave to Sally and Frank, she turned for the bar, thinking to toss a last question or two at Bart; but he was busy tending to the drinks of a whole row of thirsty patrons.

"Verity!" said Ted tightly, and took her upper arm in a grip that approached pain. "Enough of your game-playing. I want to have dinner."

"Yes, all right," she said, and let him propel her out the door.

As was his habit once he and his plans were back on track, Ted had mellowed considerably by the time she handed the Alfa over to the parking valet at San Francisco's newest and fanciest waterfront restaurant. Certainly is a step or two up from any establishment on the Port Silva wharf, thought Verity, as she eyed the carved plaster facade, the expanse of glass, the deep red awnings.

They waited in the bar for their table, drinking a French champagne Ted insisted on ordering. At her expense, Verity remembered ruefully. Ah, well; it had been a strange day, both productive and frustrating; and she was relieved when Ted's curiosity about her current job faded after a few desultory questions. What he wanted was to gossip about the law firm and complain about his father. Amos Aaron Blake was an old pirate of a trial lawyer, a stumpy, ugly man who'd worn out three wives and loudly, often publicly, bemoaned the fact that his only son preferred tennis to barroom brawls. Amos's unreserved admiration for Verity had probably contributed to the failure of her marriage.

And she herself rather admired Amos. Feeling vaguely guilty and wishing she were alone with her thoughts and her laptop computer, Verity tried to give good value to Ted in return for his exemplary— well, almost—behavior at the pub. She asked him to order for both of them, tuning out the waiter's descriptions of what baby vegetables were involved or what odd-seeming combinations of ingredients had been reduced in the production of what kind of sauce. She approved his choice of wine. Everything tasted quite good when it came.

Over the salad and in a distant corner of her mind Verity considered what she'd learned, or at least heard, about the comings and

goings of the Costellos. Over venison in red wine sauce and polenta and several glasses of a very good merlot, she gnawed at her failures and considered returning to the pub for another try.

By the time she had finished dessert wine, and dessert, and was sipping coffee, Verity had stopped mentally berating herself. She'd do better next time. She would not return to the pub tonight—too obvious. Patience had after all counseled caution.

She sipped again, smiled at the waiter who came to top off her cup, them smiled across the table at the man who had been part of her life for more than five years, as her lover and then her husband. The restaurant's soft lights drew golden glints from Ted's hair, and a glance around the room revealed no man who was more attractive. She gazed at him appreciatively, happy as she would have been while observing, say, a green and gold rural landscape, a stand of redwoods, a tanned, anonymous volleyball player on a beach.

"Let's go," he said, waving away her effort to give him a check for the bill, which he had put on his American Express card. Okay, but I'll mail it to you, she vowed silently.

Outside, at ten o'clock, the air was cool to chilly, and there was a light fog. They collected the car, Ted paid the valet, and they drove in companionable silence to the house they had formerly shared.

"Want to come in for a minute? I can make more coffee," said Ted as he climbed out of the Alfa.

"Um. No, I've had plenty. But I'll come in for a quick pee."

Verity used the toilet in the downstairs bathroom, then paused to take the remaining pins out of her slipping hair, fastening it with a clip low on her neck. As she stepped out into the hall, she heard a mellow chiming and remembered her great-grandmother's lovely old mantel clock. Something that should not be left to the movers. It would ride nicely in the trunk of her car.

Ted met her in the upstairs hall, his jacket and tie off and his hair rumpled. "Verity. It was a nice evening."

"It was. Thank you. I need to get my clock."

"Very—we had some good times."

"I know we did. But I will not change...."

"I know, and I accept that. But I'm going to miss you." He locked

his gaze with hers and didn't move closer, but reached out instead to touch her, his left hand soft against the side of her face and his right cupped high on her hip, fingers warm through her linen trousers.

"Very?" His thumb found the sharp line of her hipbone and traced it, lightly and then more firmly. Verity stood still, transfixed by the tightening of her nipples, the familiar wave of heat in her lower belly; and Ted stepped close into her, wrapping her tight in both arms and nuzzling his face against her ear.

"God, but you turn me on, you always did," he murmured. He tugged her shirt loose from her waistband and slid one hand up to the fastening of her bra.

"Ted, don't. I have to go home."

She only half pulled away, and he gripped her tighter. "Oh babe, come on. Let's have ourselves one last great fuck, to remember each other by."

Her gasp turned into a giggle. Ted grinned and brought his mouth hard against hers, thrusting his tongue deep; he pushed her bra away and clasped her breast, teasing her nipple between thumb and forefinger in a way he knew excited her. He knew every way to excite her, she thought groggily as she leaned against him. "Ted…"

"Hey, it's even moral. We're still married, after all." He slid both hands down to cup her ass and pull her hard against his erection, and she thought, well, why not? But not here in the hall, and not without protection.

"Just a moment." She stepped back and held up a cautioning hand. "We're married, we have a bed, okay? And I need a minute in the bathroom first."

He followed her into the bedroom, pulling his clothes off as he moved. Verity hurried into the adjoining bathroom, closed the door and leaned against the vanity for a moment, looking at her flushed face and enormous eyes. Why not?

She pulled open the top drawer of the vanity, where she'd kept makeup and where she'd left, she was sure…right, her diaphragm. Reaching for the round plastic case, her fingers hesitated and settled instead on a ribbed gold and black tube. An unusually large and heavy lipstick case, it was, containing lipstick of a bright orange hue

she'd never have used even in her punkish teen years. She recapped the tube and was about to drop it back into the drawer when her eyes fell on something else foreign, a box of—condoms? Ted hated the things.

"Ted?" She carried her finds back to the bedroom, where he stood naked, one hand wrapped caressingly around his erect penis.

"What are these? I mean, 'strawberry flavored'? Jesus, Ted."

"Verity, you left me three months ago. In this town an attractive straight man practically has to beat off the women."

"Or not, clearly. And where did you find these women?"

"Well, Gordon Biersch, down by the Embarcadero, is a good place. And then at the office…" He shrugged and did a little bump and grind, thrusting his cock at her. "Come on, babe."

"The office." She looked down at the tube of orange lipstick and suddenly remembered the mouth that habitually wore such a color. "Marnie Gregory. That women has taken more pricks than a pub dartboard. Jesus." She tossed the condoms at him and began to button her shirt.

"Babe, you're just jealous, that other women are enjoying what you've been missing."

"Oh, Ted, you dumb shit. Haven't you ever heard of AIDS? Or half a dozen other nasty diseases you can get from random fucking?"

"Hey, that's what these are for. Safe sex, right?"

"Right. Until one fails, or comes off, or you aren't awake enough to bother dressing for the second round. Dumb shit," she repeated, and turned to go into the bathroom, but he was after her in a flash, grabbing her shoulder and swinging her around to face him.

"Where do you think you're going?"

"Home."

"Oh no you don't. You don't take me this far and then walk out." He reached for the front of her shirt, she pushed his hand away, and he swung his right arm in a backhanded blow that knocked her sideways against the doorjamb.

She staggered but didn't fall. He came at her again; she braced her feet and closed her fingers around the lipstick tube and drove her fist straight at his face.

He fell and rolled, howling, hands cupped over his nose and mouth. She pulled back a foot to kick his unprotected testicles and then stopped, appalled at herself. And looked at him, remembering a line from a role she'd played in college: *Yet who would have thought the old man to have had so much blood in him?*

7

The Spot was on a side street in an unpolished area of town. A long room with a low ceiling, dusty corners, and mismatched chairs at scattered tables, it offered good booze and cheerful service. Tourists rarely found their way to the door; but many locals, including the younger and more sociable members of Port Silva's police force, viewed the place as a home away from home.

Tonight, Saturday, Patience counted at least ten cops in the place, women as well as men. Even Vince Gutierrez, the town's hawk-faced, volatile chief of police, had stopped in this evening for one beer and a word with Captain Hank Svoboda, his second in command. Gutierrez didn't appear here often, probably because he knew his innately authoritative presence would dampen the spirits of some; Hank, however, had managed the difficult feat of becoming a boss yet remaining almost one of the boys.

Gutierrez, on his way out, lifted a hand in greeting to Patience, who waved back. Hank, standing at the bar with several civilians (and telling them, Patience was sure, all about his Labrador bitch's recent litter), now set his empty beer mug down, nodded to his friends, and began to make his way across the room toward the table where she sat. Patience's friendship with Hank Svoboda was long-term, from early in her own marriage when she and Mike first began to spend summer vacations in the Mackellar family cottage on Raccoon Lake Road. Now, watching him, she thought he was moving well, looking good. A bad bout of pneumonia the past winter had laid him flat and reduced him to an oddly boyish boniness that had frightened his friends.

"Sorry I was so long," he said as he sat down. "But I think I got takers on at least two of my little beauties. You absolutely sure you wouldn't like one?"

"Absolutely," said Patience. "Ralph would hate it."

"Well. Too bad. But I ordered us another drink," he said, tossing a look behind him. "And here it comes."

"Thank you," Patience said as Margo, The Spot's regular barmaid, set down a glass containing amber liquid and two small ice cubes. "Welcome," said Margo, and put a bottle of ale and an empty mug in front of Hank. He laid a bill on the table, and Patience thought he winced only slightly as she did the same. As a semi-official member of the group here, she insisted on buying her own drinks and never mind middle-aged male egos. Besides, she couldn't ask a beer drinker to pay for The Macallan, the single malt Scotch that was one of her few serious luxuries.

"They're a cheerful bunch tonight," she said, glancing around the room. "Between seasons, I guess."

Svoboda shook his burr-cut gray head sadly. "We got over the rash of home-repair cons—mostly it was cheap jerks trying to get something for nothing that got took, but there were a couple of old folks I feel bad about. And the north end of town's real quiet now: the university is in finals and pretty soon most of the kids will go home for the summer. But full tourist season is about to hit. You interested in hiring on as a reserve traffic officer?"

"Thank you for thinking of me, but I'll pass. Which is more than anyone can do on the road right now." The steady stream of out-of-state cars and motor homes on narrow Highway One sorely tried local tempers every summer. Patience, out and about today, had had serious difficulty living up to her name.

"Seen more back-ends of trailers than you care to recently? Cheer up, it can only get worse," said Hank with a grin. "How's the private investigating business? Anybody try to punch you out since Thursday?"

"Not a soul, and I can't at the moment think of anyone who'd want to," Patience said more or less truthfully. Duane Heffernan was unlikely to waste energy on her, even if he should learn who she was.

"But what about you? One of my Library Friends friends told me there was a protest rally or something near the station yesterday afternoon."

His face darkened. "Damn fools. Mostly kids, nothing to do with their muscles now that school is out."

"What are they making muscles over?"

Hank looked down at the table and chose his words carefully. "There are some folks in town want us to arrest Rodney Farmer. For the hit-and-run killing of Melody Harker," he added when Patience simply looked at him.

Melody Harker, the girl whose picture had spurred David Simonov to look for his daughter. Undersized for twelve or thirteen, much older than that in face and manner, Melody had been somewhere in the middle of a fatherless brood well known in town as troublesome and sometimes thieving. "I don't think I know Rodney Farmer," Patience said.

"Rodney is a retarded eighteen-year-old who lives just down the road from the Harkers. Earlene Harker, Melody's mother, says he'd been bothering Melody; she figures he tried to pick her up and she put up a fight and either fell or got shoved under his car."

"What do you think?"

"I *know* the kid absolutely denies it and his family denies it and there's no evidence, on the car or the body."

"But?"

Hank shrugged. "I think—and this is absolutely between you and me—he might know something. Problem dealing with a retarded kid, you can't be sure how slow he really is, how much he might be hiding or how much just scared. We're trying to talk to him frequently without having somebody charge us with harassment."

"Are there no other suspects?"

"Not really." Hank topped off his mug from the bottle and drank deeply. "One of Melody's brothers says she'd taken to hitchhiking recently; and where she was found, on Route 20 just off the country road the Harkers and the Farmers live on, could be she jumped out to wave down a ride and the driver didn't see her in time. It looks like she got hit around dusk, when the light's bad."

"What a mess," said Patience softly. "For everyone."

"Mess is the right word." He waved to get the attention of the barmaid, but she was watching the darts game under way in a rear corner of the big room. With a shrug Hank got to his feet and went to the bar to collect a replacement bowl of pretzel and peanut mix. "Where's that big beautiful daughter of yours?" he asked as he reclaimed his seat. "I was planning to watch her clean everybody's clock at the dartboard tonight."

Patience felt her face and shoulders contract in an involuntary grimace that she knew Hank would read. "She went to the City. To see her lawyer and explain things to Ted." Patience held up her right hand, fingers crossed. "And that is strictly privileged information," she added, with a smile meant to take the sting out of her words. She and Hank knew a great deal about the lives and loves of their respective children.

"Kind of headlong kid she always was, I'd have figured Verity to take off with a rodeo rider, or a white-water rafter, or maybe some guy wanted her to help him study bears in Alaska. Last thing in the world I'd have expected her to do is marry a spoiled rich kid with a shyster lawyer for a father," he said.

"That's what comes of sending your kid to Stanford," said Cal-graduate Patience. She tipped the rest of her drink into her mouth, and frowned. "No, that's unfair. She and Mike were always very close; she never fought with him the way she did with me, and she listened to him. But Mike got sick just about the time she met Ted. And Ted was very sweet to her all through Mike's illness and his death, while I was no use at all.

"And so it goes, I guess," she added. "Incidentally, Amos Blake is no shyster. More of a natural force. He's an ugly, intense little man, all appetites and energy with no time for conventions. Much preferable to his son, in my opinion."

Hank's eyebrows rose briefly at this. "If you say so. Anyway, last time I talked to Verity, I got the idea she was settling in pretty good up here, turning into a real asset to your business."

"It appears that she is indeed," said Patience, and Hank looked at her for a moment, and then grinned.

"Prepared to take good care of her old gray-haired mom, is she? Hand you your cane and make sure you eat your vegetables?"

"Something like that," she admitted. "Verity is the person I love most on this earth. I'd do anything for her. But I hadn't planned on living with her."

Hank was spared the need to reply as the noise level in the bar, always high on a Saturday night, suddenly intensified, hoots and cheers erupting from the darts corner. Then came a general stampede toward the bar, with two people breaking from the crowd to head toward the table where Patience and Hank sat.

"Screw darts!" Officer Alma Linhares pushed a tumble of glossy black hair off her forehead and grinned. "Hey, Patience! Come on and show these jerk-offs how a lady does it."

"Alma, how do you manage to make a darts game sound like sexual activity?" Johnny Hebert appeared from behind Alma and towering, silent Bob Englund, two mugs of beer gripped in his left hand and a glass of red wine in his right.

"What you never learned, big John, is that *everything* is sexual activity." Alma took one of the mugs, Englund the other.

"I didn't bring my darts," said Patience. "And I never, never play with anyone else's equipment."

Alma giggled, John grinned, and Bob Englund looked puzzled.

"Captain, you feel like challenging the winner?" asked Johnny. "For the moment, that's me."

"Sorry, I've got a headache," said Hank Svoboda in his deepest voice. "Patience, can I get you another drink?"

It was Patience's turn to giggle. "Oh, I don't think so. Why don't we go on to dinner, and leave these children to their games?"

Two hours later, Svoboda sighed loudly and patted his belly as he made the turn from the highway onto Raccoon Lake Road. They'd had a very hearty Italian meal, a good thing for her lean companion but something Patience knew she'd regret the next time she stepped on a scale.

"Hey. Didn't that guy just come out of your driveway?" Svoboda hit his truck's brakes, then swiveled in his seat to look over his

shoulder, but the taillights of the vehicle that had passed them were receding very rapidly.

"Maybe he was just turning around," said Patience.

"Maybe." The long driveway was even more tunnel-like than usual on this misty and moonless night; and Patience, leaving before dark, had neglected to turn on her usual outside light. Svoboda pulled to a stop facing the house and flipped on his spotlight, aiming it first at the basement door and then at the high front door. Both were firmly closed.

"Listen, there's Ralph," said Patience. "Just his usual 'Here I am on duty' bark; there's nobody inside."

Svoboda grunted, turned off the spot and the headlights, and unfastened his seat belt. "I think I'll have a look around, anyway."

"You're quite welcome to come in. But I don't need a bodyguard, Captain Svoboda."

"Yes, ma'am." He followed her around the side of the house to the flight of redwood stairs that had replaced Mike's wheelchair ramp to the deck and the kitchen door, also closed. As she put her key in the lock, she could hear Ralph's toenails clicking on the floor; he shot out past them as soon as the door was open.

"He always in that big a hurry to take a leak?" Svoboda asked as Patience turned on the kitchen light.

"No. But he'd be as much interested in a passing raccoon as in a burglar. Maybe even more. Would you like coffee? Brandy? A beer?"

"I'm about coffeed out," he said. "Beer sounds good. After I take a look around out there. You got a flashlight?"

Patience handed him the big electric torch from her utility cupboard. She saw its beam from various windows as she poured brandy into a small snifter, beer into a mug, and carried them into the living room, where she nudged books and magazines aside to clear a space on the mission-style coffee table. The room was not large, but it was nicely laid out, with a bay window and window seat, a wall of built-in bookcases, a tile-faced fireplace. Plenty of room for the comfortable sofa, the deep wing chair, the high-backed rocker, the leather ottoman. The good speakers that went with the compact music

system in the bookcase. The big, ugly television set, but at least it was on wheels. All in all, a nice place.

Hank finished his prowl and came in, Ralph on his heels. "Nothing out of order," he said, and looked around the room as if he might search the house next.

"The locks are good," she said in tart tones. "And Ralph is a very efficient warning system; if he doesn't bark, I don't come in. So sit down, if you're staying."

"Hey, I'm an old guy stuck in old patterns. Weakened by illness, too," he added. He picked up his mug of beer and settled with a sigh onto the couch beside her. "You really ought to humor me."

"I know women are supposed to be taught humoring, but in my family that's a lesson we always skip. Genetic resistance or something." Patience's mother, Hope Smith, had found widowhood a bore and was now, at age eighty, a fire-breathing Baptist preacher in Bullhead City, Arizona. Which reminded Patience...

"Hank, do you know of any nontraditional religious organizations in the county? Retreats, perhaps, or convents or communes?"

"There's sometimes a goddess gathering up on the Albion Ridge, I've heard. But I don't know anybody who's actually been there. That's not real friendly territory."

"Goddess doesn't sound right. This person I'm looking for was involved in fundamentalist Christianity."

"I've been sort of out of touch," Hank said apologetically. "But there's always little groups setting up tents out in the county in the summer—revivals and such. Probably you should talk to somebody at the sheriff's office."

"I'll do that," she said, picking up her brandy glass. "And I'll talk to local Baptists and Pentecostals and Four-Square Gospelers and such. The pastors are not very available on Saturdays, I find."

"Writing sermons, probably. I guess you got a new case, Patience. You want to talk about it?"

She thought about that for a moment. Hank Svoboda didn't talk carelessly, and he was insightful in a way not suggested by his good-ol'-boy demeanor. Besides, she would no doubt be asking his assistance in getting the kind of information only a police officer had

access to. "My client is worried about his ex-wife and daughter; they've left the woman's second husband, haven't been heard from in a while, and he wants to offer help if they need it.

"But he has no legal grounds for involving the police. Besides," she added with a grimace, "he doesn't want them pulled over and terrified by a highway patrolman or somebody equally sensitive. So, since the ex-wife is known to be fond of this part of the state, he wanted somebody private and local to ask around and try to locate them. It sounds fairly simple."

"Probably is," he said slowly. "But you want to remember, Patience, that your kind of business sometimes annoys folks, and you don't have the protection of a badge."

"I'm aware of that," she said tartly. "And if I weren't, my mistake on Thursday would certainly have refreshed my memory."

"Yes, ma'am. But I personally think you could use a fence and a gate. Or maybe a bigger dog." Hank slid lower in his seat, propped his heels on the coffee table, and draped his left arm across Patience's shoulders; she held herself stiffly for a moment, and then settled against him, letting comfort take precedence over principle.

"I'm going to buy a new handgun," she remarked, "to replace that heavy Colt Python of Mike's. I thought you might have some suggestions."

"There's this nice little .22, called a Lady Diane. Weighs about twelve ounces."

"For shooting mosquitoes, no doubt. Or old cops who make bad jokes."

"About that. No, we'll go down to Gabe's Guns next week and have him show you some nine-millimeter weapons; some of them weigh in at about twenty-five ounces without the clip."

"Lovely!" said Patience.

"Should do the job," said Svoboda. "What's in the VCR over there, this week's 'NYPD Blue'?"

"Yes. Have you seen it?"

"Not yet," he said happily. The two of them rarely agreed on movies: Svoboda refused to deal with subtitles or what he called "us-girls" stories; Patience detested war movies, psychotic serial killers, and

special effects of any kind. But on television there were one or two cop shows, one or two sitcoms, that they could share with pleasure.

Patience finished her brandy and set the glass aside. With the warmth of Hank's flannel-clad arm against the back of her neck, her temple touching the roughness of his jaw, she followed the story with the front of her mind while the softer back corners wondered idly at her present circumstance. Up to a few months ago, she had never slept with anyone but Mike—nor Hank with anyone but Ellie, gone nearly as long as Mike.

Not that they'd been to bed that often, or on any kind of regular basis. What was happening with them struck Patience as one of life's odd, rare gifts, something you shouldn't analyze or talk about much. Quiet gratitude was the only proper response.

"Good show," said Hank when she clicked the remote control at the screen credits. "Good company," he added, and turned his head to bring his mouth gently against hers. "What time do you expect Verity home?"

"Mm." Patience pulled her thoughts together and felt, for a moment, like a teenager whose parents had gone away for the weekend, leaving her the empty house and an admonition to be good. "Probably tomorrow afternoon."

Completely wired—skin itchy and hair a-prickle, neck and shoulder muscles tight to the point of pain—Verity hadn't actually decided that she'd go into the Bull and Grizzly. Just that she'd drive by. Lights were still on inside and out, and through the steamy window she could see a few people moving about.

The decider was a parking slot right in front of the place. She could keep an eye on her tempting little car, and there'd be no picking her way alone down a dark side street when she was ready to leave.

"Hey! Annie Mack, how ya' doin'?" Bart Willoughby caught sight of her as she settled onto a stool, and came quickly to her end of the bar.

"Doin' fine, thank you. Except I need a half-and-half. Guinness."

"You got it." He concentrated on the taps, then set before her a tall glass full of dark liquid with a brief, creamy head. Seeing his eyes

widen as she took her first sip, Verity looked past him to the bar mirror, and the reddening bruise-to-be high on her right cheek. She shook her head to swing her loose hair over the mark and then winced, raising a careful left hand to the hidden but far more tender spot where her head had bounced off the doorframe.

"Thank you, Bart. I have a long drive home, and this will start me off on the right foot."

"No doubt, no doubt. But this should help, too," he added, and after a moment handed her a bar towel with something—ice cubes—tied in one end. "Just hold it against your head, there, help keep the swelling down."

She teetered for a moment between haughty rejection and tears, then reached for the towel and applied it as instructed. "Thanks."

"Welcome." He tilted his head and grinned at her, and she caught a whiff of something sweetish; Bart had improved his hours with a joint sometime recently. "Glad to see you back, Annie. And I gotta tell you, I'd really like to get a look at the other guy."

"No, you wouldn't," she told him, attempting to match his grin. Bart, and Verity in the mirror behind him, grew fuzzy for a moment as she remembered Ted's rapidly swelling nose and the welter of bloody towels with which she'd helped him mop up. Later, getting into her car, she'd found the lipstick tube in the pocket of her pants and had dropped it quickly in the gutter as her thoughts tumbled in confusion: How awful; how *useful*.

And she had a purpose here other than licking her own real or imagined wounds. "But some women are easy to push around," she said to Bart. "Dev's wife was a small person; did he hit her? Is that why she left?"

Bart's face lengthened in shock. "Oh my God, no way! Dev plain worshipped that woman, would hardly let her out of his sight. When he was down here he was always *listening*, like, to hear her move around upstairs."

Verity felt a chilly breath touch her spine; there were worse things than people slugging it out. "She must have felt suffocated."

"Well, I suppose she might of," Bart said with a shrug. "But she was a real quiet person and I guess—oh, not dumb exactly, maybe

just not in sync with the real world. Kind of woman really needs somebody to take care of her."

Which Dev seemed to need to do. "Bart. Maybe she came back."

"Huh?"

"Sure, and then they left together, without telling anybody. Just packed up and left, to go someplace where she and her little girl wouldn't have to live over a bar." She took another sip of her drink, keeping her eyes on Bart's face.

"Uh-uh. No way," he said firmly. "If she'd have come back, Dev would have let us all know, believe you me."

"Okay," she said with a sigh. "I guess I'm just looking for happy endings here, the family all back together again. Somebody told me the little girl looks just like her mother; I suppose Dev was crazy about her, too?"

Bart looked away and shifted his feet uneasily. "Well, Sylvie was— is—a pushy little kid, and bright as hell, her school skipped her right over second grade. I personally got a charge out of her, but Dev, he looked to have my old mother's view of smart—not the best quality in kids or dogs. But see, I didn't get involved there, I'm not some busybody like old Mrs. Sangiacomo upstairs, snooping into folks' lives and offering unwanted advice. 'Scuse me," he said with obvious relief, and went to the door to usher a pair of patrons out.

"Hello, pretty lady. Can I buy you a refill?"

Verity caught a whiff of manly cologne and a tinge of sweat from the large man who now rested muscular, hairy forearms on the bar next to her. "Thank you, but I'm fine," she said without looking up. Even tired as she was, she should be able to remember a name like Sangiacomo. Sangiacamo, Sangiacamo. Busybody Sangiacamo.

"That color hair really turns me on," said her neighbor breathily. "Specially with blue eyes instead of green. You from around here?"

"No," she said flatly, and sipped at her glass of ale and stout.

"Listen, San Francisco is a great town, you ought to let me show you a couple of clubs I know. You like music, maybe blues?"

"Thank you but I'm not interested."

"Or there's this jazz place, I sometimes sit in on drums," he said, and moved closer so that his upper arm pressed against hers.

Suddenly furious—bile sharp in her throat, tears hot against her eyelids—Verity blinked hard and turned only her head. "Fuck off."

"Jesus! No need to get nasty, I was just trying to be friendly."

Before she could gather herself to reply, Bart was back behind the bar, leaning forward to clasp her fisted hand. "Go hunting someplace else, Tony," he said in a pleasant voice. "This is a friend of mine just stopped in for a chat."

"Well, shit," said Tony, drawing himself up to his full six-two or so and sucking in his belly. "Excuse me all to hell."

As Tony strode toward the door and pushed through it, Bart drew a pint for himself, raised a questioning eyebrow at Verity, shrugged at her head-shake, and propped his back against the counter behind him, long legs crossed. "Tony's not some sex fiend, like—just one more sad, clumsy guy that got divorced and didn't realize how much he was going to miss gettin' laid regular."

"I'll take your word for it."

"What I figure, Annie, sex just isn't worth the risk these days. If you don't get punched out—or knocked up," he added with a nod at her, "you still might get dead. Me, I've decided celibacy's the only way to go. A drink or two, maybe a good joint, then home to the cat."

"Dog," corrected Verity glumly.

"Chacun à son goût," said Bart in an accent well south of France or even Quebec.

"Mm. But you're absolutely right about sex, Bart," she said, and tipped her head back to drain her glass. "The only safe partner now is either a virgin, or a guy who's been completely monogamous for at least ten years, and his equally faithful wife died just half an hour ago."

"Right on." Bart shook his head sadly.

Verity gazed into the mirror, and the blue eyes Tony had professed to admire. Gray-blue, they really were, more blue than gray tonight because of her blue shirt. Puffy, though, very weary-looking. She shifted her glance to the double hotplate with its two pots of coffee. "Long drive ahead. If I bring my thermos in, maybe you could sell me some coffee?"

"Just gimme a few minutes to make some fresh. And you know, Annie, I just had a thought about Dev that could make you feel better. If Lily did come back, he *might* have lit out with her without telling anybody, because," he said, leaning closer and speaking softly, "he owed the boss a chunk of money. And I'm damn sure he was in no financial shape to pay it back."

Oh ho, thought Verity. The money Lily stole. "People have done stranger things for love," she remarked, and he nodded.

While Bart made the coffee, Verity phoned her friend Erika to say she wouldn't be coming to spend the night after all. Then, thermos on the passenger seat and a full plastic travel cup in the dashboard cup-holder, she pointed the Alfa toward the Golden Gate Bridge and Highway 101 north. If the coffee wasn't enough to keep her alert, the task of shifting gears with a very sore right hand would do the trick. As she flexed her fingers around the wooden shift knob, she hoped that Ted's nose was equally painful.

Ted had paid for this car, she remembered ruefully; he'd insisted that his wife shouldn't be seen around San Francisco in the anonymous "transportation" cars she'd always found adequate. Then, characteristically, he'd decided on the Alfa Romeo—more subtle, he'd said, than a Porsche, or the Mercedes coupe. That subtlety, she hoped now, would let her push the speed limit a bit without attracting official notice and be home by two-thirty or so. Patience, somewhat less the night owl than she used to be, should be soundly asleep by that time. Verity had information she wanted to convey and some she'd just as soon keep to herself; she'd be happy to wait until tomorrow to attempt the division.

A Grateful Dead album in the CD player took her to the Cloverdale turnoff; she finished the drive through the long valley about the time she drained the last of the coffee from her thermos. If she concentrated, she could get the rest of the way home without stopping to pee.

No lights in the living room, a faint glow from the kitchen. Verity pulled up to park beside Patience's truck and found that it now had a near-twin: a somewhat older pickup with no shell. Who on earth was here? And where?

She crept up the stairs, unlocked the door and stepped into the kitchen, where a single fluorescent bulb burned in an under-counter fixture. Ralph was sitting up on his blanket, ears cocked; he wagged his tail at her before lying down again. All peace, it seemed, no intruders.

On her way out of the kitchen, Verity paused and looked at the chair nearest the back door. Big shirt hanging on it, blue flannel with long sleeves. Man's, definitely. She moved into the hall, to find a pair of large shoes, man's as well, outside the bathroom door. Nobody in the bathroom, and a good thing, too. After relieving her bladder, she peeked into her own bedroom and found nobody there, either.

She stepped back into the hall, listened hard, and heard… Goddamn. Snoring, and it certainly sounded male. From Patience's room, where the door was closed tight.

Who was in there with Patience? About to tiptoe over and quietly turn the doorknob, Verity decided that while she wanted to know, she really didn't want to see. Best bet was Hank Svoboda, old family friend and now that she thought about it, very frequent visitor. Telling herself she hoped it *was* Hank, Verity paused in the doorway of her own little bedroom, her childhood nest, and decided she couldn't stay there, right across the hall from that snoring and whatever else.

There was a sofa in the living room. And tomorrow morning, she could look up through sleep-gummed eyelashes at Hank Svoboda or some other man who had spent the night violating her mother.

Verity crept into her room, pulled the quilt from her bed, crept back to the kitchen and out the back door. There was a couch in the studio, too, an old daybed. Having conquered lust and come chastely home, she would now sleep out there, cold and lonely, while her mother shared her bed with the warm body of…whoever. Shit.

Verity had her clothes off and was wrapping the quilt around herself when the ridiculousness of it all hit her. She dropped to the couch and exploded into helpless gusts of laughter that sent tears streaming down her face and could probably be heard in the next county. She was still stifling an occasional giggle when sleep engulfed her.

8

The building that Community people called "the main house" looked like pictures of farmhouses she'd seen in books at school—really tall and plain white with a high sharp roof and big porches, and inside lots of different-sized rooms and doors and steep stairs. A place where a big family might live.

But Sylvie thought the meeting hall was something made up later and tacked on, maybe where a porch had been before. Long and skinny, under a roof that slanted from too high on one side to too low on the other, it had no curtains on the windows and no rugs on the creaky wood floor. Every noise was weirdly loud—footsteps, the screech of the metal folding chairs, notes struck on the out-of-tune upright piano. Sylvie really hated that piano.

Against the end wall, under a big bright-colored picture of Jesus with a bunch of kids around him, was a plain wooden table with a pitcher of water and a glass, a basket of torn-up bread, and a tray with little paper cups lined up on it. Right beside the table was a high wooden stand with a slanted top—a place for Brother Daniel or anybody to put the Bible while they were talking.

"Sit up!" Aunt Marsha leaned forward from the row behind and pinched Sylvie's shoulder as she hissed in her ear. Sylvie clenched her teeth but hitched herself straighter, uncurling her legs from around the chair legs to put her feet flat on the floor. Community's children—Sylvie and the other seven who weren't actually babies but weren't twelve years old yet—sat in the front rows on the women's side of the room. So they could see and hear better, Aunt Marsha said. So they could be watched and pinched, Sylvie figured.

The awful piano was safely closed up today, because Sister Jennifer, the only person who could more or less play it, was upstairs with her colicky baby. They had all sung "There is a fountain filled with blood" and "Praise God from whom all blessings flow," the voices sounding raggedy and far apart in this room.

Then Brother Daniel got up behind the speaker's stand and prayed, in a voice that swooped from roar to whisper and back again. After a drink of water and a loud throat-clearing he announced that he was ready to bring the message, something he did for such a long time that Sylvie's bottom was getting very tired from the hard metal chair. She didn't like this church. She didn't like Brother Daniel much, either. Very tall and skinny, he had this weird bony forehead that ran clear over the top of his head; his big front teeth leaned against each other; and when he came out from behind the stand and walked around, waving his arms and talking fast, the people in the front row got rained on with spit.

Finally Brother Daniel finished, wiped his face, and brought the basket of bread to be passed around; his son, Jacob, came behind him with the tray. Sylvie took a piece of bread and slipped it into a pocket, accepted a little cup from the tray, and peered suspiciously at the surface of the grape juice inside. This stuff had been out there on the table the whole time; what if some of Brother Daniel's spit had sprayed in that direction? Poison, that's what; if she drank it she'd fall right off her chair dead and stiff.

"Sylvie!" said Aunt Marsha, in a harsh whisper that carried some spit of its own against the back of Sylvie's neck. She closed her eyes and drank the juice in one gulp, thought about maybe falling to the floor just to see what everybody would do, decided that was probably a bad idea. She gagged a tiny bit not very loud.

Special meeting of the Elders' Council at eight tonight, Brother Daniel was saying; daily prayers at seven every morning as usual, Bible study Tuesday and Thursday evenings, general meeting to follow on Thursday. He went on to a list of people to be remembered in prayers, including Sister Lily Costello; Sylvie sat straighter and squared her shoulders at this.

"And remember, especially, daily prayers for our brothers and

sisters in Jerusalem, where they will witness for us in these holy times and those to come." Brother Daniel tipped his head back and stared at the ceiling for a while before sighing, wiping a hand across his eyes, and looking out again at his brothers and sisters right there in the room. "And now we'll have a fine, uplifting song from Miss Sylvie Costello."

Sylvie said, clearly, "Simonov!" as she stood up and straightened the dress Lily had made her for Easter Sunday last year, pink with flowers and a tie belt and a rim of lace around the neck. It barely skimmed the tops of her knees now, and was tight across the shoulders, but she'd defied Aunt Marsha and put it on anyway.

At the front of the room, Brother Daniel gave a little bouncy nod at her, showing those rabbity teeth; then he put his hands around her middle and lifted her to stand on a solid wooden chair beside the table. He whispered in her ear before stepping away. Sylvie took a good breath and smoothed her hair back with both hands and sang: "Beautiful Savior, king of creation…"

When she finished the second verse and focused on the room again, she was not surprised to find everyone looking at her. Sylvie had been singing longer than she could remember, following Lily's voice with hers even before she knew the words to songs or what they meant. People always listened when she or Lily sang.

"Thank you, young lady," said Brother Daniel. "That's a voice fit to glorify God. Would you give us one more, please?"

Seeing the waiting, smiling faces—except Aunt Marsha's, which was red and squinched up—Sylvie thought suddenly of Lily's favorite song of all. Maybe it would bring her back. " *'Tis the gift to be simple,'* " she sang,

> *'Tis the gift to be free,*
> *'Tis the gift to come down where we ought to be.*
> *And when we are in the place just right,*
> *We will be in the valley of love and delight.*
> *When true simplicity is gained…*

The song made her throat feel tight and funny, but she got to the end

okay. Brother Daniel swooped her down from chair to floor and patted her on the shoulder. "Thank you, Sylvie."

The other kids scattered; the grown-ups moved more slowly out the door at the back of the room, women heading for the kitchen and men in different directions. Aunt Marsha came up behind Sylvie at the door, and wrapped hard fingers around her upper arm as they went out.

"You heathen child, that wasn't a Christian hymn," she said in a low, mean voice. "There's no mention of Jesus in it at all. And I told you not to wear that old dress, the hem is practically up to your crotch."

"This is my Sunday dress Lily made it for me," said Sylvie in a rush, pulling free of that painful grip. Aunt Marsha made a quick grab and got not arm but sleeve, which ripped half-away at the shoulder. Sylvie stared for a moment at the dangling fabric, then wailed and threw herself at the woman with pummeling fists.

"Hey, kid. Are you okay?" Sixteen-year-old Lisa, Sister Catherine's daughter who had been away at boarding school until last week, tip-toed into the girls' side of the divided sleeping porch and closed the door quietly behind her.

Sylvie sniffed loudly and turned away, pulling the blanket over her head.

"Come on, don't be a dweeb." Lisa yanked the blanket down. "Look, I brought you something to eat. It's cold, but it's still good."

"I'm not hungry."

"Listen, I've watched you eat before. And it wasn't your stomach got smacked."

Sylvie lifted her head and looked at the plate Lisa carried: a whole chicken leg, a mound of scalloped potatoes, slices of tomato. She sniffed again, rolled over and started to sit up, quickly thought better of that and levered herself to her feet, smoothing her nightgown down.

"I guess I might as well eat it, since it's here."

"Damn right, the trouble I took bringing it." Lisa set the plate and a foil-wrapped something on the bedside table and fished a fork and spoon from a pocket in her dress. Sylvie snatched up the chicken leg and went to work on it.

Lisa, a tall girl with frizzy light hair, had improved her plain blue and white dress with a wide, tight belt that made her big breasts look even bigger. Now she sat on the edge of Sylvie's bed, crossed her legs, and narrowed her round blue eyes. "Even I, bitch of the world to hear my mom tell it, never got paddled, only switched. The paddle's for boys. What the hell did you do to Sister Marsha?"

Sylvie put down the half-eaten chicken leg and scooped up a spoonful of potatoes. "I hit her," she mumbled from a full mouth.

"Hit her?" Lisa's eyes got round again, a pair of white-rimmed blue marbles. "God, why would a little kid like you do something so crazy?"

"She grabbed me and tore my dress," said Sylvie, through another mouthful of potatoes. "Besides, she hates me."

"She does? Why?"

"I don't know." Sylvie swallowed, wiped her mouth with the back of her hand, and lifted her chin, to meet Lisa's gaze directly. "She just does."

"Well, if it makes you feel any better, she's in real trouble with Brother Daniel. For using the paddle on you. Any change in the rules around here is supposed to be okayed by the Elders. The men," she added, as she caught Sylvie's look of puzzlement. "In case you haven't noticed, this is a majorly sexist outfit, which is why I'm getting out as soon as I can. I'm thinking about being a lesbian."

"What's a lesbian?"

"Never mind." Lisa opened the foil-wrapped bundle to disclose a large piece of chocolate cake. She used the fork to divide it, put one-half on Sylvie's plate, and wrapped the rest up again. "I gotta go, or I'll be in deep shit right along with you."

"Okay. Thank you for the supper."

"Welcome, dummy. Just because you're crazy doesn't mean you should starve." Lisa, on her way to the door, turned with an intent look. "In this place, you've probably heard, we're supposed to love one another—'Love the Lord thy God and thy neighbor as thyself.' But people can say they 'love' you and still get real mean. You better just apologize to Marsha and then be quiet and keep out of her way."

Sylvie straightened her spine and squared her shoulders. "She should apologize to me first. She tore my dress."

"No shit," said Lisa with a sigh. "Kid, you better pray your mom gets back here pretty soon, while you're still alive."

Three of the little ones shared the girls' porch with Sylvie: Naomi Hicks, a peaceful four-year-old who hardly ever took her thumb out of her mouth; Aunt Marsha Simms's fat whiny Sarah, five; and Janey Carter. Janey was also five years old, talked mostly to a doll she never put down, and had something in common with Sylvie: her mother had gone away.

Janey, however, had a father, Brother Benjamin, a sad-faced man who wore his hair in a ponytail and always talked very softly. He and Brother Edward, stepfather of Lisa and father of Eddie the slug, were the only two people who came and went from Community more or less regularly, often leaving in the morning and not returning until evening. As if they had jobs outside. Sometimes, in the stories that filled her head when she was not quite asleep yet, Sylvie imagined herself and Janey, Brother Benjamin and Lily, living together like a real family in a place away from here.

But tonight she was eager to be free of Janey and the others as well. Go to sleep, babies, she told them, and finally sang softly to them until they did.

It was almost dark, surely after eight o'clock, when Sylvie crept out of the sleeping-porch door and down the hall. Her bare feet made no noise, and her long flannel nightgown was a faded red-and-blue print that she didn't think anybody would see in the dimness. Nobody did as she zipped down the stairs, nor as she slipped past the entry to the kitchen, where the women were still working and talking.

And out a side door. Sylvie, trained early to a catlike awareness of the world around her, had noticed that the men always held their meetings in a room in the barn. Only now did it occur to her that they did this so the women wouldn't be able to hear them.

But she *needed* to hear, because they might talk about Lily and her. If anybody knew anything, had heard anything new, it would be the men.

Besides the main house and another, smaller house for people, there were a bunch of other buildings: pig shed and chicken house and well house, and biggest of all, the barn. Inside, the barn seemed to go up forever, its top invisible in the dark. Sylvie smelled dust, the oil-and-rubber of the tractor parked just inside the door, chicken feed, hay. Manure and a hint of sourish milk from the room where the two cows were; she could hear them moving their feet in the straw. A smell of hot metal came from the room where the light was; and voices. She moved quietly closer to the open door, knelt to sit and was reminded of her sore behind, so climbed instead up the stairstep side of a low stack of hay bales. On top she stretched out on her stomach to listen.

They were talking loudly in that room, shouting even; and she thought at first they were fighting with each other. After a moment she realized that what they were doing was talking to Jesus, all together and then one, then another. Not in their everyday voices, either; the only one who sounded like himself was Brother Daniel. Weary and sore, Sylvie put her head down on her folded arms and closed her eyes.

Now they were singing, soft songs. Abide with me, that was Brother Benjamin's voice. Then a song about faith and lambs. Bible stories from Sunday school classes here and elsewhere swirled in Sylvie's sleepy mind, along with other tales from other places: Joseph and his many-colored coat, Moses floating in a little basket, a den of lions. God with a white beard wearing a long dress. God in a shining helmet, one-eyed with a black bird on his shoulder and a piece of lightning in his hand.

"...horses don't make sense." Sylvie jerked herself awake to the voice of Brother Daniel, ready to boom and not about faith or Jesus. "We don't work enough land; draft horses cost too much and we'd go broke feeding 'em. So forget it, Andrew. We're here to live clean Christian lives and shun the abominations of that Babylon out there, but we're Baptists, after all, not Amish."

Brother Andrew just grunted. He was a tall man whose long sun-burned face looked blank except when he was carrying his almost brand-new baby girl around. Next to Brother Benjamin, he was

Sylvie's favorite of the men. She had no favorite among the women, unless you counted Lisa.

"Well, that old tractor ain't going to go on forever." This grating voice belonged to Brother Willie, who so far as Sylvie could see was in charge of every machine at Community: trucks, generator, tractor. His hands were always dirty and he smelled of grease.

"No money for a new one," said Brother Daniel firmly. "Just meeting the property tax bill is gonna take every penny we've got, plus all our energy and faith. So pray for guidance, Brother Will, and I know you can keep the old Deere going a while yet. Now, there's another working day coming up tomorrow, praise the Lord, and we all need our rest. Any other business that can't wait until next week?"

"Well, there's one thing." Sylvie thought this must be Brother Fred, Aunt Marsha's husband. His voice had a squeaky sound, as if he didn't get to use it much. "My missus thinks it would be a real good idea to send that little girl, Sylvie, someplace away from here for a while at least. Maybe the summer Bible-study camp Pastor Bohr runs up at Johnsville."

No! Sylvie bit her tongue to keep the word from escaping her mouth. No no no! She had to stay here where Lily could find her, even if she had to hide out in the woods and eat leaves and bugs.

"I couldn't agree to that." Sylvie let out held-in breath at Brother Benjamin's words. "That setup is for seriously troubled kids, generally boys."

"Besides, we can't afford it," said Brother Daniel.

"Marsha was sure Lily left money for—"

"Sister Lily met with me in confidentiality." Brother Daniel's voice was louder. "She asked me to accept responsibility for her daughter, and for her own assets, until her return. I agreed, after having her put the request in writing."

When did she do that? Sylvie wondered. Lily had made her come along that day, to Brother Daniel's office. She didn't remember anybody writing anything.

"We should have had an Elders' meeting about that," said Brother Fred. "Marsha believes this little girl is evil in her nature, a moral danger to the other children."

"Bullshit."

Brother Andrew's comment brought a moment's silence. Then Brother Daniel, sounding as if he might be waving his arms and spitting. "If that's true, this is surely where she belongs, with us who know her and were entrusted with her care. We're duty bound, are *called* upon to be vigilant in behalf of her immortal soul, to supervise and chastise her and train her up in the way God wants her to go."

Sylvie, shivering now from the chilly air and from confusion— what did *chastise* mean?—realized she should get away from here and back to bed before these men came out and found her.

"But suppose something has happened to her mother? Shouldn't we inquire about that?" Sylvie thought this was Brother Benjamin again.

"Brothers, Lily Costello admitted herself to be weak and a sinner, much subject to temptations of the flesh. Seems to me she might have abandoned the child in favor of the husband."

"No," said Sylvie softly into the prickly hay. She edged her body backwards toward the edge of the stack of bales.

"So we'll do our duty by the child, and I see no need to involve any authorities. So far they've not pestered us, and the last thing we want to do is stir them up."

Feeling backwards with one foot for the way down, Sylvie overbalanced and tumbled and bounced, dislodging a bale that fell to the floor with her and startled a barn cat, which yowled and then hissed.

"What's that? Who's out there?"

When she pushed herself to her knees, brushing hay and dust from her face, she found all of them looming over her like angry giants. "Lily!" she cried, and then, "Leave me alone! If you try to chastise me, God's black bird will peck your eyes out!"

9

Verity had to move smartly to avoid chilling as she cooled down. June was doing its usual number on the north coast, heavy fog still hanging in at ten A.M. and the temperature probably not yet fifty. Fine for the long, pounding run she'd needed today, but now she was eager to get back to the car and her warm sweatpants. Christ, she thought as she paused beside a log for a brief stretch, she could use not only sweats but a parka.

That automatic "Christ" rang uneasily in the back of her mind as she scrambled up the sandy slope from the beach to the parking area. Yesterday, Sunday, she and Patience had attended three church services: a Baptist and something else evangelical in the morning, another Baptist in the evening.

Child of a lapsed, sort-of, Baptist mother and a lapsed, definitely, Catholic father, Verity had been exposed to religion in only occasional and eclectic fashion. The intensity of many, even most, of yesterday's churchgoers had taken her by surprise; very uncool, those Baptists. Gave a heathen like her a new understanding of the word "worship."

She dug a plastic bottle of water from the trunk of her car, unscrewed its cap and took several long gulps, and splashed a handful over her face. A quick wipe-down with an old towel, then she scrambled into her sweats and had another drink. What the church visits had not given her, them, was any information about Lily Medina Simonov Costello or her daughter.

Her breathing was back to normal now, her pulse nearly so. The quivers in her legs had stopped. Verity stared into the fog, listening to

the sea behind it, and contemplated the day ahead. Breakfast first, and a coordinating chat with Patience; the only decision they'd reached the night before was that pursuing Lily's possible religious connections was a task better suited to Patience than to Verity.

The sun was breaking through the thinning fog as Verity turned in past the Mackellar mailbox. Something near the road end of the driveway caught the edge of her attention; she drove on, parked, and trotted back for a look, her mind mostly on breakfast. Deer, maybe?

Moments later Patience set her mug of coffee down next to the portable phone as her daughter burst into the kitchen. "My, but you look healthy," she remarked.

"Smell that way, too, I bet. Mom, maybe I'm paranoid, but there's this spot down the driveway where the bushes are broken back, as if something or somebody had been hiding there."

"Deer, probably."

"I thought about that, but would they bed down right next to the road?"

"Well, maybe dogs or raccoons fighting. Didn't Ralph make a fuss last night? I was half-asleep, so I didn't do anything about it."

Verity shrugged. "I must have been all the way asleep; I didn't hear anything. But he was sort of strange this morning; I tried to get him to go with me to the beach, for a run, but he just hung back on the porch and whined."

"I don't think you should run him, Verity. His left hind leg was broken in several places, and he has a pin in that hip."

"Oh, right. Sorry. Anyway, there are tire tracks out by the edge of the road, as if maybe somebody parked there."

"The mail truck?" Patience asked, but she got to her feet and tied the belt of her robe more snugly. "Let's go have a quick look."

Ralph trailed them cheerfully enough, until they neared the break in the bushes. Then he sat down and barked and would go no further. "Oh, for heaven's sake," said Patience, and was reaching for his collar when he darted past her, barking furiously again.

"Ralph!"

"Hey, tough guy. You gonna eat my truck? Hi, Patience," said Wes Trueblood, the mailman. "You feeling okay today?"

Patience pushed her hands into the pockets of her robe, her cheeks reflecting the rosy pink of its quilted surface. "I'm fine, Wes. Just getting a slow start this morning."

"Well, here's your mail, nothing real interesting that I can see." He thrust a long arm out the window of his mail truck, and nodded cheerfully at Verity as she stepped forward to take the rubber-banded bundle.

"Thank you," said Patience.

"Any time. See you tomorrow. That's a real nice robe." He grinned and drove slowly off.

"So much for any tire marks," said Verity, scanning the ground. "Hey, Mom. Is this Wes somebody I should warn Hank Svoboda about?" On Sunday morning Verity had shared a hearty breakfast with Patience's Saturday night sleep-over guest, who was cheerfully unapologetic about his presence. Cops, Verity had decided, knew no embarrassment.

Patience's cheeks were still flushed. "Hush or I'll raise your rent. I wonder if Wes eats peppermints. There, on the ground."

Verity looked, then bent to scoop up the pink-and-white disk. Crushed flat by a tire, it was bursting out of its clear cellophane wrapper. "I guess we can ask him tomorrow.

"Ted doesn't, though," she added, as she set off on Patience's heels for the house. "At least, if he does, it's a recently developed taste."

"Verity, do you suspect Ted of lurking in our driveway?"

"No," said Verity as she took the kitchen steps two at a time. "Well, not really. But he was quite…upset when I left him Saturday night."

"Poor Ted," said Patience, with a note in her voice that prickled the hair on the back of Verity's neck.

"Take it easy, Mom," she said, uneasy herself. "Whew, I smell like a gymnasium. Could you put coffee water on for me, while I have a quick shower?"

Ten minutes later, clad in jeans and a clean sweatshirt with a towel wrapped around her head, Verity picked up a steaming mug and took a sip. "Wonderful. Thank you. Look, I have to call Ted anyway, to remind him that the movers are coming for my stuff today. He

promised to arrange for someone to be there to meet them. I'll call from downstairs if that's okay."

Patience, slicing bagels and envisioning Ted Blake's neck under the serrated knife, could not distinguish the words that Verity was speaking in the office below. Not that she'd have listened anyway, she told herself. But she could and did pick up tone. "Cream cheese or strawberry jam?" she asked when her daughter reappeared, wide of eye and high of color.

"Both." Verity slumped into a chair. "Thanks."

"No problem. Will someone meet the movers?"

"Yes indeed, Teddy will do that his very own self. He'll make time by cancelling the appointment with his personal attorney. Since he's decided against suing me for breaking his nose."

"Verity! Did you?"

"So it seems," Verity told her, flexing her right hand and inspecting her knuckles, bruised and still slightly swollen.

"Well. But he hit you, too."

"True," said Verity with a wide, mean grin. "And when I told him that I had not only my loving mother to testify to my injuries, but a very nice bartender as well, he just went *pffft* like a balloon on a dartboard."

Patience put toasted bagels, cheese, and jam on the table, and set about making more coffee. "Did you ask him about being here last night?"

"Not exactly. But he said he'd been staying at home until his face looked better. I honestly do feel…bad about that, messing up his lovely straight nose. Ted's looks matter a lot to him."

The note of sorrowful affection in Verity's voice made Patience bring her teeth together hard. If her daughter could still feel affection for Ted Blake, she needed more than a mother's ear and a job; she needed a therapist. "Verity…"

"I don't suppose," Verity went on, keeping her eyes on the bagel she was smearing with cream cheese, "that you and Dad ever fought."

Michael Mackellar would never in his life under any circumstances have hit me. Nearly swallowing her tongue as she swallowed those words, Patience had a mind's-eye flash of the real Mike

Mackellar, a loving but far from simple man who would be highly amused by time's gentle burnishing of his image. Do you like your halo, Mikey?

Patience sat down at the table with her coffee. "Of course we fought. But not like… Verity, do you remember your father before he got hurt?"

"Um. He was funny and used to throw me way up in the air. And carry me on his shoulders. He was big, wasn't he?"

"Mike was six-feet-four and weighed about two-twenty. He was good-looking and sweet-natured. I, on the other hand, at five-feet-one and a hundred ten pounds, had—have—a rotten temper. The only time… There was this one night, when we were out with friends and I had had a lot to drink. One of the other women was all over Mike the whole evening, wouldn't leave him alone. When we got home, I pointed out that he hadn't exactly resisted her. He laughed and said don't be silly, and I hit him, as hard as I could." Patience winced as she remembered, so young and stupid then, so old and sensible and sad now.

"Mike picked me up and draped me over his shoulder and let me hammer away at his back until I got tired. Maybe we'd have slugged it out if we'd been more of a size," she added with a shrug, reaching for a bagel half with one hand and her yellow pad with the other.

"Clearly you had better taste than I," said Verity.

"Better luck, baby, that's all. And a long time ago. But I think I'll add another name to my targets."

"Another…?" Verity knew that Patience took gun ownership seriously and went regularly with her pistol and paper targets to a firing range. She hadn't realized that the targets had names. "Who else?"

"Malcolm Lewis. The fake-hippie drug-dealing son of a bitch who shot Mike. He's been in and out of prison several times since. I like to think that some day I'll run into him, preferably when I'm armed."

Verity was speechless, nearly as shocked by her mother's language as by her revelation of a twenty-five-year thirst for revenge.

"Now," said Patience, dusting her hands together in an exaggerated down-to-business gesture, "we have people to find. Here's the schedule. I'll be in the downtown office working the phones, you'll

be on the road. That's probably Harley now," she added, as Ralph sat up, pricked his ears, and whined softly.

"Harley?"

"Nobody knows the landscape better than a boy who grew up and learned to drive in it," said Patience. "And his little four-by-four pickup will go places your Alfa can't, or wouldn't want to."

10

California is an oddly-shaped state—nearly a thousand miles long from north to south, some two hundred to two hundred fifty miles wide. Lengthwise it arranges itself more or less in strips: coast, mountains, valleys, mountains, desert. The road distance from the southern Mendocino County line to the Oregon border, traversing also Humboldt and Del Norte Counties, is three hundred miles. Even though the coastal strip of those counties, Lily Costello's purported refuge, was generally no more than twenty miles wide and often less, Verity figured this search could take a long, long time. Particularly now, when every paved road was a writhing serpent of trailers, motor homes, and vans mini or otherwise with out-of-state license plates.

"Maybe," she muttered to Harley, "we should just drive around flying banners from the sides of the truck: 'Lily, Call Home.' "

"Hey, we can find her!" Harley grinned at Verity, bright-eyed and aquiver with the look of a big puppy wishing only for a tail to wag. After Patience drove off toward town, Verity had tried to talk Harley into simply lending her his truck; he'd been so hurt by this rejection of his usefulness, and by extension, himself, that she'd given up, given in. One more male ego to be tender with.

At least, she noted, he'd applied some kind of controlling gunk to his hair, clothed his muscular, furry legs in Levi's, dug up from somewhere a giant Apple-logo T-shirt that didn't expose patches of skin. There was even a shiny smoothness to his cheeks; Verity returned his grin, patted his cheek. Yup, he'd shaved. "You're lovely, Harley."

Face flaming, he brushed her descending hand briefly, awkwardly

with his own. Uh-oh, thought Verity, stepping back. "With Harley Apodaca, Invincible Mac-Man, on the trail," she said brightly, "how can we miss?"

"Right, right. Well, unless she's gone real deep into the woods someplace," Harley added with a frown. "That's what I'd do."

"Not with a seven-year-old child along, you wouldn't. Or if you did, you'd have to come out fairly often."

"Oh, right. Kid that age probably can't go more'n a few days without TV and a pizza. So do we hit all the motels?"

"Not motels; our information is that she's operating on very limited funds." Verity stowed a tote bag of bottled water and fruit behind the passenger seat of the truck, laid a clipboard on the dash, and unfolded a map of northwestern California that she spread out on the hood of the truck. "Patience and I decided to assume she left San Francisco at a dead run, which would mean starting north on 101; the coast route would have been too slow. If she did that, but was ultimately shooting for the coast, she'd probably have come in not far south of Port Silva." She traced routes with a forefinger, and Harley nodded.

"So we'll start here, with the state forest…" she pointed again "…and then the three state park campgrounds near here. After that, we'll head north." Verity folded the map and stuffed it into the front pocket of her shoulder bag. "Okay, driver, are we ready?"

"Yes, ma'am," Harley said happily, and opened the passenger-side door for her.

Anyone who really wanted to hide—if she didn't mind poison oak and vicious blackberry vines, or skunks and raccoons and possibly bears or even cougars—could do just fine in the Jackson State Forest. The campgrounds were widely scattered, some with as few as two campsites; and those occupied were little bastions of privacy. Verity suspected that some of these folks lived out here semi-permanently, moving from site to site as necessary to evade stay-length requirements.

Although the ranger in the Port Silva office of the Forest Service thought he might have given a camping permit and a map to a woman resembling Lily Costello two or maybe three months ago, none

of the campers Verity and Harley found and spoke with had noticed Lily or Sylvie or anyone like them. The prevailing idea seemed to be that if you didn't peer in the direction of another campsite, didn't make eye contact, you could pretend nobody was there. Your very own forest.

As Harley pulled from a forest road onto Highway 20 and headed west, Verity opened her map again. "Okay, the parks. Let's try MacKerricher first; it's the biggest and so the most safely anonymous."

MacKerricher State Park is coastal, a long stretch of grassy headlands, shifting dunes, and rock-partitioned beaches. The campground is an old one, its hundred fifty or so campsites set along a series of one-way loop roads and screened from one another by well-grown trees and bushes. Verity had camped there with friends as a teenager and knew how private one could be in just the right space.

The CAMPGROUND FULL board swung from the bottom of the big state park sign at the highway entrance, as it would for most of the summer. They drove past that and along a narrow road that widened to pass on both sides of a ranger station. The tanned young woman inside the station had a telephone at her ear; she looked at them with a frown and shook her head, but Harley just grinned and waved, and pulled ahead to park.

"Good. Wait here," instructed Verity. She got out of the truck and paused to check her appearance in the side mirror: smoothly French-braided hair, discreetly lipsticked mouth, minimal eye-stuff. The deep blue cotton sweater made her look young and earnest, and the off-white jeans were trim but not tight. Not a camper, but a working woman, ready to play this one straight as Patience had advised.

The park ranger had finished with the telephone and now stood at the window counter, distaste for outlanders who couldn't read plain on her face. Verity put an accommodating smile on her own face, and made a bit of show with her clipboard. "Hi. We saw the sign and we're not looking for a campsite," she said. "But if I could bother you for just a minute?" She took a PATIENCE SMITH, INVESTIGATIONS card from the clipboard and laid it on the counter.

"I...suppose. You a private detective?"

"My name is Verity Mackellar, and I work for a private detective." Verity let her polite smile warm to a grin. "But I hope to have my own license eventually."

"Probably beats cleaning toilets for the state park system," said the other woman with a grimace. Several inches shorter than Verity, with straight blond hair and a broad Scandinavian-looking face, she had a badge pinned to the breast pocket of her brown uniform shirt, the name JANICE OLDS lettered there in white on bright green. "What are you investigating for Patience Smith?"

Lily's and Sylvie's faces, so similar in features but different in expression, gazed at Verity from her clipboard. She slid a copy of the photograph from under the clip and laid it next to her card. "We're looking for this young woman and her child, and we think—"

Janice arched pale eyebrows and stared with interest at the photo. "Why?"

"Her name is Lily Costello. She left home about three months ago, with her daughter, presumably to do some extended camping here on the north coast. Her...friends haven't heard from her in some time, and they're worried."

The ranger caught the hesitation in Verity's words, and her blue eyes turned icy. "Right. For 'friends' read 'husband.' Fuck off, detective lady. And best of luck to Lily whoever. I know how hard it is to get away from some bastard who thinks he owns you."

"So do I, but..." Verity was unwilling to get into trading war stories. "It's not her husband who is looking for her," she said, a half lie at most. "And our agreement is merely to locate her, and ask her to get in touch."

Janice inspected the photo once more, and shrugged. "I haven't seen anybody who looks like her, or her kid either, and that's the truth."

"Maybe as far back as mid-March? Driving a blue Toyota van?"

Janice shook her head firmly.

"Perhaps one of the other rangers would recognize her."

Another head-shake. "Everybody but me is summer staff, been here only two weeks. And I am personally damn sure that lady hasn't camped here in the last two weeks."

Verity sighed and let her shoulders slump. "I have the license number of her van. Perhaps your records...?"

This brought a snort. "You want to dig in Parks Department official records, you better hit the division office or Sacramento with a subpoena."

"Good thinking," said Verity sadly. "Okay, last shot. Is there anyone camping here who's been here a long time?"

"Nobody more than thirteen days; fourteen's the summer limit. Well, except the chaplain, Reverend Beamis. But he's gone home to Bakersfield for the week."

Maybe, thought Verity, cleaning toilets would be easier. More suited to her talents. "Thanks anyway," she said.

Janice picked up photo and card, to hand them back, but Verity shook her head. "Please. Keep them, and if Lily should turn up here, please ask her to call my mother. That's Patience Smith," she added quickly. She turned away from the other woman's astonished gaze and trotted back to the truck.

"Strike out?" asked Harley, popping a tape from the casette player before he reached for the ignition key.

"Right. For no doubt the first of many times. Maybe I should let *you* talk to the lady rangers," she added, and watched his cheeks turn pink.

At Russian Gulch State Park there was no CAMPGROUND FULL sign in view, but neither was there a ranger; the small building at the entrance was dark and locked, with a sign in its window instructing campers to take an envelope, choose an open site, and pay. All California's public facilities were woefully underfunded and under-staffed, the result, in Verity's opinion, of the uncivil attitudes of a long list of Republican governors. She wished she were more confident that the recent Democratic sweep of the state would bring improvement. "Just drive around," she instructed Harley.

The woman ranger, when they found her, was cooperative, but ultimately not helpful. Neither she nor her available co-worker recognized Lily Costello, and none of the campers, mostly families with children, had been in the park for more than the two-week limit.

"I think there's a few repeaters, though," said Angela, smaller and

darker, and friendlier, than Janice. "You know, people who camped here earlier in the year and are back again. You want to go talk to them, I think it would be okay."

About to say no to this, Verity reminded herself that plugging along was what she was being paid for, trusted to do. And at least she was allowed to do it in jeans. "Thanks. Can you tell me which campsites?"

One harried mother (husband off fishing), one interested retired couple, and one extended Italian family later, Verity returned to the truck possibly wiser, but with no additional information about Lily Costello and her daughter. "Okay," she said to her chauffeur, "let's hit the road. On to, what's it called? Van Damme."

"That's where the abalone fishers hang," said Harley, and right he was. The campground reverberated with the voices of large men wearing wetsuit bottoms and carrying tire irons or cans of Budweiser or both. The ranger was male (smart of the Parks Department, thought Verity) and cheerfully unhelpful.

"Nope, haven't seen anybody looks like that. I'd remember," he added, looking again at the photo and then turning his gaze, and a long-jawed, toothy grin, on Verity herself. "Like, if anybody turns up looking for *you*, I'll sure remember. You can ask around if you want; lots of these folks come two, three times a year. But to tell you the truth, Miss Smith," he said after a glance at her card, "this is probably not a campground where a woman alone would feel real comfortable. We're not rowdy, but we're, um, vigorous, you might say. Where you ought to try is MacKerricher."

"We did," said Harley, who this time had ignored Verity's instructions to wait in the truck. "They couldn't help us."

"Hey, what about Hendy Woods?" Ranger Will Dugan slapped the counter of his booth as the thought struck him. "It's quiet, off the main roads, set in trees and brushy hills. My sis is a single mom, and if she wanted to go camping, which she's never expressed an interest in doing that I've ever heard, Hendy's where I'd send her."

Verity had seen that name on a sign. "Isn't that a state park off Highway 128?"

"Yes ma'am. You take the Comptche Road right back of this

park as far as Flynn Creek Road, turn south and you'll come to 128 maybe ten miles west of Philo; turnoff to Hendy is just before you get to Philo."

Verity cocked an eyebrow at Harley, who nodded. "Thanks," she said to the ranger.

"No sweat. And if you decide to go on into Boonville for lunch at the pub there, say hey to Judy for me. She's the barmaid weekdays."

If last week's job had overtaxed her muscles, this one was going to wear out her butt. Verity clung to the door of the stiffly sprung little pickup truck and said a word of thanks to whatever goddess might be listening that she hadn't attempted this road in the low-slung Alfa.

"Oops. Sorry," said Harley as his quick braking threw her against her shoulder belt. The leggy, half-grown fawn that had caused their halt tossed them a brief, mildly curious glance before scaling the hillside in three airy leaps to disappear into the brush.

"Where's your mother, anyway?" Verity yelled after him. Her.

"Look, here's the highway," said Harley in soothing tones. "Almost there. I have a feeling we're going to get lucky this time."

"Right," Verity muttered. As the road surface smoothed out beneath their wheels, she set her trusty clipboard on her knees and stared hard at the two faces. The woman looked…exhausted. Used up, not so much physically as emotionally. The picture might have been a still from an old Western or war movie: Made it over the mountains, or through the lines, and I'm about done but my kid is okay.

"Verity?"

She gave a little shudder, as at a trickle of ice water down her spine.

"Turnoff right ahead," Harley told her.

Verity rolled her window lower; she'd dressed for the cool gray coast, not the heat of the valley. Vineyards behind them, what looked like fruit trees ahead, and off to the right, where the park must be, shine of bending river leading to a wall of green.

The park and campground lay well back from what was marked as the Elk–Greenwood Road. As at Russian Gulch, there was no one

on duty—just the "choose and pay" sign. Harley drove past the ranger station without instruction and began to cruise through the campground.

Clearly this was a family kind of place. There were more tents and small trailers than motor homes; most sites had not only cooler chests and Coleman stoves or charcoal grills, but clotheslines aflutter with little swimsuits, and tangles of wheeled vehicles from baby strollers through tricycles to geared bikes. Tethered dogs yipped or napped at many sites, and there was even the occasional cat.

"Lunchtime," said Harley, and patted his belly with a sigh. Indeed, most picnic tables were in use; Verity checked her watch, was surprised to find it was past noon, and immediately noted a hunger pang of her own. "One thing for sure," Harley went on, "with all these daddies and kids, I bet this is a really safe place. Boring and noisy, but safe."

But possibly disheartening, thought Verity, to a woman on the run, a child who had no daddy to grill hot dogs for her or carry her around on his shoulders. Might remind them of needs or losses, or even of the darker possibilities behind sunny scenes.

"There's the ranger!" she said suddenly, as they rounded a curve and saw the dark green pickup truck with the yellow-circled bear emblem on its door. The driver-side door was open, and a lanky young woman in a brown uniform was using a short-handled shovel to toss sandy earth into a smoking fire ring.

"Dumb assholes build a big old fire for breakfast, then go off sightseeing or beaching and leave their neighbors to eat smoke all day." She tossed a final shovelful of dirt and then shouldered the shovel as she came to meet them beside her truck. "Listen, George was supposed to put up the 'Full' sign when he left. I'm real sorry, but we're booked right through for eight weeks."

"We're just looking for some information," Verity assured her, and went into her spiel-with-handouts.

The ranger, Virginia Meader, was real sorry once again. She had been on the job at Hendy only since the first of the month, and the rest of the crew, except for George who had left that morning for San

Francisco, was equally new. And she had sure never seen this Lily person or her daughter, either.

"We've got the make and license number of her car," said Harley, who had clearly promoted himself from chauffeur to detective's side-kick. "Maybe, if you could tell me what kind of computer operation you guys use…"

"Oh ho!" Virginia tipped her head and squinted up at Harley, her green eyes gleaming. "Too bad, sugar, but you can't hack your way into our secret files because there aren't any."

"No computer?" Harley's voice rang with disbelief.

"Ain't that a bitch," Virginia agreed. "Nope, we just save the registration envelopes. Bundle them up every day and toss 'em in a box and keep them for seven years."

"Jesus."

"Life is dreadfully low-tech sometimes," said Verity. She asked Virginia to keep the picture and to keep an eye out for Lily and request her colleagues to do the same. Then, as an afterthought, she asked, "Is there a chaplain here?"

"Merle and I bought this rig before I gave up my church," said the Reverend Emory Harding, gesturing at the twenty-five-foot-long fifth-wheel trailer tucked neatly into one corner of the campsite. "North Mountain Baptist that was, in Phoenix. Could I get you some sugar for your tea?"

"Thank you, no; the mint is fine," said Verity. "It's a comfortable-looking trailer, Pastor Harding; and I've heard a fifth-wheel is the easiest kind to pull."

"Yes indeed, that's what sold us. We figured to take a few vacation trips to get used to it, and then spend more time on the road after I'd retired. But then," he said softly, with a sad little shrug, "Merle got sick. After Our Lord took her home to Him, the house felt too big, and Phoenix was too hot.

"But here I can be quiet and useful. I get my campsite free, I hold a Sunday service in the amphitheater, I'm around to talk to people who need somebody to listen. And I fill in for other pastors in the valley and nearby."

"People who need somebody to listen" sounded like a good lead-in to Verity; she reached for the clipboard that lay on the table next to her iced-tea glass.

But Pastor Harding wasn't finished. The pale blue eyes he fixed on her face were faded, but not vague. "First time I ever met a private investigator. Seems like a strange job for a woman, particularly a young, pretty woman."

Verity wasn't able to work up much heat over sexist remarks from a man who had to be in his seventies. "It's useful work, I've found. And so has my mother; it's her agency."

"You don't say. Your mother. I'd say you come from an unusual family, young lady."

Zap! said Verity gleefully to herself. "I'd say so, too. My maternal grandmother, Hope Smith, is an ordained Baptist minister in Arizona."

"Hope Smith. In Bullhead City. I've met her a time or two," he said, lifting his billed cap and smoothing his bald, age-spotted pate. "Fine Christian woman, Hope Smith."

Damn fine, thought Verity. Particularly from a distance of a thousand miles or so. "Pastor Harding, can you tell me anything about the woman I've told you I'm looking for, Lily Costello? Did she stay here?"

He sighed, and seemed to shrink a little inside his crisp blue shirt. "Not exactly. You see, sometimes people who are camping rough… because they have no money, or maybe because they're frightened," he added softly "…these people will come into a campground on the quiet to use the showers. Or maybe just to be around people some; children can get lonely for their own kind.

"This is against the rules, of course, against the law. But in off-season time, like March, it seemed unkind, unchristian, even, to raise a fuss."

Verity had hoped for a more recent sighting of Lily; but at least it was a start, proof that the elusive woman had been here near the coast as her ex-husband had suspected. Reaching for her glass of tea, Verity moved the clipboard so that the photo was between her and the old man. "In March?"

"Somewhere around the middle of the month, as I recall."

"Did they, did Lily, come to your service?"

"I first saw them on a Saturday; they came to the service the next morning. Very few people were there, so I noticed Mrs. Costello. I invited her and her little girl to have supper with me that night; I'd made a Crock-Pot of stew, more than I could eat."

"Pastor Harding, did Lily say where she was going from here?"

"Lily Costello is an unhappy woman. She said to me, if you can imagine, that she wished she'd stayed Catholic and become a nun." Pastor Harding's good Baptist nose twitched as he repeated this heretical notion.

"Tough to do when you have a kid," Verity murmured.

"A very bright, energetic little girl," he said with a nod. "After we talked, I believe Mrs. Costello had it in mind to mend fences with her family and try to get her life in order."

"Her family—you mean her husband? In San Francisco?"

"She wasn't very specific. I believe she mentioned her parents, her father in particular. And a sister. We were talking in terms of Christian moral health, not naming names. I am not a gossip, Miss Mackellar."

Verity ducked her head and tucked her sizeable frame into a more humble shape. "I understand, Pastor Harding."

The old man stood up, and Verity rose at once, picking up the clipboard. No need to leave a photo. "Thank you for your help, sir."

He sighed, reached out to shake her hand, and finished by clasping it in both of his. "Lily Costello is a woman full of sorrow, Miss Mackellar. If you find her, please give her my best wishes and remind her she must put her trust in Jesus."

"I will."

Harley, spotting her approach in his side mirror, readjusted his seat and popped his tape out. "Hi, boss. You get there?"

"I guess so," she said, settling into the passenger seat. She propped the clipboard on the dash and gazed at it. "Lily Costello does exist, Harley," she murmured. "She breathes, she eats, she talks. Pastor Harding says she's a woman full of sorrow. And in March she talked of making amends to her family."

"I thought she didn't have any, except her kid."

"That was my understanding, too. We'll check with Patience. Hey, Harley, we didn't score a run, but at least we got a hit. Let's go to Boonville and I'll buy you a beer."

11

"It seems like a lot," muttered Carol Heffernan as she eyed the bill Patience had just presented to her. On her lunch hour from her job as administrative assistant to a dean at the university, she wore strappy sandals with three-inch heels, a green linen skirt, and a silk blouse in a mustard-and-green print that did nothing happy for her sallow face. The clothes looked well-made and must have been expensive; probably, thought Patience, her job required an upscale appearance.

"My hourly rate is exactly as quoted at our first meeting, and my time spent is listed." Patience kept her voice soft; she also kept her hands folded atop the manila envelope containing her final report.

"I didn't know you were going to use an assistant," said Carol, stabbing a pointed fingernail at an entry on the bill.

"It was necessary; and she is billed at half my rate. The rest of the charges are expenses, all itemized: mileage, phone calls, film."

"Yes, I see. Ms. Smith…Patience…could I pay half the final amount now, and the rest next month? I'm a working woman, and…"

Clients often tried something like this with Patience; she'd decided it was partly because of her sex, but mostly a response to the appearance and demeanor that served her so well in other aspects of her work. People expect Grandma to offer milk and cookies, not a bill. "I'm a working woman, too, Carol."

"Oh. Well, I just hope this doesn't bounce," she muttered, splaying her checkbook out on the far edge of the desk and scribbling in it with hasty force.

"I hope not, too." Patience took the proffered slip of paper, glanced at it, and then put the manila envelope into Carol Heffernan's reaching hands.

Carol opened the clasp, upended the envelope, and yipped, "Oh, God!" as the photos slid to the desk. "Look how old he is! And fat! He must be still drinking."

"That, I have no information on."

"And this house is in Garberville?"

"It's all in the report, Carol." Patience took a deep breath. "The man in that picture lives in that house with a pregnant woman named Patricia and a toddler named Duane, Junior."

"I'll kill him." Carol Heffernan's eyes were a smoky light brown, almost the same color as her short, well-cut hair. Now the eyes filled, and reddened. "I'll have the sheriff on him by tomorrow morning."

"He doesn't appear to be prosperous, Carol. I doubt you'll get much of the money he owes you."

"Then they can throw his ass in jail. The son of a bitch has avoided responsibility for his real son long enough. Besides," Carol added, pulling a tissue from her handbag and dabbing at her eyes, "he's probably part of that underground, barter economy men get into to avoid child support. The bastards. He's probably doing just fine."

Jared, the "real" son, was sitting in a chair he'd pulled just outside the office door, playing with a hand-held electronic game whose beeps Patience had tried to ignore. Now he got to his feet and ambled in, baggy pants riding below the waistband of blue-and-white plaid boxer shorts, high-top sneakers unlaced. As he peered over Carol's shoulder at the photos of his father, Patience got a strong whiff of something she hadn't smelled since Verity's teenage years: pure essence of unwashed adolescent male.

"Boy, I forgot what an ugly asshole my old man is," he said. "Worse even than ol' Chuck the fuck. Hard to believe you ever let that guy…"

"You hush your filthy mouth!" Carol said, and aimed a blow at her son. Jared, who had his father's height and would one day approach his bulk, simply caught her fist in one big mitt and shook it gently, then let it go.

"Chill out, Mom. We don't need that guy. Come on, you said you'd take me to Hungry Wheels for a chili burger."

"Oh, I can pay for your afternoon snack. But how am I going to pay for clothes you outgrow every two months? Or the mountain bike or even that damned electronic chess game you think you can't live without?"

"So we'll forget the game, okay?" Jared's eyes, the same smoky brown as his mother's, touched the photos again and jerked away; he blinked hard and shrugged. "No big deal."

Patience cleared her throat. "You two may not know that Port Silva has a very active Big Brothers' group. Those I've met are nice guys; and one man I know quite well, a policeman, is a chess player."

Jared's head came up, but Carol shook hers. "We're not here for welfare information, thank you. We just want what we're entitled to. Come on, Jared, or I'll be late getting back to work."

Her son's shoulders slumped, and his big face settled into the sulky scowl that was probably its normal expression. "Right. Hey, Mrs. Smith? You know there's a guy out there watching you?"

"How do you know?" Patience asked, moving toward the door. "That it's me he's watching?"

" 'Cause I could tell, okay? Guy sits in his car, keeps sneaking these quick little looks down this way, who else would he be watching?"

"Jared, stop that! An IQ of one hundred fifty, and all he can do with it is tease and lie!" Carol wailed to the world at large as she snatched up report and photos.

"Hey, right. Car looked really weird, like the Batmobile or something and I think the guy was green, too. Probably an alien from another planet, gonna steal away this awesome brain I got and replace it with silicon." Jared crossed his eyes and sent his tongue darting in and out, lizardlike; his mother shrieked, "Jared!" again, grabbed him by the arm, and yanked him in the direction of the door.

"Oops!" Verity, in the doorway, fell back to let the Heffernans steam out. Patience followed the departing clients, put a hand on Verity's arm and stepped around her, to look toward the street. Harley's truck sat at the curb; beyond it, a Volks van and a sports

utility vehicle passed going south, and a white-orange-and purple FedEx van was close on the rear of a small, elderly car headed north.

"Someone was supposedly watching me," said Patience in explanation. "According to Jared Heffernan."

"That aromatic space cadet who just stumbled out of here? I don't think so, Mom. *I* didn't see anybody," said Verity, as she turned and waved toward the street. There was a double honk from the truck, and Harley drove off.

"Now," said Verity, following Patience into the office. "As employee of Patience Smith, Investigations, I have a minor but significant success to report."

The telephone rang; Patience reached for it, then pulled back her hand and shook her head. "Let the machine take it. I've been in this office for about six hours, and I need some air. We can compare notes at home, on the deck."

While Patience stowed things away and locked up, Verity brought the gray Ford around. "What we'll do," Patience said as she was belting herself into the passenger seat, "is stop at Johnny Wing's on the way, get something like hot-and-sour soup, maybe shredded garlic beef; I think I have his menu in the glove box. We can heat it in the microwave for supper."

"Uh, Mother, why don't I stop at Safeway instead, and pick up a few things? I'll make, oh, maybe a roasted tomato sauce for pasta, with garlic and parsley and sweet basil and olive oil. And a salad. If you don't mind, that is."

"Mind? The Lord be praised, as your grandmother would say. Verity, if you want to cook I'll deed the kitchen to you this minute. Except for the teakettle, and the wine rack. And maybe the icemaker."

"You used to be a really good cook," said Verity with a sideways look at her passenger. "I always thought you enjoyed it."

"The cooking gene has a limited life," said Patience. "Packs it in about the same time the ovaries do—one of the lesser-known advantages of menopause."

"I'll remember that," said Verity, as she pulled the truck into the Safeway lot. "Do you want to come in?"

Patience shook her head. "Put the bill on your credit card. And I'll just doze here in the sun like an old dog."

Verity was back in twenty minutes with two large paper bags that she stowed in the rear seat. "You know those posters all over town advertising the Bed-and-Breakfast Faire next weekend? There's one for a B-and-B called Oz, and the Toto in the picture looks just like Ralph."

"Ha!" said Patience, sitting up straighter. "It *is* Ralph, or was. Germaine Jorgensen is just too cheap to have new posters made."

"Ralph's former owner, I bet."

"Right. Silly woman calls herself Dorothy and wears her hair in pigtails…which I fully expect her to set afire one day, the way she waves her cigarettes around."

Fifteen minutes later the pair of them settled into canvas chairs on the deck off the cottage's kitchen. A jar of sun tea, two tall glasses, a saucer of lemon slices, and a bowl of ice cubes were on the table between them, along with Patience's yellow legal pad and Verity's laptop computer.

Verity stretched her now-bare legs out in the sun, set her little machine across her thighs, and flipped it open. "I made my notes at the pub in Boonville," she remarked, "while I was drinking a beer and Harley was inhaling two hamburgers and two pieces of pie. I'll print out later, just give you the gist now."

Her mother added another slice of lemon to her tea and sipped quietly during the report. "And then after lunch," said Verity, turning off the machine and turning on a satisfied grin, "we asked around in Boonville and then Philo, and found a woman in a little grocery store who remembered them, or actually Sylvie. So now we know for sure that in mid-March they were alive and more or less well, more or less in our territory."

"And it seems possible that they still are." Patience stared into her glass, moving it in slow circles so that the tea swirled and the ice cubes tinkled. "I spent the morning on the telephone, following up calls I made Friday and talking to people I know in the sheriffs' offices in the northcoast counties, and to friends in some of the Bay Area cities. The other night I asked Hank to check with San

Francisco and with agencies where I have no personal contacts." She paused for a sip of tea.

"So far as we could find out, there has been no report, in any of those jurisdictions, of the death or injury of Lily Costello or her daughter, or of anyone resembling them. Their van has not attracted official notice. Neither has Lily's husband, Devlin Costello; nor has he officially reported Lily missing."

"Any word from the former husband, our client?" asked Verity.

"No. But I didn't expect any this soon." A patch of shadow sped across the deck, followed by a flash of black-and-white and a liquid cascade of notes that sounded for all the world like a laugh. Ralph, dozing in the sun, bounced to his feet and barked furiously.

"Poor Ralph," said Patience. "That mocker fools him every time; you should hear its cat imitation. So—we still have a case, I believe. And my other accomplishment of the day was more positive. I found Edna Mangrum."

"Who?"

"Lily's foster mother. David Simonov didn't have her current address, and he didn't think she'd be of any use to us, because she and Lily didn't get along. But she was one of those gaps I thought should be filled in."

"Did she know anything?"

Patience shrugged. "She's in a senior citizens' apartment complex in Red Bluff. The manager there, a Mrs. Brink, told me that Edna is wheelchair-bound and cantankerous, and refuses to talk on the telephone."

"Mother, Red Bluff is about two hundred miles away. Two hundred *hot* miles."

"Yes, dear. But Mrs. Brink said that sometime in early April, she thinks it was, Edna suddenly turned 'even crankier than usual,' her words. She asked around, and one of the other tenants thought it was a visit from a female relative that set Edna off. Add that to what Pastor Harding told you, and the fact that the Mangrums seem to be the closest thing to a family Lily had…"

"Right," Verity sighed. "So I bet you want me to put on a hairdo and a power suit and pay Edna a visit."

"Thank you, dear, but I think a nice old lady will get more value from Edna than a glamorous young woman would."

"Nice old bullshit," said Verity with a grin. "But that's okay with me; I think I threw out all my pantyhose."

"So I'll go to Red Bluff tomorrow," said Patience. "And you and Harley will work your way north along the coast, with that campground book."

"Yes, ma'am," Verity replied absently. Patience's remark about a nice old lady had triggered something in the back of her memory, or someone. "Oh. Mrs. Sangiacomo. The old woman who lives upstairs over the pub in San Francisco," she said in explanation. "Mom, I think you should go to see her. If Lily was back there recently, as— what was the little girl's name? Amanda—thought, I bet Mrs. Sangiacomo would have noticed."

"I considered that, while I was going over the case notes," said Patience. "But I think my time will be better spent with Edna. An investigator friend is going to see Mrs. Sangiacomo for me, a charming middle-aged Irishman I've known for years; ladies love him."

"In San Francisco? Would I know him?" asked Verity.

"I hope not. Larry is not entirely to be trusted with an attractive *young* woman," said her mother primly.

"Larry sounds like somebody I ought to look up," retorted Verity.

12

Mid-morning Tuesday, as an unbearably cheerful Harley Apodaca negotiated a road-building detour on Highway One north, Verity spread out her map of northwestern California and was struck anew by the amount of open land out there, much of it occupied by National Forests: the Mendocino, the Six Rivers, the Shasta–Trinity, the Klamath. "My God, if you were strong and healthy and didn't mind solitude, you could live out here for at least half the year," she said. "And no quote detective unquote would find you if you didn't want to be found."

"Well, I dunno. Might be pretty dangerous out there for a woman on her own."

"No more dangerous than living with a crazy husband who thinks he owns her!" Verity heard the bitter note in her own voice and regretted it but not enough to apologize. She had slept badly the night before. Even when they were barely speaking, she and Ted had made love frequently and enthusiastically—or had sex, maybe, but by whatever name it had been part of the pattern of her life for five years.

Now she spent her nights in the high old double bed of her childhood, reaching unconsciously across chilly sheets for the warm body that wasn't there. Last night Patience had had a *date*, for God's sake—had gone out for a beer or something with Hank Svoboda. Verity had skulked around the house all evening like some jeans-clad Miss Havisham, fairly sure that Patience wouldn't bring the man home for the night but wondering whether it was the presence of her big thirty-year-old castoff of a daughter that prevented her. (And in the

nastier depths of her mind, wondering whether it was quite decent for a fifty-five-year-old widow to be having sex or making love, whichever.)

"Shit," she said aloud.

Harley let go of the steering wheel just long enough to deliver an awkward pat to her shoulder. "Listen, even if we don't find them today, there's a great barbeque place in Garberville. It's my turn to buy lunch."

My God, thought Verity, Garberville again. Be still, my heart. She slid a glance sideways at Harley, at shoulders measuring about three axe-handles across, at silken-skinned biceps exposed today by a sleeveless shirt; at muscular forearms and long legs whose furry black pelt had a reddish glint where the sun touched.

Suddenly Verity remembered her modern-sexual-options pronouncement to Bart the bartender: monogamous and newly widowed or... Harley sweetie, are you by any chance a virgin?

He turned to grin at her, and for a horrified moment she thought she'd spoken the question aloud. "Harley, I love barbeque. Here's Westport coming up, and a state beach campground. Let's check that out, go on to lunch, and then concentrate on reasonably accessible state parks and beaches.

"The point being," she added, "we'll never find her while she's actually in the woods. So we assume she'll do what she did at Hendy: come up for air and a shower now and then. And we check the places providing those things."

"Right. Patience probably doesn't want to pay us for hours of running up and down forest roads. Has she heard anything from the guy? Lily's old husband," he added in explanation.

"There was a message this morning, on the office machine. He'd come in from the wilderness where he's birdwatching or whatever— for supplies. He hopes the investigation is making progress, but he has this important job to do. He'll check back in a few days, he'll send more money if necessary."

"Everybody's out in the woods, sounds like."

"Especially us."

They asked questions fruitlessly at two state park campgrounds and a state recreation area before hitting Garberville. After lunch, the two of them looked the map over, and decided against the road west to Shelter Cove, in the area called the Lost Coast, and in favor of the big redwood parks to the north. Humboldt Redwoods State Park alone had three large campgrounds tucked into its thousands of acres.

Pretty much a wasted day, Verity noted glumly at nearly three P.M. Not so much as a nibble. She looked at Lily's face in the picture and decided it was beginning to look more enigmatic than weary: What makes you think you can figure me out and who wants you to, anyway.

"I don't know, Harley. I think these ladies are going to wind up on milk cartons or supermarket bulletin boards."

"Jeez, I hope not." As if for reassurance, he brushed his fingertips quickly across his shirt pocket, where he'd tucked a copy of the picture. "Besides, next to working on your mom's computer, this is the best job I've had."

"Oh good. Well, it's pretty here, at least," she added as they rolled on through dappling fingers of sunlight on the appropriately tree-lined Old Redwood Highway. They'd had no luck at the first two campgrounds in the area; the third was some miles ahead, off to the west along a secondary road. Verity spotted a highway sign and pushed herself straighter in the seat. "Look, there's sure to be a grocery store in this little town coming up, Weott. Let's stop there, get a Coke or something, ask our questions one more time. And head home. My mouth is worn out."

"Yes, ma'am!"

Harley's endless cheeriness might eventually seem a character flaw, Verity thought. Particularly when she was struggling hard to arrange her own face one more time in an expression conveying good temper, friendliness, and polite curiosity deserving of response. This was clearly a job for a Labrador retriever.

The store was on the edge of the little town, set in a paved parking lot that also served a post office and several unlabeled buildings. Harley pulled off the main road and then braked abruptly. "Hey, that's what I want someday!" he exclaimed, his eyes following the

smallish, nondescript (to Verity's eyes) car that was passing. "An old Mustang. They're classic."

" 'Classic' just means it probably won't start," said Verity, and then she grimaced at the realization that she was quoting her husband. "One of these days I'll lend you my Alfa."

"Deal!" said Harley. He turned into the lot and parked. Verity pulled a photo from the clipboard, slid out of the truck, and headed for the store, still working on her expression.

"Hey, look at that! A redhead!"

"By God, she's a big one, too. Just my size, ain't you, babe?"

One of them sat astride a motorcycle; two others stood up from a wooden bench as she neared. Big, not very clean, not much past high school age, she noted, and kept walking.

"Hey, Red, look at me!"

"Hey, babe, you a real redhead?" This one, the closest to the door, reached out as she passed and groped her butt.

Verity spun around, swung both arms wide, and then slammed her cupped hands against his ears.

"Ow! Jesus, you busted my ears!" he wailed, cupping his own hands over them as he stumbled several steps back.

"You should keep your hands to yourself."

"Jesus," he moaned again, tipping his head to one side and then the other. His two friends surged forward and then hesitated. "Listen, bitch," growled the one in the lead, "we can do you bad, believe me. You and your friend both," he added as Harley materialized at Verity's side.

"Maybe, but not without a lot of trouble," she said, and stood where she was until his gaze fell.

"Fuck," he muttered, and slid an assessing glance at his buddies, also hovering in indecision. "Way I see it, dumb cunt's not worth messing with."

Verity turned on her heel and strode into the store, Harley close behind her.

"Ver?"

She stopped and looked up at him. "What?"

"It's just, uh, you should probably be more careful around guys

like that. I'm big, and I'm not a coward—I don't think, anyway—but I probably couldn't handle three of them."

His face was so troubled that she bit back her angry retort, and said, instead, "Harley, sweetie, good friend, you need to understand something. You are not my bodyguard."

"But..."

"I am responsible for myself, and risks are mine to take. Especially when some dickhead thinks he's free to handle my body."

"But if you're in trouble, Verity, no way can I just stand and watch."

She looked at his worried face and acknowledged that this, too, was true. "Okay, Harley, I'll try to behave myself. You wait outside, and I'll bring you a...Coke?"

"Diet Pepsi."

"Harley, those chemicals are bad for you," she said to his retreating back.

Coke and Pepsi were available at the store; information was in short supply. The store's proprietor said apologetically that he saw too many people every day to remember each one; and he was pretty sure his wife would say the same, except she wasn't here at the moment. Verity paid for the soft drinks, thanked him, and went outside, to find that the motorcycle louts had disappeared and so had Harley.

After a moment's panic—had they shanghaied Harley in revenge for her behavior?—she decided she'd have heard the noise from any such activity, and Harley had probably gone in search of a rest room. She stood in the mild sunlight and surveyed the store's bulletin board, which offered her square dance lessons, a 1993 Ford truck with heavy-duty tow rig, a Compaq PC and deskjet printer, a $10,000 reward for information about the murder of a local man. Perhaps she should post Lily's picture here, along with Patience's card.

"Verity?" Harley came trotting down the hill behind the store. "Come and talk to this lady I found."

"This lady" was not Lily Costello, but a tall, fair-skinned woman with gray eyes and an alert expression. "Verity—Verity Mackellar,"

he added quickly, "this is Claire Ellison. She's a weaver, does these awesome wall pieces she sells in the crafts store back there."

"I do them," said Claire with a shrug, "but they rarely sell."

"Awesome," said Harley again, firmly. "Anyway, Claire saw Lily. Back…when did you say?" he asked.

"The first time was just before Easter," said Claire. "My daughter Emma brought the little girl, Sylvie, home to help dye eggs."

Verity sat down on the broad wooden steps of the shop, opened the paper bag from the grocery store, and held it out. "May I buy you a Coke? And ask you some questions?"

"Maybe you'd better tell me why, first," said Claire, but she sat down. Verity met the clear gray gaze, decided this was a time for the truth, and told it.

Satisfied, Claire explained that Emma, age eight, had met Sylvie at the information center at the nearby Burlington campground, where Emma went regularly to visit the display of local wildlife. "They're stuffed, or maybe freeze-dried: a fawn, an otter, a red-tailed hawk, lots of other critters. Emma loves them all, and always points out the sign saying they were *not* killed for the display, but met their fates some other way," Claire added.

Claire, walking to the information center to pick up Emma, had met Lily and Sylvie, and pressed by her daughter, invited them to visit. Lily stayed only long enough for a cup of tea, Sylvie for several hours that day and the next. "Emma liked Sylvie a lot. She was sorry they had to leave, and really pleased when they came back two or three weeks later."

On that second visit Lily and Sylvie had actually taken a site in the campground; but they'd disappeared after one day, with no word as to their destination. "I was mildly pissed," said Claire. "I'd fed Sylvie several meals, made an effort to be nice to both of them—not that it was a hardship, but for Emma's sake I wish they had at least come to say good-bye."

Verity got a pocket calendar from her wallet, and she and Claire worked out that Lily and Sylvie's first appearance had been on Thursday, April 1, and April 2, Good Friday. Their brief return was almost three weeks later, on either Monday, April 19, or Tuesday, April 20.

"The mom, Lily, at first struck me as short on smarts," said Claire, "but later I decided she was mostly tired. In my day—or usually night—job I'm a nurse, and I've seen a lot of stressed-out single moms hit times when they simply don't track.

"Sylvie, I liked as much as Emma did," she went on. "Smart, funny, probably full of hell when she's not trying to take care of her mom. And I'm afraid that's all I have to tell you."

As the two of them got to their feet, Verity reached out to shake Claire's hand and changed her mind, hugging the other woman instead. "Thank you! You've made our day worthwhile."

"Glad I could help. Good luck. And please, could you let me know how this all comes out? I really hate suspense."

13

Red Bluff lived up to Patience's sole memory of the place: hot as hell. And humid, too, under a slightly overcast sky; it was a river town, after all. Patience took the first off-ramp into town and stopped at the first likely-looking deli. There she ordered a turkey sandwich to go and asked directions to the nearest park.

At a picnic table set on a grassy slope overlooking the Sacramento River, she washed her early lunch down with a bottle of mineral water (wouldn't want to breathe beer on a bunch of elderly Baptist ladies) and looked over her notes. Edna Mangrum's current residence was only a short distance from the park, and lunch there would be at the coffee stage by twelve-thirty. Patience's green-and-white striped chambray shirtwaist was eminently respectable or would be when she refastened its belt; and she'd adapt her demeanor as necessary once she'd met Edna. Onward and upward, then, and thank God and the Ford Motor Company for the air-conditioning in her truck.

The Red Bluff Baptist Seniors' Home was a single-story stucco building laid out on its deep lot like an H with two crossbars. The street-facing crossbar, fronted by a visitors' parking lot, contained lobby and offices; the rear one housed a cafeteria and a recreation/meeting room. Between the two crossbars, a roof of slats and vines and a pebble-banked pond with a pump-induced gurgle made a pleasant summer spot for old people to sit.

"Nasty damp place," said Edna Mangrum as Patience pushed her wheelchair along the covered walkway. "And there's a couple of filthy cats think the place is their private sandbox. Here's my door."

Edna's door opened into a studio apartment with a bedroom alcove, a kitchen alcove, a bathroom with an extra-wide door, and a sitting-room space of perhaps ten by fourteen. With carpet, drapes, and upholstered furniture in muted earth tones, the place had the feel of a mid-priced motel. The only personal items in sight were a leather-bound Bible, a stack of desktop-printed church magazines, a large, expensive television set, and several framed photographs of a seriously overweight pug dog. Patience found it hard, or maybe sad, to believe that Edna Mangrum had lived in this room for three years.

Edna, at something like seventy years of age, was carrying— wheeling—more than two hundred pounds around on a small-to- medium frame; sparse white hair stood up like curly wires around her head, and her pouched eyes were a dark brown that had grayed at iris's edge. Now she fanned her flushed and sweating face with one hand, reached with the other to turn the air conditioner lower, then sat back in her chair and glowered at Patience. "That girl from the office says you're a detective. If you're any good, I might pay you to find somebody."

Patience sat down in the green-and-brown tweed armchair. "Have you lost someone? I'm sorry to hear that."

"Well, I don't know. Maybe lost, more likely dead. Could you find that out for me?"

"I can probably tell you how to find out for yourself. Is it some- one related to you, a daughter perhaps?"

Edna said something spitty that sounded like "Pah!" "We never had no kids, Max and me. Didn't really want none, at least I didn't. Kids are just grief. Say, would you reach over and push the button on that coffee machine? They charge extra for coffee in the cafeteria, and it tastes like dishwater anyway."

Patience got up and went to the kitchen counter, to turn on the waiting coffeemaker. "Is it Max you're interested in finding?" she asked. "Because if your husband is missing, you can get official help in locating him."

Edna's flushed face grew ruddier. "We ain't...he's not my husband no more. Divorced. Seven, eight years ago. I just sometimes wonder what happened to the old fart." She pulled a handkerchief from a

pocket and wiped her face. "But he's not worth spending money on. Why are you here bothering me, anyway?"

The coffee machine was sputtering noisily to the end of its cycle. Patience took a mug from a wooden tree on the counter, waited for the last few gasps of the machine, then lifted the pot free and poured the mug three-quarters full. "Do you take sugar or cream, Edna?"

"Sugar. Two heaping spoons."

"What about a little something extra? I have a small bottle of good rum in my handbag, something I always carry when I'm traveling." Patience had quizzed the manager, Mrs. Brink, about Edna's preferred indulgences.

"Well, I don't usually. Pastor Blomsted used to be death on drinking. 'Course, he's gone now."

Patience took this for acceptance, and poured a short ounce of aged rum into the steaming liquid. The point was to make Edna feel relaxed and indulged, not to get her drunk.

"Well. Thank you, ma'am," said Edna. "Have a cup yourself, why don't you."

Patience took her time selecting a mug, filling it, adding the barest smidgen of rum. Stirring. Carrying it to her chair. "Oh, you're nearly finished," she said to Edna. "Here, let me boost that a little."

"Mm," said Edna. Definitely not a refusal.

"I've been avoiding what I'm sure will be a painful subject," Patience said, when she handed the replenished mug to Edna. "The reason I'm here is that a friend of hers has hired me to find your foster daughter, Lily Costello."

Edna hunched her shoulders and drew her head down and in, looking for all the world like a furious troll. "Don't use the word 'daughter' to me about that slut! You can just get on your way out of here. Wait a minute," she said, narrowed eyes widening. "That Lily's got no friends except him. It's Max hired you, ain't it?"

Patience shook her head. "I can't tell you who my client is, but I can say it's not your husband."

Edna's eyes were suspiciously shiny now, the tip of her nose reddening. "Sometimes, and I know it's a sin, I wish I'd just of left him alone about the whole business. God in His wisdom made men need

more of *that* than any one woman wants, and anyway that girl had learned real early how to do stuff men like, social worker told us that when we got her. What harm could Max of done her, is what I ask myself.

"See, she's a pretty thing, too dark in my opinion, but Max was crazy about her from the start and she just twisted him around her finger, could make him do anything she wanted. Whatever happened was probably all her idea in the first place. And if I hadn't got silly and made a fuss to Pastor Blomsted, I wouldn't be alone and lonely now in my old age."

Real tears were dripping now. Patience, teeth clenched so hard her jaw ached, got to her feet to retrieve a box of tissues from the counter. She set the box in Edna's lap, retreated to her chair, and took a deep breath.

"I understand how you feel, Edna. I'm alone myself, a widow." Two truthful statements bearing no relationship to each other.

"The little slut is a liar, too," said Edna, and paused to sniff. "Before, she just kept her head down and didn't deny nothing. Now, ten years later, she has the nerve to look me right in the eye and say Max never once touched her that way."

"When did Lily come to see you?" asked Patience in her softest voice.

"Oh, well. It was sometime in the week after Easter. Is there any more of that coffee?"

"I think so." Edna was frugal with her coffee; the pot contained just one more cup. Pouring, enlivening the stuff with sugar and rum, Patience turned the picture of Lily this way and that in her mind. Who was she and what had really happened to her, now and ten years ago and in the years before that?

"Why do you suppose she came?" Foolish question, and a waste of what was probably diminishing time here. Patience handed over the mug and sat down, an expression of polite interest pasted on her face.

"Hah." Edna took a sip, sighed. "Seems like she heard somewhere about the money. That Max left for her, I don't know how much because the pastor won't talk about it, but I know it should've been

mine. Then I could've had a real apartment, with a separate bedroom. Those're much nicer."

Money. Pastor. Here, presumably. Not Blomsted, who was "gone." "I'm sorry about that, Edna. Do you have any idea where she, Lily, went from here? Where she might be now?"

Edna sat back and folded her hands around the mug in her lap. "Somebody is paying you to find that out. Seems like you ought to pay me. Maybe about...a hundred dollars?"

Clearly the rum had not addled Edna's mind. "A hundred is more than I or my client can manage, Edna. There are probably other people in town, like the minister, who'll be more willing to help."

"But you're right here. And I know one thing nobody else knows. Seventy-five?"

Patience mentally reviewed the contents of her wallet. "Fifty, if what you tell me is useful."

Edna sat straighter and lifted her chin, her eyes bright now with something other than tears. "She wanted to straighten her life out, Lily said. Start over clean with everybody. Hah," she added in comment, then paused for a sip of coffee. "Me, for one. And Max, she was looking for Max. The slut."

"And?"

"And the other one, her foster sister I guess you'd say. Marsha."

"And did she see Marsha?"

Edna's fat shoulders lifted in a shrug. "She meant to try, for whatever good it will do her. Marsha's a real strict Christian, and she's probably just as firm against adultery and fornication now as she was ten, twelve years ago."

"And where would Lily find Marsha now?"

Edna had a gold canine tooth that gleamed as she grinned and held out one hand, palm up.

Patience reached for her bag, took out her wallet and extracted two twenties and a ten. She looked at them, looked at Edna, put one bill in the breast pocket of her own dress so that its corner peeked out, and offered the other two. Edna's reaching hand hesitated, then reached again, grabbed and folded over the bills, and slid them out of sight in the voluminous skirt of her dress.

"Marsha is living with a bunch of other Christian families on a kind of farm, sounds like, real near the coast."

Near the coast? For fifty dollars? Patience raised her eyebrows. "I beg your pardon?"

"I never got the address. Maybe they got no address. But I get a card from her now and then, with a note and sometimes a picture of her kids. Had one postmarked Ferndale, I believe that's the old Victorian town got broken up so bad in an earthquake some years back. And one from someplace I never heard of called Redway."

"Would you let me see those cards?"

"Can't." Edna's voice held an edge of satisfaction: Gotcha! "Lily took 'em."

Patience made a note of the names: Ferndale and Redway. "You haven't hit fifty dollars yet, Edna."

"Well. A long time ago, the year Marsha graduated I think it was, there was this evangelist come to town. He was a real lively preacher, and Max and me and the girls went to services in his tent down by the river. The girls went to special young people's services all week." She paused for a sip from her coffee mug, her eyes watching Patience over its rim.

"End of the week, he folded up his tent and left town real fast; I heard a girl from Marsha's class left with him. Marsha was real upset, mostly because it wasn't her. And word at the church was that hardly any of the money we all offered up ever found its way to God's work."

Feeling a bit like a dog trainer, Patience took the remaining twenty-dollar bill from her pocket and held it in her hand.

Edna sighed loudly. "In one of her letters Marsha mentioned a Brother Daniel as leader of her group. That evangelist's name as I remember it was Daniel, Daniel Jones."

Jones. Wonderful, thought Patience. She handed the old woman the last bill and added the name to her notes. "Thank you, Edna. Incidentally, has Lily's husband come to see you recently?"

"Which one?" snorted the old woman. "Not that I'd know the difference, any more than Lily ever did, the slut. I just chased the pair of 'em off whenever they come sniffing around back when she was

living in my house, and I'd do the same today. They'd know better than to pester me, specially here; we got security guards.

"Now I got to lie down for my nap. Make sure the lock is set when you go out." Edna handed her empty coffee mug to Patience, turned her chair a quarter turn, and stopped. "If you should by any chance run into Max, when you're out looking for Lily...could you maybe let me know? I'd give you back your money. Or whatever's right."

"If I should encounter Max, I will let you know." Patience experienced a moment's yearning for her own youth, when judgments were clear-cut and dislikes untempered by pity. To prove she was not turning into a wimp, on her way to the door she lifted a copy from the stack of church magazines and shoved it into her handbag.

"Oh, good, you're home." Patience settled herself more firmly against her motel pillows and silently attributed her statement of the obvious to a long, hot but productive day, or perhaps the wine she'd had with dinner.

"Having busted my butt all day, Mother dear, I decided I was entitled to a little reward. So I went down to The Spot for a couple of beers, ran into Johnny Hebert, and really skinned him at darts. But where the hell are you? Ralph and I were getting worried."

Oh good, thought Patience—not about the worry, but the darts-and-beer evening and the cheerful note in Verity's voice. "I'm in a nice motel in Red Bluff. By the time I'd finished here, I decided I was too old and too tired for another four hours on the road. I've had a shower, and dinner, and now I'll sip my Macallan while you make your report to your employer."

"Clink of glasses here, Ma. We did good, Harley and I. We found a person who had definitely seen Lily and Sylvie, twice." Making something of a story of it, she told Patience what they had learned. "The second time, they turned up one day and left the next, without a word. Claire was a tad irritated about that," Verity added, "since she'd put herself out to be helpful, babysitting and such."

"I think Lily was too intent on her purpose to bother with manners or gratitude. She must have been on her way here, to Red Bluff,

on that Good Friday stop." Patience nudged the pillows into a better shape, picked up her drink, and began a report of her own successes. Her pleasure in her accomplishment began to fade, however, as she related the story of Lily Medina Simonov Costello's life as told by Edna Mangrum, and later confirmed and embellished by Mrs. Arne Blomsted, widow of Trinity Baptist's former pastor and still editor of the church magazine.

"Nothing ever broke right for Lily, Verity. No father, her mother died when she was four or five, and she came into the care of an aunt and a series of 'uncles' who abused her sexually. Social service people finally took her away and put her into foster care with Max and Edna Mangrum." Patience paused for a sip of The Macallan, which didn't taste quite as good as usual.

"Oh, shit. Let me guess," said Verity.

"When Lily was seventeen, Edna went to the pastor of Trinity Baptist and told him that Max and Lily had been having sexual relations for years. Max denied it, Lily clammed up. The final arrangement was that no one would file charges so long as Lily moved out and Max had no further contact with her, ever."

"Rotten bastard," said Verity.

"I suppose," said Patience, and then hurried on before Verity could reply. "Anyway, Lily quickly married David Simonov, a move that could have put her on the right track; I looked up the Simonovs and Costellos, since I was here, and apparently David's people were decent enough. His mother died recently and his father moved to Oregon."

"And the Costellos were not decent?"

"The Costellos are gone, too, to their former neighbors' delight. The word was that the father had some minor Mob connection; he and his three sons were known as brawlers and bad people to cross. Devlin was the youngest, and the smartest."

"Smart is clearly what Lily was not," said Verity in grim tones. "Or lucky, either."

"Wait, there was one bit of luck," said Patience. "Eventually Max divorced Edna and left town. Some two years later he came back from somewhere in Florida just to set up a good-sized trust account

for Lily, with the Baptist minister as trustee. Lily could have the money if she came to ask for it. Oh, and after ten years it would revert to the church."

"Oh ho, trying to buy his way out of his sins," said Verity.

"Well, we should probably hope it worked. Pastor Blomsted's widow, who has been trustee since her husband's death, believes Max is dead." Mrs. Blomsted had said as much to Lily as well as to Edna Mangrum; Edna, she told Patience, simply refused to believe her. "The main thing is, Lily got her money, or at least she went to the bank and took control," Patience added, and had another, better-tasting sip of single malt.

"And has handed it all right over to some renegade evangelist named Brother Daniel," Verity said with a sigh.

"That's certainly a possibility."

"So. What do we do now? Since it looks like she's okay?"

"She may be," Patience admitted. "But we were hired to find her. I think we should stay with the job until we hear from David Simonov, at least."

"Why did I know you'd say that?" There was a rustle of paper at Verity's end of the line. "Okay, here's the map. Between Ferndale and Redway we have...well. The Lost Coast. That's interesting. I've never been out there."

"Nor have I. I suppose it's likely that the foster sister's farm or commune or whatever is there somewhere."

"I'll go have a look," said Verity. "In the morning, after my stuff arrives from the City; it was due tonight, postponed till first thing tomorrow."

"I suppose you and Harley could go. I won't get home much before noon."

"Harley's classes start tomorrow. But I'll drive his truck. I lent him my Alfa tonight, for a date. Turns out dates are not frequent or casual events in Harley's life; he was so good today I thought he deserved something to give him a little edge.

"Oh!" she went on. "Meant to tell you, the crime rate in Port Silva is getting out of hand. Somebody tried to steal the truck tonight."

Patience sat up so quickly she nearly spilled her drink. "Harley's truck? From our house?"

"Nope, from downtown. I'd parked it around the corner from The Spot. But I'd brought Ralph along for an outing after a boring, lonely day; he was in the cab, and he set up such a roar that whoever it was just left the door open and ran off. By the time we got there, nobody was around."

"You should tell Hank."

"Mom, Johnny was right there. A cop's a cop, right?"

"If you say so, dear. Verity, if you do go on your own tomorrow, be extra cautious. I've heard that there are some strange people out on the Lost Coast."

"Strange how?"

"Strange in that they place an unusually high value on their privacy. So I wouldn't flash any private investigator cards without being quite sure who you're talking to. Or maybe not at all."

"Yes, ma'am. Sleep well, Ma, and I'll see you tomorrow. Or maybe the next day, depending."

14

The dark was the worst part. At a sudden rustle and snuffle, Sylvie quickly changed her mind: the dark was not the worst, those noises were.

But because it was so dark, black with nothing at all for her eyes to pick out, she couldn't tell for sure where the noise was coming from. Off to her left, she thought, along the far wall.

The door was in the center of the wall over there, across from this corner where she had pushed herself as far back as possible. She was pretty sure it was there but couldn't see it; it was closed and fastened shut from the outside with a piece of wood that turned on a big nail and there wasn't any light out there, either, to show around its edges. Unless somebody missed her and came looking—not very likely, who would care?—she'd be here until morning.

A grunting groan and an angry snort, a heavy thud, and the wooden building shuddered and squeaked and Sylvie made herself smaller in her corner, wrapping cold arms tighter around updrawn legs, hiding her face against her knees. Would it wake all the way up and remember she was in here? Come to get her?

Squeals and more rustling and scratching sounds, little things moving in the straw not the big one. Sylvie tucked her sticky cold hands under her arms and listened so hard she thought her ears must be bending out. Another flop, a sound like a huge snore, more rustlings and squeaks. Maybe, big as those babies were getting, the mother pig was not so willing to have them crowd her or suck on her, was pushing them away in her sleep.

If she was asleep. Earlier, crawling around and feeling the walls in

an attempt to find a way out of the low, narrow shed, Sylvie had stumbled over one or maybe more than one of the baby pigs, and their squeals had brought the mother to her feet with a squeal of her own, a roar. Sylvie had thrown herself backwards, scrabbling across the straw-covered dirt floor until her back met the wall, this corner, where she'd huddled, biting her tongue to keep from screaming. Be quiet, Aunt Marsha had said, be very very quiet like a mouse or you'll upset the mother pig and she'll eat you, pigs do that they really do I've seen it. Especially little girls.

Now Sylvie put her hands over her ears to drown out the sound of Aunt Marsha's voice, and the sleeping sounds of the pigs. The pigs were the scariest thing, really, she sometimes forgot that and worried—fussed, Lily would say—about less scary stuff like dark. Or cold.

The smell, at first so awful that she'd thought she might throw up and then what would the pigs do? The smell for some reason wasn't so big and thick now. She knew there was pig poop all over her, on her feet and legs and her dress, on her hands—she hadn't been able to keep out of it in the dark. Now she could hardly smell anything. But she tried to remember to keep her hands off her face, to wipe her nose or her eyes on her arm.

Rustlings and small gruntings; some of the babies were not far from her, she thought, maybe moved away when the momma growled at them.

They were near enough so she could hear them breathe. She thought she could feel some heat from them, probably sleeping together in a bunch to keep warm. She wished she could be in a bunch like that, maybe just crawl over and lie down with them.

But if they cried, and woke up their mother… Sylvie pushed herself firmly back into her corner, the wall at both sides splintery and rough but nothing could get her from behind. Knees up close, she tugged the skirt of her wet and filthy dress down and tucked it tight around her feet, bent her head and pulled the neck of the dress over her chin and nose so her breath would warm her body. Reminded herself not to go to sleep, or she might fall over and make a noise and then what?

The Community members—eleven adults, twelve-year-old Jacob Jones and sixteen-year-old Lisa Ives—had spent more than two hours discussing, among other things, the Epistle of Paul the Apostle to the Romans. Now, at almost eleven P.M., nearly everyone had gone to bed.

In the big lantern-lit kitchen Sister Catherine Ives slapped the last of the once-risen bread dough into loaf shape, wrapped the loaf tightly in plastic, then took it and seven others to the freezer where she had already cleared a space for them.

"There," she said, and swiped a long, freckled forearm across her forehead, pushing aside several carroty-red curls that had escaped her headband. "You need some help, Sister?" she asked of the birdlike brown-haired woman who had washed and dried the coffee things and was now applying a dish towel to the first of a half dozen glass lamp chimneys.

"Heavens, no. You sit down for a bit, or go on to bed."

"What this place needs is a dishwasher," said Sister Catherine, subsiding restlessly into a chair.

"I don't think those run on propane," said Sister Sandra with a grin. "Besides, I don't mind washing dishes. Hardscrabble farm I grew up on, we didn't even have running water or indoor toilets, never mind a nice big refrigerator and freezer."

"Oh, it's pretty nice here, mostly," said Sister Catherine, stretching her legs out and massaging the back of her neck. "Except I sure could do with a cigarette and a beer about now. These damn... darned Bible study nights make my butt as tired as my head."

"Um." Sister Sandra polished on.

"I mean, why don't we just let the men have their little arguments about laws and predestination and stuff like that by themselves? They don't give a...hoot what women think, don't even want us to talk."

"True," said the other woman.

"So okay, I get born again," said Catherine. "And I think, now I got the Ten Commandments and I got Jesus, that's it. I'm in. What I want to know, what's predestination got to do with it?"

"It's complicated," said Sandra, who, like several of the others at Community, sprang from Primitive Baptist roots.

"Well, even I can see that. But..."

"Sister Catherine?"

The women lifted their heads like a pair of startled deer and saw Brother Benjamin standing in the doorway, his small daughter in his arms. Catherine was on her feet at once; Benjamin Carter was both handsome and sad, a combination she'd been a sucker for in her bad old days. "Janey. Are you sick?" She reached out as if to lay a hand on the little girl's forehead, but Janey's father shook his head.

"She's not sick, she's upset. She woke up with a bad dream, and her friend Sylvie wasn't there."

"Oh, Sylvie. Probably she's in the bathroom."

Benjamin shook his head again. "I checked there. I've looked all over the house. Sylvie isn't here."

"Janey, don't you worry," crooned Catherine. "Honestly, that child," she went on in an undertone to Benjamin. "She's probably out prowling, the way she was Sunday night."

"I had a quick look around outside. Didn't see her," said Benjamin flatly. "And it appears that everybody else is in bed or getting there, except for you two."

Sister Sandra, who'd been motionless and silent during the others' exchange, now pulled off her apron and tossed it at a chair. "If Naomi wakes up, she'll be worried, too. I'd better go check on her," she said over her shoulder as she hurried out.

"Thought everybody had gone to bed. Is there any coffee cake left?" Brother Fred Simms had come through from the meeting room, where he'd been stacking chairs and putting things away.

"Sylvie Costello isn't in her bed," Benjamin told him.

"She's just…"

Benjamin cut off Catherine's remark. "Whether she's running away, or hiding, or lost, she shouldn't be out in the dark alone. For one thing, the temperature was in the forties last night. And coyotes probably wouldn't bother her, but I think there might be a mountain lion in the neighborhood."

"Oh, my!" breathed Catherine.

Fred hunched his shoulders and frowned. "That kid is nothing but trouble. But I guess we better go look for her."

"I'll put Janey back in bed," said Benjamin. "And ask Sister

Sandra to stay with her and Naomi. Sister Catherine, could you knock on doors and call out anybody who's still dressed? And Brother Fred, maybe you'd round up some flashlights?"

Sylvie was very very cold. She was having trouble keeping her teeth from chattering, and was afraid the noise would disturb the sleeping pigs. And there was that other noise, too—the howl building in her chest and pushing at her throat and trying to get out. She'd swallowed to keep it in until she had no spit left to swallow; she didn't want to put her dirty hands against her mouth, or any piece of her filthy dress.

Suddenly the big pig moved and grunted, and Sylvie flung her head back and hit the wall and bit her tongue so hard she could almost see the pain, like a bright light. Where are you Lily why are you letting this happen to me?

The pain in her tongue was making her head ring, as if people were talking somewhere far off. She swallowed salty liquid, choked and tried to be quiet about it, heard sounds again. Outside. Fixed her eyes to the place in the blackness where she thought the shed door was. Heard a real voice now, someone calling her name. Saw a bright line make the shape of the door and then go away, blackness again.

"Sylvie?"

Forgetting the pigs, she crawled forward on her hands and knees and threw herself headlong toward where the door had been. "LilyLilyLilyLily!" she shrieked, and came up hard against rough wood and pounded with her fists as the pigs, too, began to shriek.

The door burst open under her fists and she fell out and tried to crawl forward, knees tangling in the skirt of her dress. "LilyLilyLily!"

"Oh sweet Jesus!"

"Sylvie, how did you get in there?"

"Don't touch her, she's filthy!"

"Shut up, all of you," said Brother Benjamin softly as he bent and scooped her up.

She curled her arms around his neck, wrapped her legs around his body. "Oh, I'm all dirty," she whispered into the collar of his shirt. "I wet myself, I bit my tongue."

He held her tightly as he strode out of the pen surrounding the pig shed. "Somebody get the gate," he called, and then, to Sylvie, "Shh. We'll fix you a nice hot bath. Janey is waiting for you, she was worried."

"What kind of unholy mischief was she up to, creeping into the pig house in the middle of the night?" Sylvie, still shaking from cold and terror, recognized Brother Daniel's big voice. "And why did she lock herself in?"

"Don't be ridiculous." This in the snapping tones of Sister Alice, Brother Daniel's wife and a person who had no time for nonsense. "She might have gone in to play with the little pigs; that sow is good-tempered and wouldn't have bothered her. But somebody else had to lock her in."

"But she wouldn't have, Eddie says she's terrified of the pigs." Sister Catherine, Sylvie thought but kept her head down.

"Eddie likes to tease her, doesn't he? Probably he just meant it as a joke."

"No!" Sylvie pulled her face away from Brother Benjamin's warm neck and then lifted one hand against beams of light aimed at her. Nobody was moving as the lights fell away to make pools on the ground, and she saw feet in slippers or unlaced shoes, legs in pajamas, robes or coats over. Heads only shapes, faces not clear, but she knew who'd asked that last question.

"Not Eddie, it was her, it was Aunt Marsha that made me go in there. And she locked the door."

"You're a liar, little girl." Brother Fred's harsh squeak reminded Sylvie of the pigs, and she gripped Brother Benjamin tighter. "You don't like Marsha because she sees you for the evil little demon you are."

"Sylvie?" said Brother Benjamin quietly.

"She did. She said I had to be quiet or the pigs would eat me."

"She never did!" A woman's voice, Sylvie couldn't tell whose.

"Oh yes. She said it was devils in me, Jesus drove the devils out of the bad man and into the pigs so maybe he would do that to me, my devils."

For a long moment no one spoke. Then Sister Catherine said, in

a slow, shaky voice, "The story about the Gadarene swine? I think the children had that, in Sunday school, not very long ago. Probably she heard it there."

"Maybe," said Brother Benjamin, his arms tightening in what felt to Sylvie like a hug. "We can talk about it later. Tomorrow. Right now this child needs a bath and a good night's sleep."

15

She would kill him. She would take that big revolver and… No. She'd unearth the old sixteen-gauge, must be shells around somewhere, load it, and drive down and wait just inside the front door. Hi there honey welcome home *Blam blam!* Both barrels!

"Uh, lady? Listen, I gotta be going. You sure you're all right?"

The truck driver's voice finally penetrated the red fog of fury that had wrapped itself around Verity. She blinked hard and focused on the long-nosed, unshaven face, creased now in a frown that narrowed his pale blue eyes to slits. With his wiry gray-brown hair combed back and up into a kind of crest, he looked like a large, worried rooster.

"Lady?"

"I'm sorry," she said, and cast a glance around them, at the litter of cardboard and paper and…junk. "You're absolutely sure your company did not do the packing?"

"Ma'am, like it says on the bill of lading, it was all wrapped up and taped tight when I picked it up. Guy said he did it himself." He shrugged as he surveyed the littered yard. "Don't see why he bothered."

"He wanted to be sure I'd be surprised," said Verity.

"Huh? Oh, I get it. He's your old man, right?"

Verity ignored him, blowing out a long breath as she looked at her belongings, at the rolltop desk with each slat in its roller front shattered by what must have been a marching succession of separate hammer blows: *crunch crunch crunch*. At the cherry-wood tea cart

with a wide pale streak across its shiny dark surface where he had apparently poured bleach and let it stand; at the little antique rocker with its caned seat and back slashed into stiff ribbons.

"Poor guy must of felt really bad to do something like that," said the driver. "But listen, you're lucky. I've known guys, their old lady dumps 'em, they take it out on her face instead of her furniture."

And wouldn't Theodore Blake bloody Esquire be *pissed* beyond bearing to hear his behavior being discussed and rated on a machismo scale of one to ten by a truck driver. Verity felt just a tiny bit better.

"Mr., um, Gus," she said, peering at the name on his shirt pocket, "if you'll wait here just a minute, please?"

"Sure." He pushed his hands into the back pockets of his jeans and watched her run toward the house, long legs flying, hair flashing fire in the morning sun. *Guy had that and didn't hang onto it, he was stone stupid besides being a cheapskate prick.*

Verity found the Pentax camera and a notebook, and hurried back outside. "Just stand over there out of the way," she said, and began snapping pictures—six in all, and then she swung around for a quick shot of the driver just before he could get his hand up in front of his face. She set the camera atop the battered desk and flipped open the notebook, to scrawl a few lines.

"Here," she said, and thrust the notebook at him.

He took two quick steps back, shaking his head. "No ma'am, I don't sign stuff."

"It simply says that you delivered to me the goods that you had picked up already packed from this address in San Francisco; and you saw me open the sealed packing and find damaged furniture. Of which I have just taken photos."

He was still shaking his head.

Verity sighed. "Come on, it's simply the truth. Otherwise, I'll have to sue you or your company for the damage to my belongings."

"Christ, lady, you're gonna cost me my job," he said resignedly. He took the notebook, scrawled a signature, handed the book back. "Can I go now?"

"If you'll wait a minute, I'll make you a copy."

"Never mind, I'd sooner just forget all about it."

"I don't blame you," said Verity. She fished a folded bill from her pocket and handed it to him. "Thank you for your cooperation."

He unfolded the twenty and grinned. "I guess it's my pleasure."

It took him several swings and corrections to get his rig turned around. As the rear of the trailer disappeared from the end of the driveway, Verity unlocked the door of the studio and began shoving everything inside. She did not want Patience to come upon this mess; she didn't want to look at it any longer herself, or even think about it.

She found the sixteen-gauge shotgun, her father's old bird gun, in the closet in the studio. Verity looked at it, hefted it thoughtfully. Envisioned Ted's face going green as he found himself facing the twin barrels with *her* furious face looming above them. Then maybe, instead of blasting him to bloody shreds, she'd content herself with blowing noisy hell out of his stupid BMW.

Ah, Teddy, we're a wicked lot. Killers of antique rocking chairs and expensive cars. About to return the weapon to its place, she remembered that she had a real job to do, alone and in an isolated place. Might be a good idea to take this along.

In the house she went on with preparations for her trip upcoast. Cooler chest with ice, water, fruit. Hiking boots and fleece vest and Gore-Tex jacket in case she needed to do some exploring on foot and in weather. Binoculars. Notebook; she would not, she'd decided, take the useful but obviously businesslike and expensive laptop. She put business cards and several of the photos of Lily in a zip compartment of her shoulder bag; rolled clean underpants around clean socks and tucked them and a toothbrush into another zippered niche.

Verity put her gear, including her old down sleeping bag in its stuffsack and a plastic tarp for groundsheet, in the truck, and then pulled the truck-bed cover into place and snapped it down. She stowed the empty shotgun behind the seat; she'd buy shells somewhere along the way, lock them in the utility box in the back of the truck, and thus be a law-abiding person. Honest and upright and true—and at least potentially armed.

She scrawled a note to Patience sketching her route and plans and promising to check in later, and stuck it under the salmon magnet on

the fridge. She set out fresh water for Ralph, who abandoned his travel hopes with a sigh and went to lie on his blanket. Then, keys in hand and bag over her shoulder, she called San Francisco.

"Cory, I'm going to insist that the house be sold," she told her attorney. "Twenty-five hundred square feet, in prime condition in that neighborhood—it should go for a million and a half, maybe more. I want my half as soon as possible, and I won't carry a mortgage. I'll explain why later."

"No explanation necessary." Cory Benitez's cool voice made Verity feel almost like a rational human being. "I always thought a mortgage was a bad idea; just another string for a jerk to jerk. I'll have an appraiser over there this afternoon."

The drive north, by now boringly familiar, nonetheless demanded close attention from any driver who didn't wish to wind up in the ocean or plastered across the grille of a lumber truck. For the first few miles Verity concentrated on the road and Harley's Toyota truck. When she finally felt she could spare an edge of her mind for something else, she gave it over to the task before her: winkling Lily Costello out of the peculiar landscape known to northern Californians as the Lost Coast.

Last night, looking over several maps, she'd estimated that this odd chunk of land, including California's westernmost bulge at Cape Mendocino, was roughly seventy north-to-south miles long by twenty miles wide. Then she'd called northcoast hunter, fisherman, and amateur historian Hank Svoboda, who told her that the area, geologically unstable and seasonally rain-drenched at more than one hundred inches a year, had given builders of California's state-long Coast Highway such pause that they'd simply cut it off, swinging eastward just above Rockport to join 101. Thus, the Lost—or abandoned—Coast

According to Hank, the area had been a bountiful home to the Sinkyone and the Mattole Indian tribes. The white man, having disposed one way or another of the Indians, had replaced them in the Mattole River valley with orchards and livestock, in the more southerly area with lumbering.

But the road builders were right; the landscape was ill-suited to modern transportation and the coast was so treacherous that access even by air or water was difficult. Creeks were everywhere; the King Range reared to four thousand feet within three miles of the black sand coast; the famed San Andreas Fault lay just offshore. Most of the precipitous and haphazardly paved roads were traversable by sedans in summer only, by four-wheel-drive vehicles if at all during the rest of the year.

At present, so far as Hank knew, the Lost Coast was home to two publicly owned areas—the Sinkyone Wilderness State Park and the King Range National Conservation Area—as well as to a little ranching, deer and black bear and a herd of Roosevelt elk, summer hikers and campers, and unnumbered reclusive types who wanted only to be let be. Unfortunately for the present investigation, Hank had not wandered in that direction for years and had no current contacts there. Most of the Lost Coast, in fact, was in Humboldt rather than Mendocino County.

Verity thought the place sounded absolutely wonderful. Some day after this job was finished, she'd promote a long-term loan of his truck from Harley, or even buy one of her own. Get herself a fresh new sleeping bag, a one-person pop tent with a rainfly, and all the gear—tiny campstove, nested metal pans and dishes, the small water-purifying pump she'd read about. A few good paperback books. No television or CD player, maybe just a small radio for emergency information.

Verity was modifying and refining her list when she passed the remains of Rockport and approached the final eastward bend of Highway One. And right there was a turnoff: the unpaved county road that became Usal Road, leading to the Usal Beach campground in the Sinkyone Wilderness. Leading to the Lost Coast. She touched her brake, and drew squeals and several honks from behind.

"Not yet, dummy," she said aloud, putting her foot back on the accelerator and composing herself for a further fifty miles of travel. She couldn't search the whole area blind; she'd decided earlier to start from Weott, the place Lily had last been seen. Ask people there about the Lost Coast, about a religious commune. Find at least the hint of a real trail.

Lily Costello's face, infinitely weary and marked with a hopeless kind of determination, surfaced briefly from its permanent shadowed niche in the back of Verity's mind. Lily, too, had looked for peace out here in this solitary place; it hardly seemed decent to be tracking her as if she were prey of some kind. Never mind, Verity said to herself and to Lily. I'm new at this, probably won't find you anyway. And if I do, I won't tell.

There were two women in the registration booth at Burlington Campground; the curly-haired blonde smiled and shrugged as Verity approached. "I showed around the picture you left yesterday, but nobody remembered them."

"I appreciate your efforts," said Verity. "And I have a new question. Does either of you know anything about a religious commune out on the Lost Coast?"

The rangers exchanged glances and then shook their heads in near-unison. "There are no religious cults on state park land," said the blonde.

"And on private land, it's none of our business," said her partner. "Talk to the CAMP guys; they might have noticed loud praying while they were looking around for pot farms."

It took Verity a moment to realize that the woman meant not camping, but the state Campaign Against Marijuana Planting. Not a likely source of information for her present inquiry.

"Okay. Thanks."

"Oh, wait." The blonde slapped herself on the forehead. "I forgot about the monastery. Out near Whitethorn, or maybe Briceland. Anyway, it's on private land and it's run by this group of nuns, people go there on retreats."

Verity thanked them and set off for the park's visitor information center, unsure what to do with this last bit of information. Lily had told Pastor Harding that she wished she could be a nun; but he'd seen it as a cry of complaint rather than intention. And it didn't seem likely one would take a seven-year-old child to a Catholic retreat.

The woman at the information desk knew of the nuns, also. "But I don't know much else about what's out there," she said in a hushed

voice. "Probably perfectly nice people, but I'm told by tourists that they're very *watchful*, you know; stop along the road for any reason at all, and first thing you know someone in a dusty truck will pull up and look you over and ask if you're lost.

"If you do decide to drive out there, you should probably stay right on the main road," she added, and went on to help a sun-burned, shorts-clad man who had several booklets in one hand and a twenty-dollar-bill in the other.

None of the other workers in the information center had anything to offer; most were summer help only, and lived elsewhere. Might turn into a blind search after all, Verity told herself glumly as she climbed back into her truck.

There were half a dozen vehicles in the parking lot at the Weott store. Reminding herself that it might be a long time between restaurants or even grocery stores, Verity went inside and collected more mineral water, a chunk of cheddar cheese, a small jar of mustard, and a loaf of sourdough bread in a plastic wrapper. The friendly man behind the counter had been replaced by an equally friendly woman; she knew, too, of the nuns, but nothing about any cult or commune. "Not to say there might not be one, or several," she said cheerfully.

Verity thanked her, paid for her purchases, and headed out the door and around the corner, past the post office. The crafts shop was open, but Claire Ellison was not there; with a wave at the owner, Verity hurried on up the hill and over its crest to the small green house Claire had yesterday pointed out as hers.

"Verity, hello! Emma, say hi to Verity," Claire added as an aside, and the gray-eyed child perched on the top step nodded her smooth brown head and greeted her.

"Hi, Emma."

Claire had set up a table on her front porch, and was at work gluing minuscule lacy dresses and feathery wings to small faceless figures made of Styrofoam balls. "Christmas is only six months off, and people are going to need tree angels," she said with a grin. "Need them lots more than they need handwoven wall hangings, I can tell you."

"People mostly have no taste," said Verity, who had seen one of Claire's hangings in the shop the day before.

"Well, there's money, too," said Claire. "These guys don't cost much. Hey, I was just about to get away from the glue fumes and make some lunch. How 'bout I give you a tuna sandwich and you tell me the latest in the life of a detective."

While Claire spread a mixture of tuna, onion, celery, and mayonnaise on hamburger buns, Verity related an edited version of her efforts, and their lack of success.

"There are always stories about weird stuff out in the Lost Coast," Claire said, as she set sandwiches and a pitcher of tea on the table and then sat down across from Verity. "Sometimes they're even true, like about a bunch of survivalists five or six years ago, or the ongoing war between the troops and the dope growers. But I haven't heard anything lately. Fact is, the only people that know much about what goes on out there are the ones who live there."

"I haven't come across any of those," said Verity.

"I suppose not." Claire frowned as she took a bite of her sandwich. "Maybe you should just go on out to Honeydew. They have a store and a school, and a ball field where people seem to get together. Somebody there might know about a religious commune; whether they'd talk about it, God only knows."

"So I've heard." Verity thought that this job, too, was better suited to her mother; everybody talked to Patience. All she herself seemed fit for was the physical stuff, like road crews.

"Dirty Mary lives out there sometimes," said Emma, who had been silently working her way through a sandwich and a mug of milk. "And she'll talk to you if she likes you, or if you give her money."

"Emma, it's rude to call her that," said Claire sharply. "And I've told you not to hang around her; she's not...a suitable companion for a child."

"Sylvie's mama hung around her, and gave her money, too. I bet she just spent it on booze," added Emma virtuously.

Verity raised her eyebrows at Claire, who made a wry face. "Mary—if she has a last name I've never heard it—is an old derelict panhandler and, oh, kind of a hermit, I guess. Well, she looks old; her hair is white and what teeth she's got left are bad. I suppose that

could be from a steady diet of Green Death. Rainier Ale," she added in explanation.

"And she lives around here?"

"She lives in her old car, and after she's picked up her disability check or whatever it is, and panhandled for extras, she heads for the woods. Probably out to the west, now that I think about it."

Verity focused her mind's eye once again on the map—that large, empty expanse. "Claire, can you be more specific? If I were to look for Mary, where would I start?"

"Um. Probably Honeydew. You could say you're her long-lost daughter, she mentioned having a daughter one time but I've no idea if that was truth or tale."

"In summer, she likes to be on the water," said Emma. "She says she really enjoys a good fresh fish."

Verity had an image of herself trudging along miles and miles of coastline, some of it map-marked with names like "Mistake Point" or "Point No Pass."

"I believe there are some walk-in campgrounds, for hikers," said Claire. "And I know there's a private one at Shelter Cove. But that costs money, and they wouldn't rent space to someone like Mary any-way. No, you want something you can drive to, near the water, that's free."

Verity looked at her watch. "I'd better get moving. Thanks for lunch and information, Claire. And you, too, Emma."

"Just get back on the highway north, and the first turn left will take you to Bull Creek Flats Road—to Honeydew," said Claire. "And listen. Be careful."

"I will." She went back down the hill to the parking lot, pausing for a last look at her jumping-off place. A big motor home was pull-ing in from the road; a shiny-red square Jeep or some such was nos-ing to a stop right in front of the store. Several older, dusty, probably local vehicles, two pickups, and a small sedan sat in the shade on the far side of the post office. No motorcycles on the scene today. Verity climbed into the truck, took a quick look at her map, and set out for Honeydew.

16

Bull Creek Flats Road begins as a paved trail ambling between the mammoth, grooved trunks of redwood trees, their green-gold shade so deep that the state had put up signs: TURN LIGHTS ON FOR SAFETY. Drive slow for safety, too, thought Verity, yielding cheerfully enough to an approaching car whenever the passage was particularly narrow. Trees reigned here, with their great size, their sense of timelessness and peace.

At a turnout a man was measuring himself against one of the trees, his arms wide in mock embrace; it would have taken four or five like him to encircle the trunk. Beside him, a woman simply gazed upwards. It occurred to Verity that perhaps disturbed and angry persons, even minor criminals, should be sent to the redwoods, for meditation and restoration of spirit.

A few miles of this, and then the terrain steepened. The road, a narrow ribbon of black asphalt buckled here and there by weather or by shifts of the ground beneath, slashed its way upward across scraped rock faces and along the edges of sheer drop-offs. Verity crept on at very low speed, pausing now and then to gaze across what looked like endless rumpled reaches of forested mountains. This was not really a large chunk of country, but it seemed endless, an old green world far from anything familiar.

On this stretch she encountered two vehicles coming toward her, passed none going her way. A time or two, on a switchback, she caught sight of one or maybe two cars behind her; but they never got closer. At the 2700-foot summit she left the boundary of Humboldt Redwoods State Park and began a sweep down into the Mattole

River valley, descending via a series of hairpins and switchbacks that kept both hands on the wheel and her foot hovering near the brake. Trees still, maples and live oaks mixed with Douglas fir; a grassy meadow now and then, or a deep little valley cradling a house and barn. The land was fenced and firmly posted: No hunting fishing swimming camping trespassing for reasons of any kind. No looking no breathing this means you. Folks along here didn't seem friendly.

Glimpses of the winding, sunlit river on the right now; and finally the end of the descent at a single-lane bridge. Verity paused, took a deep breath, and drove over the river into the hamlet of Honeydew. She was unsurprised to note that the twenty-five-mile trip had taken her well over an hour.

The Honeydew Store and Post Office sat behind a row of gas pumps and a large dirt parking lot. It was a longish building with a roofed porch across its front; lined up on benches there were a pair of obviously sore-footed young hikers, backpacks beside them; two grubby little girls eating Popsicles; a gray-haired man in jeans and sandals, fanning himself and sipping mineral water; and an obese woman in a long dress and straw hat.

Verity parked, got out and stretched, and looked around. She saw cars and trucks of varying ages; but nowhere in view was the rusted-out Volkswagen squareback that Claire Ellison had told her was Dirty Mary's live-in vehicle. With a mental shrug, she set off for the store, past the pumps where a large man in overalls and a billed cap was putting gas in a new American sedan.

"No, ma'am, I wouldn't take this big boat off onto any little un-paved detours," he told the elderly woman behind the wheel. "But the road from here north to Ferndale is okay, twisty and narrow but well paved, and takes you down right along the edge of the ocean. Windy and colder'n hell down there, though."

Nodding at the bench-warmers, Verity stepped into the store, a dim and cavernous place with a creaky wood floor and a rustic atmosphere that she suspected was partly for show. Tourists did stop here, after all.

There were two or three shadowy figures exploring the store's aisles, and a gray-haired, denim-clad woman at the counter along the

back, paying for whatever was in the paper bag before her. Behind the counter was a woman older than Verity but not by much; wavy dark brown hair was tucked behind her ears, and the eyes that looked up to meet Verity's were a cool greenish hazel.

Verity had been turning over in her mind the three objects of her search—Lily Costello, a fundamentalist religious commune, a woman called Dirty Mary—trying to decide which she could most fruitfully toss out for discussion. One and maybe two but probably not three, she decided. Best to avoid provoking local loyalties. And probably best to follow Patience's advice and keep the business cards in her bag. She paid for the can of Coke she had pulled from the store's cooler and took a long drink.

"Ah, that's good. My name is Verity Mackellar, and I'm looking for a friend."

"Aren't we all," said Hazel-eyes, with the barest hint of a smile.

Verity smiled back. "But this is an old friend. Her name is Lily, and we were going to do some camping out here, she and I and her little girl. And maybe look up another old friend who's supposed to be living somewhere near here in a church group."

"So, did you and this Lily have a fight or something?"

Verity gave a palms-up shrug. "I couldn't get time off from work. Then, when it turned out the last minute that I could, Lily had already left. She's about your height, olive-skinned, with long, straight black hair. Sylvie is seven, tall for her age, and looks a lot like her mother. They're driving a blue minivan."

The woman, who had listened intently, shook her head. "I haven't seen them. Let me ask Doug," she added, pulling up a hinged portion of the counter and stepping through. Verity followed her out to the porch, where they met the overalled man from the gas pumps.

He listened to the woman's quiet-voiced question and then looked past her to Verity. "Nope, don't sound familiar to me. Sorry."

"Me, too," said Verity, letting her shoulders slump. "Maybe she located the farm where Marsha is staying. It's supposed to be a kind of Christian commune, I understand."

Doug pulled his cap off and ran a big hand through gray-streaked black hair, his nearly black eyes reflecting no expression Verity could

read. "There's plenty of privately owned land out here, some of it lived on by groups that don't fit what the census-takers would call family. The only time there's any trouble is when some outlander comes busting in across posted land and then pees his pants at the sight of a shotgun."

"Spoken like a native although we've only been here six months," said the woman dryly. "Just running the place while the owners take care of some business back east. If there are any communes or cults or covens nearby, they haven't bothered us."

Doug grinned. "Babe, you're forgetting that jack Mormon with the three wives."

"He was only interested in converting *me*," she retorted. "I'm sorry, Verity, but I guess we can't help you, except with supplies if you plan to camp anyway."

Verity hesitated, then took the plunge. "Somebody told me that the person who knows this area best is an old woman named Mary something who lives in her car."

Doug's face remained impassive, but his wife bristled. "*Dirty* Mary, you mean. Light-fingered Mary, I'd call her. And you couldn't believe a word she said even if you happened to catch her sober. Filthy old witch."

Doug laid a gentling hand on her arm. "Live and let live, Babe." And to Verity, "We haven't seen her in weeks, luckily. Probably she's parked somewhere on the water, is all I can suggest."

"That's pretty much what I'd like, myself. I heard there was a Bureau of Land Management campground not far from here, right on the ocean?"

"Those campsites are primitive, just like some of the campers," replied Doug. "But you're a big girl. Just take the road north toward Ferndale, right along the river, fifteen miles or so till you come to Lighthouse Road. That'll take you down to the river mouth."

"Thanks." Verity went back inside the store, to buy two more cans of Coke and a bottle of wine, an overpriced zinfandel that would warm her a bit if she wound up sleeping out. Remembering Claire's words about old Mary, she reached for a six-pack of Rainier Ale, then changed her mind and picked up the whole case. Plenty of

room in the truck and a long way between stores out here. On her way back to her truck, she paused to speak to the porch bench's sole remaining occupant, the obese woman, who had either had too much to drink (or maybe smoke) or chose to behave as if she had: Don't know nothing about nobody.

The road followed the winding river at an easy pace past small farms, orchards, fields where cattle grazed. Once Verity paused to wait while a flock of large, odd-shaped birds unhurriedly crossed the road before her: *tame* wild turkeys? There was little noise except for the quiet engine of the truck; there were no towering buildings, no jetliners crossing that chilly blue sky. She felt that she might have stumbled into a time warp, a little piece of life left over from an earlier era. She spotted some power poles and wires and concentrated on them to reorient herself.

Lighthouse Road proved to be a narrow, more-or-less paved track opening out at its west end to a sandy parking lot and the Pacific Ocean. Verity drove into the lot, joining a pickup, two passenger cars, and a white van, all of them obviously mobile; and a scatter— six, she counted—of what looked like derelict vehicles. Occupants of most of the latter had staked claim to spaces adjoining their vehicles by means of beach chairs, tarps slung on ropes, plain ropes marked with fluttery strips of fabric, even a low fence for a small, noisy dog.

Primitive, indeed. She parked the truck near the entrance to the lot and climbed out, locking the door in what she hoped would not be taken as an unfriendly gesture. Bag slung over her shoulder, she trekked head-down past the non-mobile homes toward the ocean, where a brisk surf was roaring in and then whispering back over dark sand.

Wonderful endless view. Cold wind. After several minutes' chilly observation of nature, she took a big gulp of sea air and turned back toward the lot and its inhabitants. Tall overalled man beside one ancient car, dreadlocks lifting in the wind as he gazed at her. Two hefty guys in jeans and T-shirts near a rusted-out pickup, one of them bending so low over the remains of a boat that Verity could see more of his pale hairy ass than anyone could possibly wish to. A man and

a small child on a freestanding car seat, the child with a nippled bottle in his or her hand, the man with a can of Bud.

If there were women here, they were inside the cars and trucks. Verity chose to make a quick, unfocused eye contact with each person she passed as she made her way through the sand toward the far end of the lot, and the car she'd spotted from the road. A college friend had owned a Volkswagen squareback, elderly even then; there weren't that many of them left around.

"Hey, Red!" called one of the men.

Verity lifted a hand and waved over her shoulder but kept moving, looking mostly out toward the water. There was another call, the exact words lost in the wind. Then the door of the little Volks opened and a wild white head poked out.

"Shut the fuck up, you bastards!" the old woman shrieked. "Can't a lady take a walk in peace around here? Hi, honey," she said more softly to Verity. "Don't worry about them, they're all noise, no bite— at least, until they get real liquored-up. Say, would you maybe happen to have a beer on you?"

Verity sneaked another look at her watch. "Mary, I'd better go. Otherwise, it'll be getting dark before I find the…group." Mary—all the name she had or needed, she'd said—persisted in calling the commune "them Christers."

Mary giggled and lifted the green can to her mouth. Although she complained that the company had recently cut its alcohol content, Rainier Ale was still Mary's favorite tipple (not the way she'd phrased it) and the one in her hand was number—five or six, Verity thought. She'd been quite generous in wanting to share; Verity, needing to appear sociable, had nursed one and then a second. Vile stuff, in her opinion.

"Right, you want to get there before dark," said Mary, and giggled again. "After dark, them Christers will be busy either prayin' or fuckin'. No booze, no smokes, no cards, no dancing—what'n hell's left, eh?"

"You said you didn't think they'd refuse to let me in." Coy and sly at first, evading Verity's questions while asking plenty of her own,

Mary had relaxed at about the third can of ale and become loquacious and helpful. She knew every inch of the Lost Coast you could drive to and a lot you couldn't; she'd met or at least seen practically every person who actually lived out here as opposed to just camping or snooping. "Except for them fascists down at Shelter Cove," she'd added. Rich, ugly people who screwed up the landscape with their big, ugly show-off houses right on the water. The Pacific would get them, or the San Andreas would, and she hoped to live to see it.

But in her opinion the Christers were okay, if you didn't mind being prayed at. Their land was fenced and posted and they had long guns, but they weren't mean, more like standoffish. Like everybody else who lived out here. They'd never shot at her, after all, although she had come right up to the fence and talked to them.

"I believe if they was to turn away a lone ranger—oops, I mean lone stranger—they'd lose their license." Mary spoke slowly, shaping her words with exaggerated care. "It's required, ain't it? Didn't Christ say, even as you do it unto one of the least of these my brethren you do it unto me? Or something like that. 'Course they never invited *me* onto their property, but folks in the towns usually don't, neither," she added with a shrug.

Verity pulled her feet close and managed to push herself up from the low sand chair she'd been occupying for more than two hours. They'd sat outside, because Mary liked to smoke while drinking, and didn't smoke in her car. They'd sat on the far side of the Volks, in the vain hope that the other permanent residents of this parking lot (the camp proper was over the ridge) wouldn't realize Mary had a supply of booze.

"Now, you got those maps I marked for you?" Mary didn't rise, simply squinted up at Verity.

"Yes, ma'am. And I thank you. Back to Honeydew, then south on the dirt road…"

"It's gravel, and real steep. Then it'll be paved off and on, biggest problem is when you go from paved to gravel, gotta watch you don't brake too quick." Mary paused for a gulp of Rainier, and Verity waited.

"There's that jog west, then the road goes on south. Through this

chickenshit little town and don't you stop there, honey—and past a school. Then a crossroads, after that this little gravel quarry, and the road you want is next after that on the left. Looks as if it's gonna peter out right away but it don't, not till you get to the gate. Maybe two miles in. Kind of a nice little creek-bottom valley there."

"Mary, I'm grateful to you," said Verity.

"Glad to help. Hope you find them. That lady, Lily, was hell-bent on getting to those folks, so I told her how; but in my personal opinion that's no fit place for a kid to grow up. No way to find out how the real world works. No freedom," she added, and cast a satisfied look around at the sand and the brush and the bit of ocean visible from her chosen spot.

"Right," said Verity. She hunched her shoulders against an increasingly bitter wind. "Mary, I have an extra sweater in the truck that might fit you."

"I got plenty of clothes, blankets, even a slicker," said Mary. She set down her empty can and reached for the backup she'd stashed in the sand. "I got more'n half a case of beer left, thanks to you. 'Course, that'll run out sooner than you might think. So if you maybe could spare a little cash?"

Verity fished two twenties from her wallet, all she thought she could spare this far from auto-teller machines. She handed them over, then reached out to grasp Mary's grimy, clawed hand. "Maybe I'll see you again."

"Sure. You watch out for them Christers now."

"I will. You watch out for your neighbors."

Verity had pulled her truck down the lot to park it beside Mary's car. Now she climbed in, hooked up the seat belt and locked the door, and started the engine. For a moment she feared the truck had settled too deeply into wind-drifted sand; then, slowly, the tires bit and she backed out onto more solid ground.

She drove very slowly past the permanent residents, eyes forward; the visitors' vehicles there when she arrived had departed one at a time as the afternoon wore on into evening and the wind picked up. Mary had told her that the permanent people were not usually any problem to her, that she was ugly enough and mean enough to take

care of herself anyway. But what about when you're blind drunk, old woman? Verity thought. And what about the fact that they have to know you've got booze now, and might suspect you have money?

She hesitated at the lot's edge, wondering whether she should try to convince Mary to come away with her. Knowing Mary wouldn't willingly do that, knowing as well that she didn't want to take responsibility for the old derelict. One of the squatters, the dreadlocks guy, was framed in her side mirror now, climbing into an ancient sedan that appeared to have been sandblasted beyond paint into pure rust; as she sat there dithering, the old car shuddered and belched black smoke from its exhaust.

Shit! That thing could move after all. He probably wasn't coming after her, but... Her tires spat sheets of sand as she stepped on the gas, swung out of the lot, and sped more quickly than was comfortable down the narrow, rutted trail.

It was not yet dark, only dusk; but the road wound and twisted, and often ran under overhanging trees, so she couldn't be sure there was no one behind her, only that there were no headlights back there. By the time she reached Honeydew her shoulders and neck ached from tension.

She'd gassed up in Weott, and besides, she didn't want further conversation with Doug or the woman he called Babe. She drove past the store, stopped under a tree some distance down the road, and sat for a few long minutes watching her back-trail. Nobody; then a stake body truck whose wide-hatted driver slowed to glance at her and drove on. Then nobody.

She sighed, rotated her shoulders against the ache in her back, reached into her cooler for a Coke, and thought better of that. Best to keep both hands free for the wheel. The feeling that someone was following her was probably imagination, juiced up by her time in the squatters' lot. But there was nothing wrong with being ready for trouble.

She'd been traveling the length of a low valley that chilled and darkened early because the King Range to the west blocked the late-day sun. As she reached the gravel section and began to climb, she found the road hanging with dust from earlier travelers; like the sun,

the ocean wind did not reach into this tunnel of overarching trees. Verity picked her way along in the gathering gloom, wishing she'd been smart enough to get away earlier. Wishing she'd thought to stop at the Honeydew store for a pee; she'd wimpishly avoided the foul-smelling chemical toilet at the beach.

Lots of what looked like side roads, this one bolting up the side of a steep hill, that one disappearing over a brushy edge into a dark canyon. There were no friendly lights twinkling out there, as you'd expect from dwellings; maybe the people at the ends of these lanes lived without electricity. Or maybe they were just too far back in the brush to be visible from the road. Verity did not find these thoughts cheering.

The pressure on her bladder was approaching the intolerable. She had not yet turned her lights on, in what she supposed was an instinctive attempt to be invisible; but she could make out another of the side roads just *there.* She swung across the road and edged down a narrow lane she might never get out of. Pulled as close as possible to the trees on the right and leapt out and was very glad that her jeans had a zipper instead of buttons.

She was still squatting, light-headed with relief, when she heard an engine. She stood up, pulling her clothes together as she looked toward the road. A vehicle was passing slowly, without lights; she didn't actually see it, just heard its throaty rumble. Maybe a local, knowing the road so well he didn't need to see it.

And maybe not. She waited until the engine sound had completely faded before opening the door to her truck. Wincing against the brightness of the overhead light, she fumbled with its surface and found the switch that turned it off. Reached into the cooler and fished out a bottle of mineral water. Cupped a handful of the cooler's melted ice and used it to wash her hands; cupped another handful to splash on her face. Uncapped the bottle and sipped and listened.

Nothing. She climbed into the truck, started it, and eased forward; the track widened slightly and she began the tedious backing-and-forthing necessary to get turned around. Her last turn brushed a fender against a tree trunk with a sound that made her wince; Harley would be heartbroken and she hoped the damage was only to the paint.

Ready to pull out onto the main road, she saw lights approaching from the south—the way she'd be headed. No problem, she thought, and then she caught the engine sound and dropped the truck quickly into reverse, rolling backwards. Verity knew next to nothing about cars, but she had acute hearing and near-perfect pitch: this was the same car, coming back.

Alone in a strange wilderness as night approached, she wasn't interested in searching for logical explanations. She lowered both windows and crept forward to road's edge, following the car with eyes and ears. When it was no longer discernible to either, she shot out onto the road and headed south as quickly as she dared, lights still off.

Eyes glued to what she could see of the road, she reached into her bag and felt around until the small flashlight met her grip. She had come—she turned the flash on the dashboard—only eight miles from Honeydew. Seemed ridiculous, but that's what the odometer said. She turned the flashlight on her watch and discovered that it was nearly nine o'clock.

And nearly full dark; there was a half moon up there, but most of the time it was obscured by the trees and by a developing misty cloud cover. She slowed to a crawl and felt her way along.

Her teeth came together hard as lights appeared in her mirror. Same car? She couldn't hear it, so she couldn't be sure; but the lights were single and not very bright, the right one misaimed as if it had been hit. Old car, most likely. As she tried to watch both the darkness ahead and the rearview mirror, the lights came closer and then just seemed to settle in back there. Near enough to see her? A curve in the road brought her foot to the brake, and she winced at the sudden flare of her own taillights. Behind her, the other lights disappeared.

Somebody who lived here and had turned off. Logical and probably even true but not sure. Shotgun behind the seat; if she pulled over right now and grabbed it and quickly unlocked the box in back… There might not be time and anyway, would she dare shoot? But if that were ol' Dreadlocks back there, she could at least scare him.

She scraped brush as the road turned abruptly and she didn't, quite. Lights behind her again sent her to the edge of panic; she concentrated on penetrating the darkness ahead with her unaided eyesight, speeded up and turned and turned again, a sharp turn that time, and made it and the next. No lights visible behind her now, what could she... Lights ahead, coming toward her and outlining her truck to her follower but also lighting the road: a fence post way down on the right side, some kind of opening nearer on the left. Headlights very bright now.

Verity sped to meet that vehicle, drove into its dust cloud as they passed each other, squeezed her eyes tight-shut for a moment and opened them, and saw the side road. She swung the truck hard left, bumped downward, and jolted along for forty yards, fifty, more; turned her lights on and off quickly to see that she'd run out of road, up a rough dirt slope and crunching through brush and another bump; her foot hit the brake, her head hit the cab roof, and she and the truck stopped. As she grabbed for the ignition key, she was groggily aware that the sticky liquid dripping down her face was blood.

17

Timid rays of sunlight had finally crept over the eastern ridge and were being greeted raucously by several thousand birds. Verity snaked her left arm out of the warm sleeping bag and blinked gummy eyes at her watch: almost eight-thirty. Time to find out whether she could move, and then whether she could move the truck.

The night before, after she'd stopped the bleeding from the cut in her scalp and determined that she couldn't extricate the truck in the dark, she spent what seemed an eternity huddled in dry-mouthed panic, her back to a tree and the loaded shotgun across her knees.

But panic, she'd found, was not self-sustaining. It needed to be fueled, and nothing came to bother her but wind high in the trees and once, after a rustle in the brush that nearly stopped her heart, a large raccoon that reared up in indignation at the blaze of her flashlight beam and then took itself off. After its departure, she sat there drawing deep breaths and berating herself for behaving like a wuss over nothing at all and possibly wrecking Harley's truck in the process.

Finally, exhausted but reasonably calm, she'd made a supper of bread and cheese, sipping a little wine for the spirit's sake as well as for warmth. Then she unrolled her sleeping bag in the bed of the truck and slid into it, the shotgun within reach beside her. Plastic tarp pulled up over all as protection against the damp, she made a silent, solemn vow to awaken at the first snapping twig, and went to sleep.

Now she groaned softly as she pushed the bag aside, levered her

stiff body upright, and peered around. The truck rested against a little hill, nose buried in underbrush. Behind the truck was the real hill she'd come down last night, not so steep as it had felt then; but trying to get the truck up that trail backwards would not be a lot of fun.

So get moving, city girl. Verity had a few quick swallows from the bottle of mineral water she'd brought to bed with her, then wriggled free of the sleeping bag and inspected her right ankle, sprained or at least banged around during last night's abrupt stop. Surprise, it was swollen. And painful. But the swelling had been contained somewhat by the elastic bandage she'd had in her bag.

Same ankle that had played a role in her drama with Dr. Sundermann, she noted wryly as she loosened the wrapping just a bit. Proof of her grandmother's dictum to a less than truthful grand-child: Lies you tell will haunt you by coming true.

Gotta pee, gotta brush the nasty green moss off my teeth, gotta wash my face. Her ankle capable of bearing weight if she was on and off it quickly, she tended awkwardly to the first need, then hobbled back to the truck and took care of the second, watching herself in the truck's side mirror as she brushed and wondering what she could pos-sibly do to make herself presentable. Blood had flowed copiously from her scalp last night; she'd mopped up in the dark, and in the clear morning light she looked like someone who'd just crawled out of a train wreck.

She fetched a couple of paper towels from the truck, wet them in the chilly water in the cooler chest, and dabbed some of the worst smears from her face. Never mind, she told her reflection; we'll use it. Who wouldn't feel sorry for that face?

Her pale blue sweatshirt was beyond any help but that of a wash-ing machine; but her fleece vest, she found, would cover the worst of it. Less gruesome-looking now and definitely warmer, she brushed her hair and plaited it into a single braid. After looking for a long moment at the shotgun, she broke it, removed the shells she'd in-serted the night before, and put them back in the box. She slid the weapon into its canvas case, tucked the box of shells in at one end, and put the whole package behind the truck seat.

Then, with a sigh, she looked the truck over. If she gathered some brush to lay behind the wheels, and put the truck in four-wheel mode, and was very lucky…

It took a sturdy dead branch doubling as crutch and rake, plus a lot of sweat and pain, but she finally got Harley's truck out of the hole it had dug for itself. Then, in a series of small maneuvers that strained her patience and her sore ankle, she even got it turned around, ready to approach the road headfirst.

So. Onward. After all the damage to herself and the truck, she'd damned well better find Lily and tell her for Christ's sake to call home. The compound or commune or farm or whatever was no more than seven or eight miles from here. Surely they'd take her in, an injured and weary wanderer. If not, surely they'd at least hand her a cup of coffee through the fence; she hoped coffee was not against their religious principles.

No one lay in wait for her at the top of the hill—not Dreadlocks, not some opportunistic Lost Coast serial rapist. Not Lily Costello's distraught, abandoned second husband, who might be feeling even more possessive of a wife who had come recently into money; this possibility, which had brought her bolt upright in the middle of the night, was less compelling by daylight, but still…

She pulled herself back to the world at hand. Truck running normally so far as she could tell. World a misty gray, fog smothering most of the sunlight. No vehicles in sight on the road, no other engine sound in the odd silence fog seems to create. Verity drove slowly and watchfully, was past a fog-shrouded tiny town almost before noticing it, found the crossroads Mary had described and then the quarry and immediately after, the turnoff to the left. She crept down the narrow rutted road with her windows down, hearing birdsong and then possibly a creek. And an engine, somewhere.

A curve to the right, and there was a broad pipe-and-wire gate, held shut by a heavy chain and a padlock. Verity turned off the truck and sat where she was for several minutes, listening. When the engine sound came no nearer, and no person appeared, she took a deep breath and pressed the heel of her hand firmly against the truck's horn. Then she scrambled out and hobbled toward the gate. If these

were people who met visitors with guns, best they see clearly that she was a lone, lorn woman.

Two minutes later a figure came into view, moving steadily down the trail toward her. A tall, lean man in jeans and a blue shirt, light brown hair pulled into a ponytail, he carried a long gun under his right arm, muzzle pointing down. A .22, Verity thought.

She hooked both her hands chipmunk-fashion over the top pole of the gate, right there in full view. "Oh, please. Can you help me?" she called, surprising herself by the quavery note in her voice. "I got lost in the dark, and had an accident."

He moved more quickly, taking a ring of keys from his belt as he neared the gate. "We don't have a doctor here, but one of the women is a pretty good nurse. Let me get the gate open, then I'll drive you up to the compound."

"Thank you," said Verity in her new shaky voice. Probably she was just faint from missing a meal—two meals. She retreated awkwardly to the truck, but instead of getting inside, she leaned against it and watched him grip the heavy chain and turn the padlock up.

"Brother Benjamin! Brother Benjamin, who is it?" A girl was running down the trail toward them, legs long and skinny under a loose dress. "Is it Lily?"

The girl skidded to a stop several feet behind the man she'd called Brother Benjamin. Her face, younger than her height would have suggested, twisted in disappointment, and she squeezed her eyes tight-shut. Open again, they were huge and dark in a thin face surrounded by hacked-short black hair. She looked like one of the child-victims of whatever war was currently showing on the evening news. Well, little kid, we're a pair, Verity told her silently.

The man half turned, and put an arm across the girl's shoulders. "No, Sylvie, it's not Lily. It's someone who's had an accident and needs our help."

"Oh, I'm sorry." Sylvie darted ahead of him through the gate and came to Verity's side. "Can I help you?"

So the girl was here, but the mother was not. And Sylvie clearly didn't know where Lily was, but did Brother Benjamin?

Wouldn't hurt to pretend the need of a little assistance. Wouldn't

even be pretense, Verity decided as she put her weight on the bad ankle. "You can be my crutch, if you don't mind, and help me get around the truck."

In spite of her underfed, unkempt appearance, Sylvie provided a steady shoulder for support and even, shyly, looped an arm around Verity's waist as they moved to the other side of the truck. Verity opened the door, then pulled herself up and in, grimacing in not-entirely-feigned pain. Brother Benjamin paused at the back of the truck to set his rifle in the bed; then he got in behind the wheel.

"Sylvie, would you please get the gate?"

"Okay, but wait for me!"

"Who is Lily?" Verity asked, turning to watch out the back window as Sylvie pulled the gate into place.

"Sylvie's mother."

"Oh. Has something happened to her?" Verity thought this a reasonable question in the circumstances, even from a stranger.

"We hope not," he replied in chilly tones; he brought the truck to a stop, opened the door, and stepped out to let Sylvie slide in past him.

As Brother Benjamin drove slowly along the trail, Verity gazed around her at a landscape that was worlds away from her own life. To one side was a stand of smallish trees, apparently an orchard of some kind. To the other was a broad field, very green; alfalfa, maybe? Beyond the field was a smaller field, fenced; two cows lifted their heads and gazed at the truck with mild curiosity.

"There should be horses," she said, and then felt her face grow hot.

"We've talked about that. But Brother Daniel vetoed the idea."

Okay, thought Verity, a boss named Daniel. Tying up things neatly, except for the absence of Lily.

They eased around a gentle curve and came upon a cluster of buildings. A big, dark barn loomed on the left, several smaller buildings visible beyond it. To the right a tall house gleamed white as errant rays of sunlight penetrated the morning fog. Two stories and an attic over a basement, Verity thought; wraparound railed porch, tall windows with broad frames and pediments. It was the classic grandmother's

house, even to someone whose grandmother had lived in a 1950s cinderblock tract in Phoenix.

Brother Benjamin pulled the truck around to the rear of the house. "The women will be in the kitchen," he said to Verity. "They'll help you. I'm Benjamin Carter, Brother Benjamin here at Christian Community; this is Sylvie—"

"Simonov," said Sylvie firmly, from her perch on the skinny middle seat.

Hewing to her basic principle of truth-telling when possible, Verity said, "I'm Verity Mackellar. I appreciate your help."

Brother Benjamin led the way to the back door, opened it, and ushered Verity into a high, warm room full of heavenly smells: coffee, baking bread, the memory of bacon. She thought she might fall to her knees and lift up empty, begging hands.

Four women, varying in size and age but similarly dressed in skirts, blouses, and aprons, turned to look at them. Verity saw curiosity, as well as concern and distress.

"Verity, meet Sisters Jennifer, Sandra, Catherine, and Alice. This is Verity Mackellar, who needs help," said Brother Benjamin.

"But we can't... Brother Daniel isn't here." Sister Jennifer was a round-faced young woman whose blouse showed damp circles over her heavy breasts. Verity had no difficulty pegging her as mother of the infant dozing in a nearby carrier.

"Verity had an accident," said Brother Benjamin. "Sister Alice?"

The oldest woman in the group, face sharp under a crown of graying braids, eyed the not-very-welcome visitor for a moment, then nodded and pulled a straight chair out from the table.

"Sit down here and I'll have a look."

Sister Alice's fingers were thin and strong, her touch as impersonal as her narrow pale eyes. "The scalp cut won't need stitches," she announced. "But the bruise..." She pushed strands of hair back from Verity's temple, and prodded the sore spot high on her cheekbone. "That's an earlier injury. Did someone hit you?"

Verity felt her face grow hot. "I had an argument with my husband. We're, uh, we're divorcing, and he was upset."

"Young woman, Christian Community is not a battered-wives'

refuge." Sister Alice stepped back and folded her arms over her chest. "If you're being pursued by an angry, aggressive husband, I'll ask you to be on your way. We do not want that kind of trouble here."

"No!" Sylvie, who'd been hovering near the door, ran forward to take up guard duty next to Verity's chair. "She's hurt, she can't walk!"

"Mind your manners and your mouth, young lady!" said Sister Alice.

Reaching a blind hand out to the little girl, Verity stared wordlessly up at Sister Alice and remembered her terror of the night before, her sense of being pursued. Her paranoia, she'd decided once there was daylight to think in. But Ted?

"No," she said after a moment, shaking her head. "My husband can lose his temper, but he'd consider it beneath his dignity to chase me down. Besides, he can't possibly know where I am, where I was headed. I didn't know myself."

The older woman held Verity's gaze for a moment, and then gave a small nod. "Put your leg up here, please. Sylvie, go sit at the table."

Verity propped her foot on the small stool, and Sister Alice pushed the jeans leg as high as possible and unwrapped the elastic bandage. She probed with those strong fingers, and Verity set her teeth against a yelp of pain.

"Not too bad, as sprains go," pronounced Sister Alice. "You should have applied ice, of course, as soon as it happened."

Verity had a quick image of herself in that dark, cold little gully, shotgun in hand and one foot in the icy water of the cooler chest as she awaited assault. Not bloody likely, she thought, but silently. This was not a woman who invited a sharp response; she reminded Verity of the headmistress of a particularly strict school, or maybe a bank examiner.

"Well." Sister Alice straightened. "Since you're here, we'll ice it and have you keep weight off that foot for a few hours. After you've had a bath and a change of clothes," she added, mouth tightening in distaste. Verity had observed that no woman in the room displayed any jewelry beyond a plain wedding ring, nor any hint of makeup. It wasn't the bloodstains that offended Sister Alice; it was the jeans, the lipstick, and probably the gold hoop earrings.

Well, maybe they would feed her once she was presentable. Using the crutches provided by Sister Alice, she hobbled after a cheerfully helpful Sylvie down a long hall whose white-painted walls were spotlessly clean and completely empty of any decoration. The bathroom at the end contained what might have been the original fixtures, but the claw-footed tub was well-scrubbed and was long enough for a six-footer.

"Sister Alice told me to bring her your dirty stuff," Sylvie said, "and she'll give me something you can wear. It'll be really ugly, though," she added with a grimace. Verity peeled out of her jeans and sweatshirt and handed them over; she was just easing her aching body down into still-flowing hot water when Sylvie reappeared, closed the door, and took up a perch on the toilet lid, skinny legs tented up and equally skinny arms wrapped around them.

Verity had small experience with children, and even less interest. Generally she thought round, smiling children, like Sister Jennifer's baby and the doe-eyed small girl who'd come into the kitchen as she and Sylvie were leaving, were the ideal. Now, sliding a glance sideways, she judged that Sylvie, all long limbs and sharp edges and intensity, had probably not been softly round even in the womb. The little girl struck an odd note in this community of humble conformity.

"This seems like a nice place," she said in conversational tones. "Have you lived here long?"

"It's sexist," proclaimed Sylvie. "And boring. I don't live here, I'm just staying until Lily comes back for me."

"I see." Verity sat up reluctantly and began to soap her arms and shoulders. "Where is Lily?"

"She went to see the Devil."

"Ah." Perhaps the child belonged here after all—or had been here too long. Although she didn't seem, even at the tender age of seven, a very good prospect for evangelizing.

"Are you going to stay here?" Sylvie wanted to know.

Verity slid down in the tub and propped her legs up to scrub them and her feet. "I might stay a day or two, if Brother Daniel approves. Is he a nice man?"

Sylvie shrugged. "He's okay. He spits when he talks, so you don't want to get too close."

Lovely. Verity took the band off her braid, finger-combed it loose, and managed a quasi-shampoo under the faucet. As she sat up spluttering and twisted her hair into a rope to wring it out, she found Sylvie beside the tub with a towel.

It felt strange to be toweling off and dressing under the attentive eyes of a child. Clad finally in a loose full skirt and long-sleeved blouse, Verity unwrapped the towel from her hair and dug her hairbrush from her bag.

"Your hair is so pretty. I always got to brush Lily's hair."

The huge black eyes were intense. Verity sat down on the toilet lid and handed Sylvie the brush.

As the little girl wielded the brush with care, Verity asked, "Sylvie? What happened to *your* hair?"

"Aunt Marsha cut it off."

"For heaven's sake, why?"

"She said it was because I liked it too much, and God despises vanity. But it was really because she hates me. And because my hair was full of pig poop and she didn't want to bother getting it clean."

"Pig poop?"

"From the night she locked me in the pig house with the pigs. It was really dark in there and I couldn't keep out of the poop."

The little girl's voice was matter-of-fact. She took two last strokes with the brush and said, "There. It's done. It's pretty."

Locked in the pig house? Either Christian Community was a meaner place than it appeared, or this child had an unusually vivid imagination.

In her proper and surprisingly comfortable clothing, seated in an out-of-the-traffic-lanes chair with footstool and ice pack, Verity did her best to blend into the scenery. This was a well-kept old house, the little she'd seen. The kitchen was old-fashioned but spacious, well-suited to accommodating several workers at once, and these three were clearly easy maneuvering around each other. Quick-brown-bird Sister Sandra scraped piles of chopped carrots and onions into two

steaming stockpots that Verity's experienced nose told her contained chicken. Sister Jennifer moved out the door in the direction, presumably, of the dining room, a nursing baby in her right arm and a pile of plates in her left. Red-haired, freckled Sister Catherine (who somehow reminded Verity of Dirty Mary although she looked quite clean) set a small folding table next to Verity's chair and put a large mug of coffee on it.

"From breakfast, and probably thick as mud. But you look like you need it," she remarked. "Sugar or cream?"

"Oh no, thank you. This is lovely." Verity clasped the mug in both hands and inhaled deeply. Sister Alice had taken herself off somewhere. But where was Sylvie's *bête noire*, Sister Marsha?

"So, you're ditching a mean husband. Where'd you live, you and him?"

"San Francisco."

"Wow. Maybe you ought to think this over."

"San Francisco is an evil city." Sister Jennifer had come back into the room, and now spoke with more firmness than she'd shown before. "It's full of perverts and sinners and worshippers of Mammon."

Verity thought she'd give her two out of three on that. "It's full of temptations, at any rate," she said, and sipped her coffee and regretted the sharp edge to her words. San Francisco flavor, she was, and should tone it down.

"So how did you wind up here?"

"I was just driving, heading away from cities with no particular place in mind. Trying to figure out what I was meant to do with my life, praying for guidance." (Here she mentally crossed her fingers.) "I have to confess that I'm not a very religious person," she added, "even though my grandmother is a Baptist minister. But I'm very grateful to you all for your kindness."

"I didn't know Baptists had woman ministers!" Sister Jennifer's eyes grew even rounder.

"Arizona Baptists definitely do," said Verity. "Anyway, I apologize for intruding here. But if I could stay for just a day or two, until my leg is stronger and my head's maybe in a better place…" She let her voice trail off.

The three women looked at each other, glanced at Verity, looked away. "I don't know," said Sister Sandra. "We can't—that is, Brother Daniel would have to make that decision." Sister Jennifer nodded, and carrot-haired Sister Catherine shrugged and spread her hands in a gesture of helplessness.

Sylvie had tucked herself into the space between Verity's chair and the wall and stayed there, a silent but somehow electric presence. Now she stood up and said, "She won't make extra work. I'll take care of her."

"Sylvie Costello! What are you doing here, young lady? You're supposed to be in the study room reading Proverbs."

The woman who'd come in from the hall was short and heavy, with dishwater-blond hair straggling around a broad, reddened face.

"Brother Benjamin said I could be here," said Sylvie. "Besides," she added in a stronger voice, "you're not supposed to boss me anymore, Brother Daniel said so."

"You nasty little imp of Satan!" As the woman launched herself in Sylvie's direction, Sister Jennifer gave a squeak of distress and Sister Catherine took a step back out of the way, eyes wide with interest and lips pressed tight as if to contain not a scream but a smile.

A cup of coffee smashed on the floor, dropped from Sister Sandra's suddenly awkward fingers. "Oh, I'm sorry. I hope I didn't burn anyone."

Everyone stopped as if in a freeze-frame; and then the room was simply a kitchen where a minor accident gave everyone something to do. Except, thought Verity, Sister Marsha; this had to be Sister Marsha. The woman's face was so full of rage that Verity reached out from her chair to put an arm around Sylvie's waist: *Not through me you don't.*

Footsteps on the back porch brought everyone else's eyes around, and Brother Benjamin came in.

"I'm ready to leave for town. Is the shopping list ready?"

"Yes, here it is. And Brother Benjamin, maybe you should take Verity with you, and help her find a place to stay," suggested Sister Sandra as she handed him a folded sheet of paper.

Not yet! Letting go of Sylvie, Verity folded her hands in her lap,

put a slump on her shoulders and what she hoped was a look of weary pain on her face. Not yet.

Brother Benjamin glanced at her, and at Sylvie beside her. "She's not in shape to drive that rough road," he said firmly. "And if I drive her in, someone will have to come after me."

"But Brother Daniel isn't back yet," said Sister Jennifer.

"I'm sure he'd want to offer hospitality to a stranger at the gates," said Brother Benjamin. "I'll take responsibility, if you're worried."

Okay. Verity took a deep breath. "Brother Benjamin, may I ask a favor of you? Could you call my mother for me, please? She knows how upset I've been, and by now she's probably having visions of me lying dead in a ditch."

Sister Sandra was shaking her head. "We do not advertise our presence here, nor invite visitors."

"You wouldn't need to tell her where I am," Verity said, to Brother Benjamin. "Just say…say I've had a small accident, but found some kind people who were willing to take in someone's poor lost lamb of a daughter. And I'll be home in a day or two."

18

"Nope, nothing. Of course, I did grandma duty all day yesterday, so by two A.M. I probably wouldn't have heard a helicopter landing right in the yard. And Brutus is so deaf you need to wake him up and point out anything you want barked at." Liz Cimeno, Patience's neighbor and friend, nudged her ancient sheep dog with a sneakered toe, but he slept on. "Have you talked to Jeff?"

Patience sighed and nodded. Jeff Jeffries, a contractor who lived on the other side of the road about halfway between her place and Liz's, had gone to bed early the night before, needing to be on a building site at six; he hadn't heard a thing until his alarm went off. But the lots on Raccoon Lake Road were each several acres in extent, the houses set well back from the road; people who lived here valued privacy and got lots of it, usually.

"Nothing," she told Liz. "But Ralph doesn't go off for no reason, and several times this week we've thought there was someone hanging around. By the time I got all the way awake last night I was ready to take off after the—whoever—but I'd left my truck in town for a lube and oil change."

"Listen, thanks for letting me know." Liz, a few years younger than Patience and long-divorced, lived alone except when one of her four offspring turned up for consolation, rent relief, or baby-sitting help. "I think I'll clean my .22, just in case. After I have another cup of coffee," she added, glancing up at a sky still heavily overcast at almost ten A.M. "Come in and join me?"

"Thanks, but I'd better get home; Benny Martinez's boy should

be bringing my truck back any minute. Besides, I'm in such a vile temper I'd spoil your morning. Another time?"

"Sure. God, Patience, I just *hate* wasting time and energy worrying about the crooks and bastards out there. Maybe I should get a Rottweiler."

"They're very expensive," Patience said quickly. "And they eat a lot." Possibly even small neighboring dogs.

"I suppose. Well, be sure to let me know if anything else around here looks funny."

After agreeing to this request, Patience trudged homewards, to her own coffeepot. She'd had a long, hot trip from Red Bluff yesterday, arriving home to find several messages on her machine: old business from Claude Bernillo, the paving contractor; new from one woman who wanted to check up on a recently acquired boyfriend and another who wanted to locate a support-delinquent husband. Patience talked to Claude and set up appointments with the women, wondering as she did so whether she might be approaching a boring rut in her work.

Finally she consoled herself with a steak for supper, and most of a bottle of good merlot, retired early with the Elizabethan/Jacobean volume of the poetry collection she'd found in a used book store— and was catapaulted into bleary-eyed, head-throbbing wakefulness by Ralph's fierce barking.

And Verity, out on the road doing the interesting job, had not called as promised. Or at least she hadn't half an hour ago. Images of coffee mug and message machine alternating in her mind, Patience had almost reached the house when something by the studio door caught her eye: a torn piece of heavy brown paper, with a chunk of bubble-wrap stuck to it by brown tape. Maybe Verity's furniture had arrived, although her note had said nothing about it. Maybe Mike's old rolltop desk, which Patience was scheming to reclaim for her own office, was in the studio. Maybe she'd just go in and have a look.

"Could have been worse. Could have taken it out of her skin instead."

Tempted to put down the telephone, Patience simply held her tongue.

There was a gusty sigh at the other end. "Sorry, Patience, my dear. Totally crass and stupid thing to say. You're trying to tell me my son is heading for trouble."

She leaned back in her chair and gazed out the window of her downtown office, where fog still billowed and bushes still dripped at something after eleven A.M. "That's part of it. The sense of malice was startling, Amos. He murdered those poor pieces of furniture." At the memory of the rolltop desk, which had belonged originally to Mike's grandfather, she felt the back of her neck grow hot.

"Patience, let's not be carried away by drama."

"If you like, I'll send you copies of the pictures Verity took." Patience was sure—well, fairly sure—that Verity had taken such photos with the Pentax she'd then left in the studio with the furniture and her notebook. The film was presently at the developers.

"Ah. Pictures."

"She also has this, signed by the truck driver," said Patience, and read the brief statement aloud to Amos Aaron Blake, Esquire, Verity's father-in-law.

"Christ, law school was wasted on that boy," groaned Amos. "Okay, sorry again, I mean it. Just my litigator's reflexes, and you know I love Ver."

"You need to remember how much *I* love her," said Patience very softly. "Enough to interfere in her life even though I know she'll be furious with me, and to do whatever is necessary to protect her. That's not a threat, you understand."

"You mean I should turn off the tape machine," said Amos. "I did already, Patience, the minute I knew it was you."

"You're getting soft in your old age."

"Aren't we all," he replied in glum tones.

Not me, she said to herself. Not me.

"But probably not you," he said, and she could almost hear his grin. "Okay. I know a good furniture restorer here, I'll have him get in touch."

"I know a better one *here*. I'll send you the bill when he's finished."

"Your call. Now, is there anything else I should know?"

Patience pondered this for a moment; on her short list of possible prowlers, Ted's name was well down. But still.

"Someone has been prowling around out here," she said slowly. "Hush and listen, Amos, this is not an accusation. Someone was here Sunday night, again last night, maybe other times. I'm going to have to do something about it."

"My son would absolutely *not*—"

"Hush. Probably he wouldn't, but why don't you ask him? If he convinces you he couldn't have been involved, please call and let me know, and I'll be able to cross one possibility off my list."

There was an uncharacteristic silence. "I'll think about that," he finally said. "About his failed marriage, Patience, a subject God knows is well within my area of expertise, I will definitely talk with him. And damn his eyes, I'll even try to make sure he gets some quote professional help unquote. Fucking therapists will own this fucking city before long."

"Not until the lawyers give it up," said Patience.

"Ah. True. Trust me, Patience, and I mean it. Give my love to Ver. And keep some for yourself. My invitation still stands, you know. A night on the town, and I'll put you up in my suite at the Hunting-ton. We'd have a good time."

"We probably would. I'll keep it in mind. And you keep the rest of this in mind, Amos."

"You have my word."

As she hung up the phone, Patience permitted herself a small grin. Nice to know somebody out there lusted after her pudgy, aging body. Sometimes Amos almost tempted her.

The mournful note of a foghorn called her back to the real world. Possessed of a voracious curiosity honed by her years as a professional snoop, Patience was no respecter of privacy. She'd considered it her maternal duty to keep close tabs on Verity during her youth, stopping short of diary reading only because her daughter hadn't kept one.

So she didn't feel guilty about having explored the locked studio this morning. She didn't feel guilty about calling Amos, although she knew there'd be a blowup when her interference was discovered. But she was growing increasingly nervous about the lack of word from

Verity, who had promised to check in. Whatever their other failings, the Mackellars kept their promises.

Patience had left home to come to town less than an hour ago. But if Verity were to call there and get no answer, surely she'd call here? "Oh, for heaven's sake!" she said aloud, picking up the telephone to punch out her home number. When the answering machine picked up after only two rings, she muttered, "About time!" and cued it to give her the messages.

"Mrs. Mackellar, I have a message from Verity. She had a little accident but she's fine, got out of it with just a sprained ankle. To make sure you wouldn't worry, she asked me to tell you she found people kind enough to take in someone's lost lamb of a daughter. She'll be home in a day or two, as soon as she can drive comfortably."

The caller, a male with a soft but clear voice, hung up. Click. There were no more messages. Patience set the telephone down very carefully. Verity had found the people, presumably the commune people, kind enough to take in a daughter. Presumably, again, Sylvie as well as Verity. Did this mean Sylvie was there but Lily was not? Not necessarily; but the manner of the message meant Verity had not felt free to identify herself or her purpose.

Patience rolled her chair back against the wall, got up, and began to pace and try to think. Her first impulse was to track Verity, to go to Weott and talk to the woman there; that's where Verity would have started yesterday.

Stupid idea; she's doing her job and it's not a two-person job. There's no real reason to think these helpful people are dangerous. Verity is big and strong and smart. Yes, but...

The telephone rang; she snatched it up, sure that it would not be Verity, and it wasn't.

"Hi, darlin'," said Larry, her San Francisco P.I. friend. "I did that little job for you, called on a sweet old Italian widow lady."

Patience turned on the recorder. "Larry, you lovely man. Tell me all about it."

Larry did not reveal by what technique he had won entry to Mrs. Sangiacomo's house and heart; these were professional secrets. But he had learned that she was the still sorrowing longtime widow of a fine

man, she had two grown children who neglected her, she disliked children in general, and nearly everyone else in particular, except Devlin Costello.

"He was a fine man married to a wife who thought she was too good to help out in the bar. He adored the woman, worked himself half to death to give her everything, tried to be a stern but loving father to that loud brat of hers, probably a bastard although no one ever said as much. And then the bitch left him after all, breaking his poor heart."

"Larry…"

"Getting to that, love. After poor old Dev had mourned and carried on for weeks, drinking too much and missing work now and then, the wife, 'that Lily,' came back. Mrs. S. says this happened on a Friday almost three weeks ago—May twenty-eighth. Dev didn't work that night, and as it got later Mrs. S. could hear them talking loud, even yelling. It's a solid old building, by the way; I'd say Mrs. S. must have had her ear right to the wall.

"Anyway, they finally quieted down and Mrs. S. went to bed, and probably passed right out from the cheap dago red she swills." Larry, who loved good wine, made a little sound of distaste; probably he'd had to force down a glass or two of Mrs. Sangiacomo's inferior stuff.

"Next morning all was quiet, she says. It was rainy and foggy, her daughter was coming to take her to Sonoma for the weekend, and Mrs. S. didn't notice whether the Costellos' van was still in the back lot. When she got home Sunday night, she found out that the Costellos were gone bag and baggage, to coin a phrase. Cleared out completely.

"Mrs. S. said she was very happy for poor Dev and wished him and Lily well," Larry added after a moment, "but she was lying in her wine-stained false choppers. I'd say her idea of a good marriage is being the sole survivor. Wouldn't surprise me to find out she'd done in her own old man."

"Hush, Larry!" Patience snapped, and quickly recovered herself; it wasn't her friend's fault that she'd become personally involved with this case and found all its possibilities uncomfortable. "Sorry. Do you know whether she actually saw Lily Costello that Friday night?"

"She did not. But she was sure it was Lily she heard."

"Did she discuss the situation with the pub's owner?"

"He's the building's owner as well, local guy named Jack Arbegast, and she doesn't talk to him. She says he wants to force her to move, so he can raise the rent. Would you like me to look him up and see what he has to say?"

Larry's time wasn't cheap, and David Simonov's money was going fast. "I don't think so, Larry. But thanks. You do good work."

"All compliments gratefully accepted, especially from a respected colleague. Also money; I'll send my bill."

"I'll pay it."

Patience put the phone back, propped her rear on the edge of her desk, and stared out her window. She set her hands palm-to-palm under her chin, as if in prayer, then flexed her fingers and began to tap them lightly, rhythmically against each other in silent arpeggios that seemed to help her think.

Apparently Lily had gotten herself and Sylvie to Brother Daniel's little group, wherever and whatever it was—the people who took in lost lambs.

Apparently—according to two witnesses, Mrs. Sangiacomo and the little girl Verity had spoken with last Saturday night—Lily had returned to her husband's apartment on or about May 28. Apparently without Sylvie; Mrs. Sangiacomo's tale had not mentioned Lily's daughter as part of the Costello reunion, and the child in the other apartment saw only Lily, not Sylvie.

Hands clasped tightly now, Patience reconsidered the telephone message and was quite sure that precise, clever Verity had meant exactly what she said: the kind people had taken in a daughter, singular. So Sylvie was at the commune, Lily was not. It seemed that Patience Smith, Investigations, had completed half the work asked of them by the self-deprecating David Simonov: they had located his daughter. She could tell him that when next he called.

"Be damned if I will!" Patience said aloud. Not without Lily's acquiescence; that had been *her* agreement with Simonov. Perhaps the woman had simply stashed her daughter (in a presumably safe place, after all) and trotted off to rejoin her attractive if crazy husband; but

that didn't sound like the Lily they'd been tracking, nor the woman whose face looked out from that photo.

She sighed and sat down at her desk, to open the folder with all her notes on this case and printouts of Verity's notes as well. She read everything carefully, then spread the sheets out and began to jot down dates on a yellow pad.

Christmas card from Lily to David Simonov, presumably in December, says she is thinking of leaving a husband who is "making her crazy." In early March, Lily announces on a birthday card that she is actually leaving Dev Costello. And she does; Costello comes to question Simonov about it "two or three weeks later"—end of March, early April?

Patience wrote on another sheet: "If Lily had van, how Costello cover three hundred miles S.F. to Susanville? and back? Maybe ask Hank check auto regs."

Back to the notes. No further contact, Lily to Simonov, though he says he may have missed her. Mid- to late March, Lily turns up at a campground in Mendocino County and talks to the chaplain there. Just before Easter weekend, on April 1, Lily and Sylvie are in the big redwoods park on Highway 101; witnesses, a weaver/craftsperson/ nurse named Claire Ellison and her daughter.

Then, the week after Easter—April 5 through 9, that was—Lily is in Red Bluff, seeing Edna Mangrum and the Baptist minister's widow. And a banker.

On April 19 or 20, Lily and her daughter are once again in the redwoods, seen by Claire Ellison and Emma.

And that's it, until Lily is reportedly seen, and heard, in San Francisco on May 28. A gap between the last two sightings of almost six weeks. And following that, a gap of two weeks until David Simonov turns up in Port Silva to hire Patience Smith, Investigations. A glance at the calendar and she added six days since.

Patience looked at all these dates and did not like them. The six weeks' gap possibly—probably—meant a stay, a safe haven, with the Christian group. Rescuers of lost lambs. Rest, recuperation, restoration. Decision-making.

But the two—really three—weeks since San Francisco made

Patience very uneasy, sent her up from her chair again to pace the room and stare into the mist. Damn and blast.

Best case, the woman was back at the commune; hold that thought. There was simply no further to go on this until Verity came back or reported in, a fact that made Patience clench her teeth. And then shake her head, with a strained chuckle. When she'd worked with Mike, and then later on her own, she had been the legs, done the roadwork, gone after what she was looking for. Now she was reduced to sitting here like a fat gray spider in the center of a web, tossing out lines and trying to pull in others.

Verity was perfectly capable, damn it. Patience wasn't worried about her; she was envious of her.

Looking at the silent telephone, she thought of one more line the spider should spin: one seeking Dev Costello's recent movements. He'd have credit card records, surely; and she had a source who could dig those out if she had Costello's social security number. Which she could probably wrest from this Jack Arbegast. She played clever telephone games, got the job under way: efficient spider.

Finally logic repressed ego and suggested she stop dithering about this and dither instead about something more manageable, say their prowler. She ran a mind's-eye rogue's gallery past, people she had recently irritated: Walter Tully, still upset about being found out and then felled by a crutch. Duane Heffernan, possibly led to her by Carol. Dr. Sundermann or his youngest son: Claude Bernillo reported that the pair of them were resisting the proposal, accepted by the rest of the family, that the doctor should retire for his own good and that of the public.

Only the last made sense, and that just barely. Another faint possibility was David Simonov; perhaps he was hanging around to watch the investigators instead of pursuing his own investigation of wildlife sanctuaries. Making a mental note to have Hank Svoboda check Simonov's auto registration, as well as Costello's, Patience reached for the telephone.

Harley's answering machine replied with a burst of absolutely vile quasi-music. Patience held the receiver away until the beep sounded. "Harley, Patience here. I want to set up a watch at my house tonight, to catch an intruder. If you're free, let me know."

19

When Sister Sandra went out to ring the bell that would call everyone to lunch, Verity knew no more about Lily Costello than she'd known from the start: she wasn't here.

About Christian Community, she'd learned that the adult members worked hard, were pleasant to each other within what seemed a mild hierarchy, and did not gossip, at least in the presence of an outsider. There were eleven all together, according to Sylvie, with only Brother Benjamin not part of a couple. "And there are nine other kids and a baby," she'd added.

The big kitchen was clearly Community's crossroads. Over the course of the morning Verity had met all the women, all the men except Brother Daniel, and most of the smaller children. The children, like their parents, seemed healthy, well-fed, and ordinary. All except Sylvie.

Sylvie, who had left Verity's side only to fetch ice or coffee or water, was an edgy, unhappy presence who clearly made others uneasy. Verity thought Lily Costello's choice of refuge ill-suited to her daughter. But whether that choice should be countermanded by a formerly uninvolved father was a call Verity didn't feel qualified to make. This she'd leave to Patience.

In the dining room, adults and older children ate at a long table, the smaller ones at a round table of their own. The blessing was lengthy. The chicken soup was excellent, as was the fresh bread. In lieu of conversation there was a reading from Proverbs by huge, blond Brother Edward, Sister Catherine's huband.

Verity, who'd read some of Proverbs years ago in a Bible lit class,

had forgotten or failed to notice how forceful was the book's tone. Lines like "I will also laugh at your calamity; I will mock when your fears come," struck her as unhappy lunchtime music for small children. She kept her head down and ate and was glad when the meal was finished.

"Did you enjoy the reading?" she could not resist asking, when she had said her thanks and escaped out into the sunlight with Sylvie once again at her side.

"I like the stories, like Joseph's coat or Jonah and the whale. I don't listen to the other stuff."

"Oh wise child," said Verity. She stretched her spine to its fullest length and looked up at a sky of pure blue. "Pretty day. Let's stay out here for a bit and enjoy it."

"Just a minute, young lady!"

Verity swung around, braced herself, and shifted her lefthand grip, prepared once again to turn a crutch into a weapon. A red-faced man who might have sprung out of the ground loomed over them, one hand thrust out to seize...no, to point. At Sylvie.

"Young lady, you will go to the meeting room and kneel down for an hour and pray God to teach you Christian submission!"

Sylvie, who'd been chattering happily as she showed Verity around the compound, now squared her shoulders and stuck her chin out. "I didn't do anything."

"You defied Sister Marsha!" he shouted, spittle flying. "And now, when you should be helping her get the smaller children down for their naps, I find you..." He gulped breath and stood back, realizing belatedly that he had an outsider for audience.

Verity took a deep breath of her own, easing her stance from vigilant to humble. This spitter had to be the big boss, Brother Daniel. "I'm Verity Mackellar, and it's my fault." She brushed the back of her hand lightly against Sylvie's shoulder, trying to telegraph affection and caution. "I asked Sylvie to help me walk around a bit."

He drew himself up to his full six-feet-four or -five, making a business of settling his poplin jacket on his shoulders. "That's

kind of you, Mrs. Mackellar, and I'm glad Sylvie was able to be helpful. But it doesn't excuse her rudeness to her aunt. Sylvie, do as I told you."

"Thank you, Sylvie," said Verity softly. The little girl shot a look of fury at Brother Daniel, and one of reproach at Verity, before trudging away.

Brother Daniel put a hand out to Verity, registered her crutches, and withdrew it. "I'm Brother Daniel Jones, leader of Christian Community. Brother Benjamin told me you found your way to us after an accident. May I help you back to the house?"

On the side porch, which was vine-shaded from the warm early-afternoon sun, Brother Daniel settled Verity into a padded wicker chair and pulled a second chair close for himself. "It was kind of you to befriend Sylvie," he told her. "She's had a ragtag kind of life, poor child, with no proper home, and I'm sorry to say, no discipline."

"She says she's waiting for her mother to come for her."

"Sylvie's mother has declared her intention to become a member of Community, once she has resolved her worldly problems and responsibilities. While she's attending to those obligations, she left her little daughter in our care." He leaned closer and patted Verity's hand. "We're deeply dedicated to living God's good life, and because we are so few, we must all be energetic and cooperative. Being a loving, God-fearing Christian in today's world is hard work, and it's our duty to see that even our youngest children come to understand that."

The eyes he fixed on hers were a luminous silvery gray, fringed with incredibly long, dark lashes. Nearly hypnotic, those eyes, and his voice was a warm, deep baritone. Here on the quiet porch Verity could sense the seductive quality that had overcome the gangling build, receding hairline, and large front teeth and brought people to open their hearts and pocketbooks to this man. If she hadn't seen him in action with Sylvie, she might have been charmed herself.

But probably not.

Brother Daniel delivered a few more platitudes, gave Verity's hand a lingering clasp, and went off to prepare himself for the after-supper Bible study—in which she was more than welcome to join them, he assured her as he left.

No thanks. She'd be as out of place as poor Sylvie. Struggling to her feet, she wondered how the little girl was faring, somewhere in the house on her knees.

In the kitchen, Sister Sandra was drying the last of the lunch dishes, while Sister Catherine was putting the top crust on the second of two big pies. "Is there anything I can help with?" Verity asked.

Sister Sandra set a bowl of something green on the table, along with an empty colander. "You could shell these nice early peas. They'll go into the chicken soup, along with some frozen green beans, for supper."

Verity nudged a chair next to the table and sat down to her task.

"I guess your little buddy Sylvie ran into trouble from Brother Daniel," remarked Sister Catherine. "That kid asks to get her head handed to her about three times a day. Sometimes I wish my Eddie had her nerve, though."

If this wasn't an invitation to gossip, Verity needed new antennae. "She seems sad. Has something happened to her mother?"

Sister Catherine slid the pies into the oven, then settled into a chair on the other side of the table and stretched her legs out comfortably. "What happened, her mother came here, gosh, about two months back. Wanted to get born again one more time—you can do that over and over—and make a good Christian life for herself and her kid. Then a couple weeks ago she dumped the kid on us and trotted back to this sexy, good-looking husband she'd been telling us she was scared of."

"Sister Catherine!" Sister Sandra's voice rang with disapproval, and she came across the room to join the conversation or perhaps squelch it. "We don't know that," she said to Verity. "She left to clear up business and let her husband know she was filing for divorce. I suppose she might have got sidetracked, like; we're none of us safely above the temptations of our lustful flesh." Her glance at Sister Catherine carried daggers of meaning. "But she's a loving mother."

"You haven't heard anything from her since she left?"

"Not yet. But it isn't easy to get in touch with us, and it's not simple to arrange a divorce. She'll be back."

Sister Catherine was undaunted. "See, Verity, Sister Marsha was

sort of related to Sylvie's mother, Lily—grew up with her. Marsha says Lily was always crazy about this guy, this Dev Costello, that she only married her first husband because she was in trouble and Dev wasn't around. Then she left the guy—maybe Sylvie's father, maybe not—soon as Dev came around again."

Sister Sandra, agitated but obviously at a disadvantage in knowledge, just shook her head and plucked a fat peapod from the bowl. "I know she would not willingly abandon that little girl," she said, and snapped the pod open, to let tiny green peas rattle into the metal colander.

Would not willingly abandon: the phrase sent a chill down Verity's spine. It was a moment before she realized Sister Catherine was speaking again.

"…so I need to ask you this big favor."

Verity owed her one. "Please, ask."

"I have to get into Garberville to see my doctor, and both trucks are gone. How 'bout I borrow yours? I'll be real careful," she promised.

Before her encounter with Brother Daniel, Verity had been thinking about heading home this afternoon. Now, with an image of Sylvie's hacked-off hair and defiantly tilted chin sharp in mind's-eye, she flexed her sprained ankle and decided that she really shouldn't drive until tomorrow. "The truck belongs to a friend, but I don't think he'd mind your using it. The key is on a plastic Apple tag in the front pocket of my bag, over there in the chair."

Sister Catherine grinned, retrieved the key, tossed it high and snatched it out of the air with one hand. "Thanks. I should be back in a couple hours."

Verity reached for her crutches and hauled herself up from her chair, to follow the other woman to the door and watch her hurry across to the barn's foreyard where big, white-blond Brother Edward was splitting logs. He rested on his axe while Sister Catherine spoke, nodded after a moment, and returned to his labors as she trotted over to Harley's truck and climbed in.

"Did she have to ask his permission to leave?" Verity wondered aloud.

"Here at Community we live according to the Bible as the literal word of God," said Sister Sandra from behind her. " 'Wives submit yourselves unto your own husbands, as to the Lord. For the husband is the head of the wife, even as Christ is the head of the church.' That's from Ephesians."

"Oh," was all Verity could think to say. She returned to the table and her assigned job.

"We came out here and created Christian Community because we believe the modern world is an evil, unkind, and ungodly place. We want something better and safer, morally and physically."

Sister Sandra picked up a mechanical timer from beside the stove, turned its dial, and set it back; the tick was loud in the quiet room. "You've probably noticed we don't have electricity or telephones, but that doesn't mean we're superstitious or weird about science or technology. We just think what pours out now from television and computers and the movies and even the schools is rotten. Evil. We don't want to dirty ourselves or our children with that filth."

"Well. I couldn't say you're wrong," Verity remarked after a moment.

Sister Sandra turned to look directly at her. "Couldn't say right, either, I bet. Why're you really here?"

"Because I got lost and had an accident," said Verity flatly.

"Right. Are you a reporter?" she asked suddenly.

"No. I'd swear that on my grandmother's Bible."

Sandra sighed and crossed her arms over her breasts. "Whatever you are, you need to understand one thing. We're not some cult, okay? Brother Daniel thinks he's the leader, and he is, sort of; but we, or the men anyway, make the decisions together, after lots of discussion and plenty of input from the women. We share all our worldly goods, and all our skills. We don't worship anybody but the Lord God and his Son. Nobody has sex with anybody but his own spouse. We take good care of our children; we chastise them, but we don't abuse them. Don't you *dare* bring the world down on us."

Mesmerized by this oration, Verity blinked and took a moment to collect herself when it was finished. "I won't. There are many things about your life I envy. I promise I'll leave first thing tomorrow."

"Good. Now, Sister Catherine's trip to town leaves me short-handed. When you finish with the peas, if you want to try standing up for a while, there are salad greens to wash."

Working in a kitchen nearly always smoothed Verity's ragged edges. By the time she hung up her apron in late afternoon, she and Sister Sandra had become, if not exactly friends, at least comfortable co-workers. As the smaller woman set off for a walk, Verity pushed one of the wicker chairs into position and propped her bandaged ankle on the lower porch railing. Didn't hurt much, really, but Sister Catherine, no surprise, was taking her time about bringing the truck back. So travel would definitely wait until tomorrow.

For the moment, the late-afternoon sky was brilliant, and what looked like Community's entire contingent of children was enjoying freedom and sunshine in the open space between house and barn. An energetic and noisy lot they were, not notably repressed.

Dolls were apparently acceptable here. Three very small girls, and one nervously orbiting small boy, had set up a housekeeping corner under the vaguely watchful eye of a blond teenaged girl. An older boy, just barely preteen to Verity's inexperienced eye, was doing something to the chain of a bicycle; he was so gawky-tall he had to be Brother Daniel's son. Three slightly younger boys kicked a soccer ball around.

"Do you need more ice, Verity?"

Verity looked up to see Sylvie standing beside her chair, and felt a hitherto unnoticed tightness in her shoulders ease. "Hi, kid. No, I've decided I'm almost better. The bandage, and some rest, will do it."

"So are you going to go home?"

"Maybe tomorrow morning."

"Okay." Sylvie's mouth made a straight line, and her chin was out. "I guess I'll go talk to Gertrude the goat."

Rejected! thought Verity, and was surprised at her sense of loss. She watched Sylvie march off past the tinies, past the bicycle mechanic toward the slight slope where the goat was tethered. As she neared the soccer players, the ball came in her direction; she turned, planted herself and kicked it hard, over the head of the pursuing boy.

Good kick! thought Verity. The boys milled around, Sylvie in their midst, apparently part of the play. Then one boy stepped back, and two were scuffling with Sylvie, shoving her back and forth between them. As Verity lurched to her feet, one of the pair gave Sylvie a two-handed push, and the other, larger boy grabbed her by one arm and swung her around once, twice, a third time—and sent her flying.

Verity vaulted over the porch rail, felt her skirt catch and rip, hit the ground stumbling and righted herself. Her shriek of anger and pain immobilized everyone in sight except Sylvie's hulking, overall-clad assailant, who let out a howl of his own and raised both arms to ward her off.

"I didn't hurt her! She's a witch anyway.... *Ooof*!"

Verity knocked him backwards with one elbow-thrust and limped on to where Sylvie lay sobbing. The boy crouching next to her, the one who'd stepped out of the way earlier, looked up with a troubled face. "I'm sorry," he said, as Verity dropped to her knees beside them. "I didn't know what they were going to do. I should have stopped them."

"Think quicker next time," she snapped. "Sylvie? Where do you hurt?"

Sylvie rolled over and sat up, clutching her right shoulder; blood welled from a cut on her forehead, where a knot was rapidly forming and darkening. She wasn't sobbing after all, but gasping to catch knocked-out breath, her face white, her eyes clear and blazing. Eyeing her now, Verity knew that Patience had been right in her picture-judgment; this was a tough little kid. Probably not tough enough, though, not at age seven. Somebody should get her away from here.

"I'm telling my mom you hit me," came a wail from behind her. "She's got no right to kick our ball like that. Girls aren't allowed to mess with boys' games!"

"Listen to me, you bloody little savage!" Verity stood up and turned, to tower over the boy who was clearly Sister Marsha's son. "If Sylvie's shoulder is dislocated, I'll come after you and pull both *your* arms out of their sockets with my bare hands."

"Let me have a look." Sister Alice had materialized, or perhaps

been fetched by a frightened child. "Move back, David," she said to the crouching boy, and over her shoulder to the howler, "Zachary! Be quiet!"

Sylvie scrambled to her feet, wrapped her good arm around Verity, and buried her face.

"Sylvie, it's all right. You and I and Verity will go inside, so I can put a bandage on your forehead and examine your shoulder. If I'm going to have to hurt you, I'll tell you first."

The little girl lifted her head but stayed tight against Verity's side as the three of them moved toward the house. "The rest of you, go find something useful to do," said Sister Alice to child and adult on-lookers. "Zachary, go get your mother. Brother Daniel will want to talk to both of you."

Verity was back on the porch, sipping tea and thinking longingly of her bottle of wine, when Harley's truck finally rolled in and Sister Catherine rolled out, more or less, and headed her way with a wave.

"Hey, Verity! The doctor couldn't see me right off, so I just win-dow-shopped for a while and went to a Taco Bell for lunch, those places used to be my favorite. Then after I saw the doctor, don't tell anybody but I went to a movie."

Window-shopping in Garberville? Bar-hopping, more like; Verity got a good whiff of beer and cigarette smoke as the woman neared. Which was no business of hers, as long as her truck was safely back.

"Hey, listen, I had lots of time to think today, waiting around, and I got something to tell you. To suggest," said Sister Catherine in lowered tones. "Walk a ways out toward the barn with me, okay?"

"Better be quick. Supper's almost ready," Verity said, and fell into step beside Sister Catherine, hitching along in her recently adopted one-crutch fashion. "What is it?"

"We already talked about how your little pet, Sylvie, is having a real hard time here. The other kids don't like her, and quite a few of us older folks find her a constant pain in the…rear end. What I'm getting at, why don't you take her with you when you leave?"

Verity stopped, braced her crutch, and looked at the woman. "Kidnap a child? I don't think so."

"Come on, it wouldn't be kidnap. I mean, Brother Daniel's got no legal right to her, not while she's got a mom and stepdad out there somewhere. You could even take her to her own father."

"What do you know about her own father?"

"Nothing, how would I?" said Sister Catherine with an extravagant shrug. "But I really believe getting her out of here would be for her own good. I could help."

I bet you could, thought Verity. This woman was a type she knew well: the bored mischief-maker. Whatever she had in mind, it was unlikely to be to Sylvie's benefit, or Verity's either. "I'm leaving tomorrow morning, and Sylvie's in bed with a sore shoulder and a knot on her head, from an assault by Zachary Simms."

"Zachary? Really? Shoot, and on my one afternoon away. But see," she added hastily, "that just proves my point."

"It was nasty," said Verity flatly. "Sister Alice is taking care of her, and she's far better trained than I am. Oh, while I'm thinking about it, may I have my truck key, please?"

"Touchy bitch, aren't you," said Sister Catherine. She slapped the key into Verity's outstretched hand, turned, and flounced off.

Sister, hell, thought Verity. I wouldn't put it past her to have had the key copied. Wondering what on earth the woman was playing at, Verity clomped over to the truck, opened the door, and after a glance behind the seat to make sure Catherine hadn't hocked the sixteen-gauge to pay for her beer, reached under the dash and removed the miniature circuit board that was the key to Harley's Pro-Lock. *Now* let anybody else try to drive off in this truck.

"Verity?"

It was Sister Sandra, from the porch steps. Supper call, no doubt. "I've eaten," she said. "With Sylvie."

"Yes, I know. But Brother Daniel has called a general meeting before supper, to discuss what happened this afternoon. He wants you to join us."

Verity made her way slowly up the steps, head down. Considering. Sister Sandra led the way through the front door and into the living room, where most of Community's people were waiting. Verity stopped in the doorway, and shook her head. "I don't think so."

"I beg your pardon?" Brother Daniel towered over those near him: Sister Alice. Sister Marsha and her bulky, grizzled husband, Fred. Brother Benjamin. Brother Andrew, Sister Jennifer's husband, cradling their sleeping baby.

"What I did this afternoon was intervene when I saw a skinny little girl assaulted by a boy who must be twice her weight. That's all."

"Zachary says you hit him and called him an evil name," said Fred Simms.

"I called him a savage. My Baptist grandmother would have said heathen, but she'd have meant the same thing."

"And where do you get off, namin' it 'assault'? It was just kids fightin', not rape or like that."

Not yet. But Verity kept her mouth shut, and Brother Daniel said, "Brother Fred, that's enough."

"If you want someone else's description of the events, you should talk to David...Hicks?" Verity looked at Sister Sandra, who nodded. "He was there, and he didn't like it."

"We'll do that. But you..."

Verity interrupted him again. "I can't be involved in a discussion of the meaning of this, because I don't share your beliefs."

"Our beliefs don't condone violence against children by larger children. That's part of what we've tried to leave behind in the cities." Brother Benjamin's face was flushed, his voice tight. Several others made murmurs of agreement.

"I understand that. But I don't believe men are superior to women—or boys to girls. I don't believe in witches."

"The Bible speaks of witches," intoned Brother Daniel.

"And that means something different to you than to me." She spread her hands. "My sprain is better, and I'll be on my way early tomorrow, with thanks to all of you for your help. Oh, I'm sorry, but I tore the skirt you'd lent me. I left it in the laundry room and took back my own clothes."

The members began to talk among themselves, and Verity edged past the group and finally escaped into the hall. There she propped her crutch against the wall and moved forward on her own, limping slightly.

Near the end of the hall was a small room, probably once a hired-girl's room, where the teenaged Lisa Ives usually slept. Presently Sylvie was in bed there, and asleep, Verity hoped.

But she was awake, sitting stiffly against the headboard with eyes fixed on the door. There was a fresh bandage on her forehead, and her right arm was in a sling. "I thought you'd gone home already," she said as Verity entered.

"I wouldn't go without saying good-bye to you. I'm leaving tomorrow morning." She put a hand on Sylvie's forehead beside the bandage, which was silly because she didn't think she'd know a fever if she felt one.

"Will you sleep with me tonight?"

"No."

"Why not?"

"Because it's a single bed, and besides, I snore."

"Phooey. Where are you going to sleep?"

"Probably in my sleeping bag, in my truck."

"It'll be too cold."

"Not in the sleeping bag."

"Can I come out there, too?"

"No, Sylvie. You need to be careful of your shoulder."

The huge dark eyes filled with tears that began to spill. It was the first time Verity had seen her cry.

"Sylvie, don't worry. Things will be...okay."

"Will you come to see me in the morning?"

"I will. I promise. But when I come in, Sylvie, you must be very, very quiet. It will be really early, and we don't want to wake the house."

She blinked, and used her left hand to wipe her eyes. "Okay."

 20

"That is not humanity at its loveliest out there," said a short-of-breath Patience as she slipped inside the back door of the Port Silva police station.

"Assholes of the universe," said Officer Alma Linhares cheerfully, closing the door. Alma paused for a moment, to smooth her rumpled blue-black hair and tuck in her uniform shirt where it had been pulled loose from her belt. "We've got four of the worst cuffed to chairs in the squad room. And if the dozen or so that're pissing and moaning out front don't break it up real soon, we'll find chairs for them, too."

"Hank Svoboda asked me to..." began Patience, and Alma nodded.

"Help him talk to Rodney Farmer, the retarded kid," she said. "His grandmother—she's the one who basically raised him, his mother mostly lives in the Bay Area with this or that guy—is away on a day trip with a church group. And our local heroes decided to corner him in his own house and throw rocks."

Patience glanced into the squad room as they passed and saw four boys in middle-to-late teens slumped around the long table.

"So a neighbor called us, the captain went out and got Rodney, and Englund and I took the van and collected those sorry specimens. Two of 'em are Harkers, Melody's brothers," Alma added.

Patience had no trouble telling which two. With lank black hair and narrow, olive-skinned faces, they were male versions of the dead girl whose resemblance to his daughter had pricked David Simonov's conscience.

They had reached Captain Hank Svoboda's closed office door. "Was Rodney hurt?" asked Patience.

Alma grimaced. "Physically, just some superficial cuts on one side of his face, from flying glass when a rock broke a window. But he was so terrified he peed his pants, poor sad guy. Captain's made some progress with him, but he thought a nice, warm female person with gray hair and a cool head could speed things up."

Alma rapped on the door and said, "Captain? Patience is here. Oh," she added, turning, "that DMV check you asked for? The guy in San Francisco, Costello, had just the one vehicle registered to him—'94 blue Toyota minivan. The guy in Susanville, Simonov, also just one, a white '98 Subaru hatchback."

"Thank you, Alma," said Patience, as the door opened. Hank Svoboda, unofficial-looking in a T-shirt and his uniform trousers, nodded at her and stepped aside. The big office was dim, blinds pulled on the double window and only the desk lamp burning.

"Patience, come in. I want you to meet Rodney Farmer. Rodney, this is our friend, Patience Mackellar."

As Hank turned on the overhead light, a figure huddled in a chair beside the desk straightened, and Patience saw shaggy brown hair, smeary round glasses, a child's expression on a man's face streaked with tears, blood, and snot. Rodney unfolded like a carpenter's rule to what seemed about seven feet and wailed something and launched himself at her.

"Lord, Patience, I'm sorry," Hank Svoboda said for what had to be the twentieth time.

"Hush. It all worked out and I'm fine. Good heavens, do you suppose he treats his own grandmother that way?" Rodney Farmer's intent had been embrace, not attack, a fact Patience had realized just in time to stop Hank from coming forcefully to her aid.

"His own grandmother is a sweet-faced, gray-haired lady about your size," said Hank. "She's got a tongue soaked in battery acid, and she never lets anybody mess with any of hers."

"I'm honored to have been mistaken for her," Patience told him. The office door opened, and the two of them rose to greet a Rodney

who had had his face washed, his hair combed, and a can of Coke put into his hand. "All set," said Alma, and departed.

"I'll talk to you now, okay? Just ask me stuff," he said, and sat down in the chair beside the desk.

No, he had not run down his neighbor, Melody Harker, but he had seen it happen. "He hit her on purpose," Rodney insisted. After hitting her, the man—medium size, medium age, neither bearded nor bald—had stopped his car and got out to look at Melody. "Then he just rolled her like she was garbage into the ditch there by the road, into the weeds." And got back in his car and drove away.

Rodney did not know the man. He did not notice the license plates; he never paid any attention to numbers. The car was small, old, dusty; he thought it had only two doors. He thought it was maybe gray, or green.

"I didn't look very hard, I was too scared," he said simply. He waited until the sound of the engine was no longer in his ears before tiptoeing over to look at Melody. She was broken and bleeding, and that frightened him more, so he ran away and hid. "I didn't tell Granny," he said, ducking his head. "She might have thought I done it. She always thinks it's me that broke stuff."

Hank thanked Rodney, Patience kissed his cheek; then they moved to the door, leaving the boy to his Coke.

"Will you be able to convince the Harkers of all this?" asked Patience in low tones.

"I think so. We always figured that whatever hit her that hard had to be marked, and his grandmother's car—which he has driven a time or two, not legally—showed no damage. Good Lord, it's almost six o'clock. I'll find somebody to keep an eye on him till his grandmother arrives. You come on down to The Spot with me and I'll buy you as much single malt as you can handle."

Patience got to her feet, noting that she was stiffening up already. Being lifted off your feet and hugged desperately might not qualify as assault, but it had much the same effect. "I need to register for an exercise class," she muttered. "Thanks, Hank, but not tonight. I have some work to do yet."

"Talk to you tomorrow, then," he said, and kept one big hand on her shoulder as he walked her to the back door.

Jared Heffernan flung his front door open almost before the sound of the doorbell had faded. "God, I thought it was my mom, she'd forgot her keys. What do *you* want, anyhow?"

"Thank you, I will come in," said Patience, stepping past him into a dim and dusty entry hall. She found a light switch and flipped it, and turned to inspect Jared, who didn't look much better than Rodney Farmer. "What's the matter, Jared?"

"I'm afraid she's gone up to see him, my dad." Jared slumped to the bottom step of the nearby staircase. "She keeps saying the cops aren't doing anything, and every morning she goes to work with her gun in her bag, like she might just drive on up and take care of things herself."

"Should she be home by now?"

He looked up at the tall case clock against the wall. "Well, maybe not. On Thursday nights she sometimes has a drink after work with this woman from the same office."

Terrific. Armed *and* loaded. "Jared, does she have a license to carry a gun?"

"Shit, I don't know." He put his head in his hands. "No, she can't have. She's got no reason and she's never said anything about it. It's a gun, a revolver, my dad had. Listen, I'll pay you if you go take it away from her," he said, looking up hopefully.

From Grandma to gunslinger, thought Patience. And she had other things to do. "Jared, where is your telephone?"

"Huh? Right over there," he said, pointing. "Why?"

"Because I'm going to call the police and have them take away your mother's gun."

He stood up with a roar and leapt at her, second time in as many hours and she wasn't having any this time. She stepped aside, and as he stumbled past, she seized his left hand in her right, swept the arm up behind him, and applied a wristlock, hard.

"Ow! Quit that, you're gonna break my fuckin' arm!"

"Hush!" she snapped. "She won't go to *jail.*" Patience shifted her

grasp, pushing her left hand under his elbow to grip and bend his fingers. "It's a misdemeanor, she'll pay a fine. And she'll be much *safer*." She whacked the back of his head smartly and released him with a hearty push toward the staircase.

He subsided to the bottom step again, cradling his arm and shaking his head. "You better watch out, lady. I'm a lot bigger than you." He paused, sniffed. "I dunno, I guess she will be. Thing is, she'll think it was me that called the cops."

"No, she won't. Now, where does she go for this after-work drink?"

Jared named two places. Watching him for signs of renewed energy, Patience called the station, got Hank, and told him the story.

"There," she said to Jared, who had slumped back against the stairs and was rubbing his face like a weary old man.

"Uh, thanks, I guess."

"You can repay me with some information."

He frowned up at her, and she hurried on.

"Remember the day you came with your mother to my office?"

"Shit, yes. That stuff you gave her, that's what really set her off."

"Jared, I'll talk to her again. Tomorrow, maybe. But do you remember telling me someone was watching me, there at my office?"

"Sure. But you didn't believe me."

"It was your mother who didn't believe you." Patience regretted that tack, and tried again. "I agree, I didn't take time to go into the matter then. But I'd like you to tell me about it now."

He propped himself on his elbows and cocked his head at her. "Tell you what?"

"Who was watching? And from where?"

"Some guy, that's all."

"Old or young? Black or white?'

"Hey, how many black guys you see in good old Port Silva? He was white. I don't know how old; he had hair, and it wasn't gray."

Patience kept her mouth shut.

"Brown, his hair was, I think. Not real long or anything. And he had dark glasses on. I don't know how big; he was just a guy sitting in a car on the street."

"What kind of car?"

"That's how come I noticed him. He had this classic old Mustang, probably a '67. Like my dad's."

It was a few minutes after seven when Patience opened her kitchen door. Ralph trotted out past her, eager but not frantic; she left the door open as she set the bag containing her supper—shredded garlic beef and shrimp with vegetables—on the kitchen counter beside the microwave oven.

The answering machine blinked: one message. The caller was not Verity, but Harley; he had received her message and would come by sometime between seven and eight.

Patience let Ralph in, looked at the food containers, and felt a large lack of interest. She fixed herself a drink instead, and sat down at the table with the folder of notes she'd brought home with her. Claire Ellison, that was the name of the weaver, Verity's information source. In Weott.

Where there was, of course, another answering machine. Patience identified herself and asked that Claire call her. Then she freshened her drink and went out on the deck to survey her domain. Her original plan for catching the prowler was still a sensible one, if her extension cords proved long enough. And if Harley got here before dark, to do the work. She was feeling stiff, and old, and not very useful.

She was still out there, leaning on the rail, when Verity's Alfa arrived—giving her a jolt that faded at once as she realized who was driving it: Harley. She went down the steps to meet him.

"Any word from Verity?" he asked, as he unfolded himself from the low car.

"Just a secondhand message this morning," she said, and repeated it. "And don't worry about your truck; if it was damaged, we'll take care of it."

"Sure, okay, no problem. I shouldn't have started this stupid class," he muttered. "I should have gone with her."

"No, you shouldn't. This was a one-person job, and a woman was the best person for it."

Harley hunched his massive shoulders uneasily. "I guess. So the kid's probably okay, but what about the mom? What about Lily?"

"Nothing," said Patience. Her most recent tugs on the lines of her spider's web had brought in nothing new; neither Lily nor her van had come to public attention in the San Francisco Bay Area or the adjoining counties.

"Too bad," said Harley. "I guess, anyway." He knew what kinds of inquiries Patience had under way. "So, what's this about an intruder, and what are we going to do about it? Shoot him?"

"I have this standing frame for lights," she told him, leading the way behind the house to the small garage. "Mike used it when he was painting walls or whatever. And I have a motion-sensitive floodlight. We'll mount the flood on the frame, and put the frame beside the driveway."

"Hey, great! We could mount a camera, too."

"I thought we'd simply take turns watching," she told him. "It's late already, and our technical resources are limited."

"Not mine. I've got this Polaroid camera, I could rig a tripod or just sling a kind of platform in a tree. Wouldn't even need night film with that light."

And she wouldn't need to stay awake. "Harley, it's your job; do it any way you want. Let me show you where the gear is."

He followed her to the back of the garage, where the footed metal frame stood against a wall. "You never told me about any intruder, Patience. Got any idea who it might be?"

She sighed as she bent and laboriously lifted the long, heavy-duty extension cord. "For a while today I thought I had it solved. I thought it was a man I've tracked on a child-support case. But his son convinced me that his father was forced to sell his '67 Mustang years ago, during his divorce.

"So it could not have been Duane Heffernan who sat watching my office from a green Mustang recently. And it probably isn't Duane Heffernan who's been hanging around here driving Ralph crazy and worrying me. Come on, I'll plug this in at the front of the house and see whether it will reach. You bring the frame."

"Patience? Here's something really strange," he said as they walked.

"Is it too heavy?"

"Thing is, there was this old green Mustang behind Verity and me on, um, Tuesday it was. We turned off for Weott and it drove on. I noticed it because I want one—or I did before I drove that Alfa."

Patience unplugged her cord and set the whole big coil down. "Harley, come inside."

In the kitchen, Harley ate fortune cookies and inspected the containers of Chinese food while Patience made a quick call to Larry Mulrooney, her San Francisco P.I. friend.

"However you do it, Larry, I need to know whether Dev Costello had a car of any kind while his wife was away. Especially whether he might have had a Mustang. He's not recorded owner of anything but the van, but he may have been driving someone else's.

"So," she said as she hung up. "Larry will take care of that right away. And you can handle the other one."

Harley spooned a cold shrimp into his mouth and tried to look as though it had happened while he wasn't looking. "Yes, ma'am. How?"

Patience got herself some ice and poured another shot of The Macallan. "I'm not driving anywhere," she said aloud. "All right, here it is. The other man in this story, David Simonov, doesn't show as registered owner of a Mustang, either. But in Berkeley, we had a neighbor, a young man, who was slowly repairing and customizing and generally tarting up an old MG, I think it was, and he didn't drive it, so it wasn't registered. Here's what I want you to do."

From her file folder Patience retrieved the telephone number of David Simonov's neighbor, whom she had called early in this case for information on the man's home and life. "You met Professor Simonov at school several months ago," she told Harley now, "and he told you he was thinking of selling his old green Mustang. You've finally gotten the money together, and you've been trying to get in touch with Simonov, with no luck."

"Gotcha! And I'm wondering if he, the neighbor, knows whether the car might have been sold already."

"Harley, you're brilliant."

Patience, too restless to sit still, paced between kitchen and living room with the portable phone while Harley made the call. Should

hook a recorder up here, too, as well as downtown, she told herself, her palm firmly in place over the mouthpiece.

The neighbor was friendly. Sure, he knew that Mustang, Professor Simonov had complained about not having time to work on it. He, the neighbor hadn't heard about any proposed sale, but he'd run next door and have a look if the young man didn't mind waiting.

Either the neighbor was in his underwear and had to dress before going out, or these houses were a half mile apart. After what seemed fifteen minutes, Patience released the mouthpiece to pick up her glass, took a too-large sip of Scotch, and had to set the phone aside quickly lest her sputtering be heard.

"I see," said Harley. "Listen, that's okay. I appreciate your help."

"It's gone?" asked Patience before the receiver was back on the base.

"Yup. He kept it out back of his house, on blocks. All that's there now are the blocks."

21

When the telephone rang, Patience was trying to surface from a confused but somehow important dream of multiple Duane Heffernans driving old cars through fields of broken furniture, a camera serving for hood ornament on the nose of each car. She rolled over and peered through sleep-fogged eyes at her clock as she reached for the instrument beside her bed. Four forty-five A.M.

The dream still tugging at her, she said "Hulmmm?", cleared her throat, and tried again. "Hello?"

"Is this Patience Smith? Patience Mackellar?"

It was a woman's voice, sounding both weary and hurried. "Yes, to both," said Patience.

"Patience, this is Claire Ellison. You called me last night."

And you're calling me back at this hour. Patience lurched upright and threw the covers aside. "Yes. What is it?"

"I'm just about to get off night shift—I'm an on-call nurse at the hospital in Garberville—"

"Verity?" Patience croaked the name through a mouthful of dry cotton.

"Oh, no. Not that I know of, anyway. But this old woman was brought in yesterday afternoon by her friends, badly beaten, and she was somebody I knew Verity had gone looking for. As a possible lead to that woman, Lily, and her little girl, Sylvie," she added.

"I haven't heard from Verity directly. Tell me." Telephone to her ear, Patience padded barefoot into the kitchen and heard about Dirty Mary while she filled the kettle and set it to heat.

"…apparently in really bad shape when she got here, not able to say anything coherent. I'd guess her attacker left her for dead, but she's tougher than anybody'd think. Anyway," Claire went on, "when I learned she'd been admitted, and went in to see her, she insisted on talking to me. She was so *ashamed* of herself, that she'd told the man what he wanted."

As Claire Ellison reconstructed the old woman's story, she'd gone outside just before dawn to relieve her bladder and was grabbed silently from behind and carried down by the ocean, where any sounds she made were unlikely to be heard. The man kept hitting her until she told him what she'd told Verity the afternoon before, and Lily before that: how to find the people she called "them Christers."

"Could she give *you* the directions, do you think?" asked Patience.

"She has, sort of; she's pretty foggy. Do you have a pencil?"

Patience wrote down Claire's instructions. "And from where you are, the best way would be to go in from here, Garberville, by the Briceland–Shelter Cove Road," Claire told her.

"Good. Thank you," said Patience. "Has anyone called the sheriff?"

Claire sighed. "They're spread thin up here. They think old Mary is crazy, and they weren't too sure about me. They said they'd check."

"I'll talk to somebody," said Patience, and hung up.

"Patience?" Harley came in the back door, rubbing his eyes. "I saw your light on. I guess I dozed off out there. Did the prowler get past me?"

Patience had forgotten the prowler, and had forgotten all about Harley, who had clearly kept last night's promise to return after his date and camp on the deck in order to keep a watch on his light-and-camera setup. Reassured by a window reflection that her flannel nightgown could pass for decent, she jerked her mind into gear: Verity and the Christers. The Humboldt County sheriff's people, via Hank Svoboda. And her dream, she had it now, cameras and photos. She focused on Harley. "Never mind the prowler. Is there plenty of gas in Verity's car?"

"Yes, ma'am."

"Good. I'll be needing it, as soon as I make a couple of calls." She

concentrated briefly on the coffee cone, pouring boiling water with care; then she picked up the portable phone and carried it to the little kitchen desk and her Rolodex. Chet Engeberg, the editor of the Port Silva *Sentinel,* would be still in bed at this hour. But he was a good newspaperman and a good friend, and the person most likely to have the answer to her question.

Harley brought her coffee to her when it was ready, and made a mugful for himself. "What was *that* about?" he asked when she'd hung up.

"According to my client, David Simonov, it was a newspaper picture of Melody Harker, along with the story of her hit-and-run death, that spurred him to begin the search for his daughter. Because of the resemblance between the two. Wait here, Harley, while I dress." She headed for the bedroom, coffee mug in one hand and telephone in the other.

He leaned against the counter and sipped carefully at very hot coffee while Patience spoke to someone else on the telephone. When she stopped talking, he called out, "What difference does it make? About the picture?"

"When I saw two Harker boys at the police station yesterday, with that stamped-from-the-same-mold Harker face, it struck me as odd that I didn't remember seeing that face in the paper."

"Maybe you missed it."

"Chet Engeberg just told me that Melody's mother didn't have any pictures of her except the ones from school, those end-of-the-year line-ups of a whole class. None of them was distinct enough to use."

"Oh. Shit."

"Indeed." Patience came back to the kitchen wearing jeans, sweatshirt, and sneakers. "Somebody, probably David Simonov, is trailing Verity; he beat up an old woman to find out where she'd gone. And where Lily and Sylvie had gone before her. I've talked to Hank Svoboda, who will take care of lighting a fire under the Humboldt County sheriff. Now I'm going up to the Lost Coast. Do you want to come along?"

"You bet!"

Verity woke just before five-thirty, unzipped the sleeping bag, and slid quietly from the truck bed. There were no lights in the house, no sign of movement. Wouldn't be long, though, she told herself as she reached back into the truck for her bag and her fleece vest. Which was okay, because she needed somebody to be around to unlock the gate.

As she'd expected, the kitchen door was not locked. She stepped quietly inside, and softly down the hall. At the room where Sylvie slept, she knocked very lightly with just her fingertips, fished her penlight flash from her bag, and opened the door.

And stifled a gasp of surprise as the light beam found Sylvie upright on the edge of the bed wearing socks, dress, and too-large jacket, her shoes in her lap. That's it, then, Verity told herself, and clicked the flash off.

"Where's your sling?" she asked softly.

"It got in the way."

Probably it did. Deal with that later. "Okay. You carry your shoes, and I'll carry you."

With Sylvie astride her right hip, Verity retraced her steps, limping only slightly. In the kitchen she pulled the door wide, edged herself and her burden outside, and stood for a moment looking for movement in the misty dark, seeing none. She pulled the door toward her until she heard the quiet click of its latch, then stepped carefully down the porch steps and hurried to the back of the truck.

"Okay, kid, you ride back here for starters. Roll up in the sleeping bag and be very, very quiet."

"I know how to be quiet."

And where did you learn that, I wonder. "Good. Once we get going, I'll try not to hit too many bumps; and I'll stop and let you get in with me when I think it's safe. Okay?"

"Okay," Sylvie whispered. She tossed her shoes inside, then crawled after them, and Verity eased the tailgate up. "I have a couple of things to do up front. Then I'll be going back inside for a few minutes. Don't worry."

"Okay."

Verity snapped the cover into place and went to the cab, to replace the Pro-Lock circuit board and to squeegee fog-moisture from

the windshield. As she moved around the truck to get the other side, she saw the first light in the house, in the kitchen. Good. She finished the job, wiped the squeegee off, and put it away.

The early kitchen worker was Sister Alice, who looked only mildly surprised when Verity appeared. "My ankle is much better," Verity said, and demonstrated by standing squarely on both feet. "So I thought I'd get on the road early." The older woman inclined her head briefly in a nod that Verity took to mean "Good luck and good riddance."

Verity used the bathroom and gave her teeth a quick brush. As she came back through the kitchen, Sister Alice gestured at the stove, where the coffeepot steamed. "Would you like a cup, to take with you?"

"Lovely. Thank you. I have my own cup," she added, and fished the plastic insulated cup from her shoulder bag. "I wanted to tell Sylvie good-bye," she said, as she accepted the filled cup and snapped its top into place. "But she's still asleep, and I didn't want to wake her. Will you please tell her for me?"

"I will."

"Thanks," Verity said again.

Here in the valley the summer sky was brightening even before six A.M., and there were breaks in the misty fog. Verity tapped her fingertips lightly on the side of the truck bed, as she had earlier on the bedroom door, before climbing into the cab. She started the engine, ran the windshield wipers briefly, and then turned on the headlights and backed the truck around to head out. She planned to go home via Garberville, where she'd stop to call Patience and find out whether David Simonov had been in touch and perhaps even left a number where he could be reached. It was time the careless bastard started acting like a father.

The house was still mostly dark and quiet, but she caught a glimpse of a man, maybe Brother Andrew, in the entrance to the barn. Milking time, probably. She drove slowly down the trail, and as she neared the gate, another man loomed out of the fog: Brother Benjamin. At his gesture, she braked to a stop and rolled down her window. Would Sylvie realize that this stop was only for the gate? And if she recognized the voice of this man, her friend...

"On your way, I see," he said. "I'll get the gate for you."

She smiled at him, her ears straining and hearing only silence from behind her. "Thanks. And thank you for giving me a refuge." She'd had a pleasant if guarded chat with this man the night before, and was uneasy about being less than honest with him. He was attractive in a lean, outdoorsy way, and seemed to be a good person, too; the kind of life Sister Sandra had described earlier might be satisfying with a man like Brother Benjamin. For someone whose character was suited to solitude and deference, unlike hers. Or Sylvie's.

Now Benjamin took a deep breath and turned to face her. "God help me, I feel like a traitor. But I was wondering if I could ask you to look up Sylvie's father when you get home."

She was startled into temporary speechlessness. "I beg your pardon?" she said, when she got her wits back.

"I watched you with Sylvie, I could see you connected with her in a personal way. So you know this place is not a refuge for someone like her. Here we bend and adjust and defer. It's a lesson not everyone learns."

"True," said Verity.

"Her father lives in Susanville. I looked him up in the telephone book yesterday, and wrote down his address and phone number." He handed her a slip of paper. "If you feel right about doing this."

"I'll feel fine about it," she told him with perfect sincerity.

"Good. Now, like I said last night, you go right at the top of the hill, and right again at the intersection eight miles on. That road will take you to the Shelter Cove–Garberville Road. After that—I'll pray for you to find your own best way."

Surprised to find tears in her eyes, Verity blinked them back, nodded, and put the truck in gear. Brother Benjamin pulled the gate back, and she drove through. Good girl, she said silently to her still-silent passenger.

Verity left her window down as she drove through the gate and headed back to the real world. No, the *other* world. She wouldn't come back here, and she hoped Sylvie's future, and Lily's, could be worked out without bringing that world down on Community.

She crept along the rutted trail at a pace that barely moved the

speedometer needle, climbing slowly out of the little valley. When she reached the narrow gravel road she'd turned from—God, only twenty-four hours earlier!—she pulled the truck as far right as possible, stopped, and set the brake. Here it was, the line to cross. Turn onto that road and she was a kidnapper. She opened her door and stepped out.

There were swathes of fog out there ahead, tangled in trees crowding the road, drifting across the road itself. Verity took a deep breath, and another, and turned and walked to the back of the truck. "Okay, kid," she called, as she pulled the bed cover loose and then dropped the tailgate.

Sylvie sat up quickly and scrambled forward, to throw herself into Verity's arms. "Oh, I'm really glad to see you! It was really dark, and noisy, and I thought I was back in the pig house."

"Oh, Sylvie." A knot she hadn't known was there loosened in Verity's chest. So what's a little kidnapping? This kid needed rescue, and to hell with the consequences. Besides, she knew dozens of lawyers. "Come on, it should be safe now for you to ride up front."

She lifted Sylvie off the tailgate and set her on her feet. The cooler chest was against the bed-wall just behind the wheel well; Verity opened it and pulled out a plastic bag containing two apples, a chunk of cheese, and a sorry-looking banana. "Hooray, breakfast. Now help me close everything back up and get out of here before somebody finds out you're gone and comes after us."

"They won't come. They'll be glad," said Sylvie.

All buttoned up and belted in, they set off down the narrow, bumpy gravel road, patches of fog limiting visibility to an extent that would have been dangerous had they been traveling at more than ten miles an hour. Verity sipped coffee while Sylvie ate an apple down to the tiniest remainder of core, then broke off a piece of cheese and wolfed that. Verity saw her eyeing the banana and said, "Go ahead. I'm not hungry."

Finally Sylvie sat back with a sigh, tucked the banana peel back into the bag, and said, "I'm full."

"Good."

"Verity, where are we going?"

"To Garberville, and a telephone. And then home. To my mother. She'll know what we should do next."

"You have a *mother*?"

"Listen, kid, I even have a grandmother. But she doesn't live with us." Belatedly Verity wished the word "mother" had not passed her lips. She didn't know what she could say to this child about Lily Costello.

"How far is it? To your house?"

Verity relaxed. "Only about ninety miles, maybe ninety-five. But a lot of it is pretty slow going. It might take us three hours."

"I like driving," said Sylvie. "When I was with Lily, we used to drive a lot." The child's voice had an oddly distant note, as if she had somehow relegated her mother to the past. Verity was trying to decide how to respond when Sylvie leaned forward in her seat to peer out the windshield. "Verity, who's that?"

Verity peered in her turn. On the road ahead, touched by vagrant rays of sunshine that were beginning to penetrate the fog, she saw a small, low car. Facing them with headlights on, driver's door open and driver's seat empty, it was parked closer to the center than the side of the very narrow road.

Verity stopped the truck twenty feet short of the empty car. With a steep drop-off to her right, she might possibly skin by this obstacle, but not without closing that jutting door. And wherever the driver was, he wouldn't have a battery much longer; the headlights were dim. One of them, the right, pointed askew from its setting in what might be a crumpled fender. "Sylvie…"

"Look, there's somebody."

A man stepped out of the trees on the passenger side of the car, buckling his belt as he walked. Tallish and trim in chinos and a close-fitting leather jacket, he moved like a young man although a khaki rain hat and wraparound dark glasses made his face difficult to see. He stopped as he spotted them, and lifted a hand. "Hi, are you folks from Community? I'm David Simonov, and I was coming to see my daughter there, check on how she's doing."

"I'd say it's about time!" snapped Verity, slinging her bag over her shoulder as she stepped down from the truck. "And I can tell you how she was doing: not well at all."

"I'm really sorry about that, Sylvie. I hope I can make it up to you."

"Sylvie, wait."

But Sylvie, who had bounced out of the truck, was trotting in his direction. Halfway there, she slowed, stopped; he held out a hand. "I'd know you anywhere, Sylvie, you look just like your mother. Come along, she's waiting for you."

Facts and suppositions whirled in Verity's head, but her only conclusion was that this did not feel right. She took two steps back, reaching for the truck door. "Sylvie, come back here!"

Sylvie, standing stock-still and watching the man now slowly approaching her, suddenly stiffened with a full-throated shriek. "It's Dev! It's Dev it's Dev it's the Devil!" she screamed, and spun around to run.

The man lunged and caught her, grappled with her briefly, pinioned her against his body with one arm. "Shut up, you little bitch!"

"Where's Lily? What did you do to Lily?" Sylvie screamed, flailing her legs. "Devil Devil Devil!"

"Lily's where she wanted to be," he snarled, "and she wants you with her." His vicious, open-handed blow caught Sylvie full-face. As the little girl sagged in his grip, Verity was yanking the gun case from behind the truck seat, the words "Dumb dumb dumb!" roaring in her head.

"And you, blondie," he called to Verity, "never mind. Your cannon's there, but the shells aren't."

Catherine! Her mind registered this betrayal and set it aside as she turned and stepped clear of the truck door. He had Sylvie slung head-down over his left shoulder, his left arm gripping her legs. His right arm was extended, so that she could see clearly the revolver he was pointing at her.

"Whatever has happened," said Verity slowly, clearly, "you'll only make it worse by hurting this child." She kept her eyes wide, afraid to blink. "Too many people know about you, you can't possibly expect to…"

"Shut up," he said softly. The struggle with Sylvie had cost him his hat and glasses, revealing a white and furious face with eyes that

glittered hard blue. "I don't expect anything but what I've got right here. And it's all I want."

Sylvie was stirring, and he clamped his arm harder across her legs. "Now, we'll all go for a little walk in the woods. Right over that way," with a motion of the revolver, "where I just came out."

Uh-huh, right. "I don't think so," she said, and stayed where she was, feet planted and shoulders squared.

"*Goddammit,* you *will…*" He took a breath, shook his head, and lifted the revolver. "Have it your way."

"Sylvie, dive!" Verity shouted as she thrust a hand into her bag.

Sylvie howled and kicked her legs and eeled free of the grasping arm, to plummet headfirst to the ground and roll away.

"Sylvie, run!"

Dev aimed a kick at Sylvie's rolling body and stumbled but righted himself. He turned his snarling face to Verity, and the Freeflight tungsten dart, flung with all her strength and skill, buried its spike in his eye socket and clung there.

"Sylvie, run!" she screamed again as Costello, howling with pain, dropped his gun and reeled backward, slapping at his face with both hands. Verity flung herself this time, in a headlong grab for the gun that Sylvie, too, was diving for.

Verity rolled over and up onto her knees, trying to hold Sylvie against her body, trying to get control of the gun. Above them, Costello yanked the dart out with a shriek of pain and threw it aside, lurched to his car and reached inside and came upright brandishing a three-foot-long tire iron. He swung it high and came roaring at them.

The first bullet hit him mid-chest, knocking him into a backwards stagger. The second took him off his feet. Verity surged from kneeling to standing in a single motion and pulled Sylvie with her, back and away toward the truck. Her ears rang, her knees wobbled, and in her mind's eye was her policeman father's dictum, like words flashing on a screen: Aim for center-mass, second shirt button. Thank you, Daddy.

22

"I killed him."

Sylvie was clinging tightly to Verity, her face drained of color and her eyes enormous. "I killed the Devil."

"No, you didn't." The quick response covered a melee of confused thoughts. Verity knew she herself had pulled the trigger, although Sylvie had certainly done her best to get her hands on the gun. An act of self-defense on Verity's part, it would have been vengeance on Sylvie's for the murder of her mother that Costello had effectively confessed to. Could a child need, was she in any way entitled to, blood vengeance? *Gaah.*

There was a gurgle of sound from the man on the ground, and Sylvie pulled free of Verity and craned her neck. "He's not dead!"

He's as dead as we're going to make him. Verity looked at the revolver in her hand, suppressed a wish to lob it into the trees, and instead put it in the front pocket of the leather bag that was still, miraculously, slung from her shoulder. "You *didn't* kill him. I shot him, Sylvie. For both of us. Because he was going to harm us." Closer and more manageable truth, she thought, with a shudder that made her tighten her shoulders.

Costello was lying on his back with his knees cocked up, as if he'd tried to rise. He was breathing rapidly, shallowly; blood was welling through two neat holes on the front of his leather jacket.

She knew she should try to stop the bleeding—pack the wound, turn him and pack the exit wound if there was one. She moved closer and saw that his face was grayish-white, his eyes half-open. Different color eyes, the right one blue and the left a blood-streaked green, its

colored contact lens knocked askew. Probably by her dart, she thought, and swallowed hard.

"He's the Devil, Verity! Keep away from him!" Sylvie tugged urgently at the hem of her vest, and Verity took a step back, her eyes still on the man who'd intended to kill them. His very short hair had an odd, rumpled look. Trying to curl, that's what it was. And a stray beam of sunlight touching that dull brown hair drew a gleam of something brighter.

Red curls beneath the brown, and green eyes. This was the Devlin Costello she'd heard described at the pub, by Frank, the darts-player, or maybe by his wife. Was there in fact an actual David Simonov, or was there only this man, this actor?

Her spinning thoughts were pulled up by a groan and then a mutter from the injured man. "Bitch. I'll…get up…minute."

Verity swooped Sylvie up and ran for the truck, to plop her inside and shut the door. "You stay right there!" she snapped. "Please. I'll see if I can do anything for him, and then we'll go. Sylvie?"

"Okay."

Costello was still breathing. Moving his arms a bit, as if trying to swim. Muttering. Reliving his murderous activities, thought Verity. "Where's Lily?"

"Lily," he said in a hoarse whisper. "Oh, God. It…didn't…burn."

"Verity? Are you coming?"

Shit. She turned, to see Sylvie sliding out of the truck. "Sylvie, stay there! I'm coming."

She had nothing to stanch the bleeding with anyway, except her own clothing. What she had to do was get him to help. No, he was too big for her to handle and too dangerous and besides, being moved by an unskilled person would probably do him more damage. Get out of here for help, that was the only answer.

"Take her…brat… Then…burn." His voice was growing fainter with each word, the pauses between words longer.

"I'll be back," she told him. "You just keep breathing. Or not, you bastard. I'm coming," she called, to Sylvie.

Back to Community, or on to Garberville? Probably Garberville, Verity thought, if she could get her truck past his car. "Please get back

in the truck," she said to Sylvie, trying to keep her voice even, "and fasten your seat belt."

Sylvie, who had almost reached her, stopped, lifted her head, turned. "Listen, Verity. Somebody's coming. Should we run?"

The sound of engines, magnified by fog and the overhanging trees, swelled louder and seemed to surround them. "Oh, baby, I don't think so," she said, and wrapped an arm around Sylvie and turned with her to face whoever was coming. "Let's figure it's the good guys."

The first car, a utility vehicle with a star on its nose and a light bar on its roof, screeched to a stop behind Costello's car, whose lights by now showed only the faintest glimmer. Like Costello, thought Verity. Suddenly aware of the weight of the revolver in her bag, she retrieved it and bent to lay it on the ground, then stepped back, pulling Sylvie with her.

"Humboldt County Sheriff's Department!" barked the brown-uniformed man who surged into their dusty, rutted arena. "What's happened here?"

"The Devil was going to shoot us, but we shot him instead."

The deputy stared open-mouthed at Sylvie. Verity, hearing stark truth, decided against embroidery. "He stopped us on the road, and meant to kill us. I need to get this child away from here." She tightened her grip on Sylvie, who sighed and subsided against her.

"There's the weapon," Verity added, with a gesture. "I didn't check, but I assume there are still bullets in it."

The deputy sheriff, taller than Verity and built like an aging linebacker, picked up the revolver and ejected the remaining cartridges, then moved to a quick survey of the injured man. As a second vehicle pulled to a stop behind his, he straightened and bellowed, "Medics? Over here."

"Now," he said, stepping out of the way of the two men and their stretcher and turning his attention to Verity and Sylvie, "you better tell me all about it."

Verity opened her mouth and then closed it, unable to think where to start. "I think I need, we need, to sit down. In my truck, maybe? And a drink of water?" She also had a sudden need to pee.

"Lady, I need to know your name, her name—" pointing at Sylvie "—and especially his name," he said, gesturing at the man being bundled onto the stretcher. "I need to know what you were doing out here with this piece."

Sylvie followed his glance at the revolver. "We didn't bring that, that's the Devil's gun. He's had it for about a zillion years; he likes to point it at me to scare Lily."

The sheriff was staring again at Sylvie, and Verity thought maybe she was in the middle of a lunatic movie running at double speed. Maybe her brain was melting, like her knees. The medics carried the stretcher past, and bile rose in her throat and threatened to invade her mouth and spill right down her chin. Maybe if she just sat down here in the dirt...

"I beg your pardon," said a familiar voice, and Verity locked her wavering knees and peered down the tunnel past the lineup of vehicles. Here came Patience, unusually pale of face, Harley right behind her. Both of them stepped aside to permit passage of the laden stretcher, both looked down at it, and Verity thought Patience's color improved immediately.

Stretcher past, Patience moved forward like someone who expected the waters, or the police, to part before her. "I'm Patience Smith, a licensed private investigator and the person who notified your office of potential trouble," she said to the deputy. "My daughter and her charge there, the child we were hired to find, are obviously in need of medical attention. Perhaps in Garberville? Sheriff Roncalli of Mendocino County and Chief Gutierrez and Captain Svoboda of the Port Silva police will vouch for me."

Hired. Yes indeed, apparently by that man I just shot. Who is in no condition to pay our bill. Verity bit back a giggle that might lead to God knew what, and straightened her own spine in imitation of her mother's. *Goddamn, Ma, if you can get us out of this one...*

"Mrs. Smith. Humboldt County Sheriff's Deputy Bill Brown. I know Hank Svoboda from the academy. I, uh, well, why don't you and your daughter follow the ambulance to the hospital in Garberville, and I'll come along after, talk to you there."

"Thank you," said Patience, coming dangerously close to

graciousness in Verity's opinion. "We'll go in my car, back there at the end of the line. And Harley…" she looked up at her young companion "…can bring the truck when the road is clear."

There was nodding, shuffling of feet. Verity gave Harley as much smile as she could muster, told him the keys were in the truck, noted for the first time with a touch of panic that Sylvie's mouth was bloody. Remembered events and decided Dev's blow had split her lip. *Gaah*. Tried unsuccessfully to peel the child loose so the two of them could walk, finally picked her up and trudged off in Patience's wake.

Past Costello's car, past the county vehicles, and there by God was her own car. "Give me the keys, Mom. And I'll give you the kid. Sylvie, this is my mother, Patience Mackellar."

"I want you!" wailed Sylvie, nearly strangling Verity with her skinny arms.

"Verity, are you sure you're up to driving?" asked Patience.

Verity smacked Sylvie lightly on the butt and set her down. "Stop that. My mother has a much nicer lap, which is where you'll have to sit in this car. And even with a banged-up ankle, which I've not had time to think about, I am the only one who can get this machine out of here backwards and fast. Okay?"

 **23**

"Look, I figured it might be Dev who took the Mustang," said Simonov, "but I wasn't sure, and I didn't report it. So I don't see why you've dragged me down here."

"Because it was used in the commission of a crime," said Deputy Brown.

"To kill Lily?" Simonov half whispered, his tanned outdoorsman's face showing white around the lips.

"Devlin Costello had killed your wife...."

"*His* wife. My former wife," said Simonov quickly.

"Right." Brown's heavy face was impassive except for a brief tightening of his mouth. "He claims he killed your *former* wife almost three weeks ago. Alameda County has found her vehicle down a brushy arroyo in the East Bay Regional Park District, about where he said it would be, and they're gonna call me when they get the body out."

"He killed her *before* he came to see me? But—he was so miserable, he loved her so much." Simonov shook his head in disbelief, blue eyes wide. "When the car was gone, I thought he'd taken it so he could look for her. That's really why I didn't report it."

"Uh-huh. Well, with your Mustang for transportation, he was able to run down and kill a young girl, beat up an old woman, then waylay and try to kidnap with intent to kill a young woman and another young girl, your daughter." Brown paused for breath. "You happen to remember her?"

"Sylvie? Of course I do, but I haven't seen her for a long time. I'm not sure I'd even recognize her."

"Oh, you'd recognize her," murmured Patience, drawing an irritated glance from Simonov.

"Look," he said to Brown, "I've got nothing to do with any of this, hadn't seen or heard from Dev or Lily for almost five years until he turned up and stole my car. And I've been working seven long days a week for the past month, there are people who can attest to that. So if you don't mind…"

Deputy Brown got to his feet. "In a few minutes we'll take you over to the hospital to give us a formal identification of a comatose man, except he'll probably be dead by the time we get there. Only other person might be able to help us out that way is a seven-year-old girl who's a mite too upset to be a witness."

"I…okay, I can do that," said Simonov.

"Then, when I get word from Alameda County, I'll take you down there to identify the body of your former wife. In the meantime, I'll check your story with whatever names you'd care to provide; and you'll stay right here in town."

As the door closed on Brown, Simonov slumped in his chair and put a hand over his eyes.

"Mr. Simonov, do you want to see your daughter?" Patience asked in her gentlest tones.

"Uh, well, I think that would probably just upset her more."

"Sylvie is your daughter?"

"Oh my God, yes. Lily's looks sometimes give people the wrong idea, but she's…she *was* a real puritan. Sex only with the guy you're married to and then only in the missionary position after you've prayed together."

Patience made an effort to keep distaste from her face and voice. "But she left you."

"Yeah, well. We were having trouble by then, she wasn't interested in my career, didn't have anything in common with my colleagues." He shrugged. "I think it was Dev she always wanted, anyway. And he promised to marry her."

"I understand you're planning to marry again?"

"Oh, no, not me. I got married the first time way too young, as you can probably see from the mess that's resulted. I'm going to wait

for a little more wisdom before trying again," he added with a crinkle-eyed, boyish grin.

"Sensible of you. What do you plan to do with Sylvie while you're waiting?"

The question, or the new edge to her voice, snapped him to attention. "Listen, Mrs. Smith or whatever you call yourself, my daughter is none of your business. Anyway, I understand from the deputy who flew me down here that Sylvie's mother had found her a home in some kind of religious community. I'm sure she'll be fine there."

The physical resemblance between David Simonov and Devlin Costello was not a simple matter of colored contacts and hair dye, Patience had decided there in the interview room at the county sheriff's substation in Garberville. It had to do more with body attitude, angle of head, wide earnest gaze. While an inch or two taller, and leaner, Costello had managed to convey perfectly the surface, maybe even the essence, of David Simonov: self-deprecating, uninvolved, humble in a way that simply meant he didn't care about anyone else.

Slouched now in a canvas chair on her own deck, she watched the lowering sun paint a few cloud-streaks with pink and gold and silently absolved herself of at least half her current load of guilt. She'd been taken in by a very good actor, and she, and Verity, had done the best they could with what they'd been given. Maybe she'd go to church on Sunday; as a mostly fallen-away Christian, she felt better about dropping back in to say thank you than to ask favors.

For the moment, though, she was trying to give shape to the day's events—at the sheriff's station, the hospital, even, briefly, at Christian Community—by discussing them with Hank Svoboda, who cheerfully fetched her a fresh drink whenever her throat got dry. She thought she had maybe two or three hours left before alcohol and emotional exhaustion dropped her flat. Then, if somebody would kindly toss a blanket over her, she'd sleep for a week.

"Here you go, lady," said Svoboda, and set a glass of pale amber liquid on the low table beside her. With a bottle of ale for himself, he

settled into the canvas chair on the other side of the table and propped his boot heels on the deck rail.

"Sylvie's still asleep," he told her, "with Ralph right there tucked under her chin and looking real pleased with himself. I listened for a couple minutes, but she didn't do any of that hiccuping little kids do when they're still not finished crying."

"Sylvie knew her mother was dead, from the moment she recognized her stepfather out there on the road this morning," Patience said, keeping her voice low. "So when we told her about Costello's confession, she cried, but she didn't fall apart. Then, when she and Verity and the therapist at the hospital talked about it, Sylvie said it was okay because Lily was in heaven and didn't have to be sad any more. And Dev the devil was going to hell."

"Among life's simple but satisfying concepts, hell's got a lot going for it," said Svoboda. "But what beats me," he added, "is that Costello left a trail a mile wide and didn't even try to cover his tracks. How did he figure he was going to get away with all this?"

"He didn't. Not after assuming a disguise that couldn't possibly serve for long, and then hiring help to locate his victim."

Patience looked out at the darkening sky and thought that even after a lifetime as a cop, Hank Svoboda was too straight and honest a man to understand obsession and vengeful guilt. Maybe you had to be a woman, watchful from necessity. Or an evangelical Christian, taught early of the existence of evil.

"He had nothing reasonable to gain from killing Sylvie," she went on. "She didn't see him kill Lily, and the suspicions of an abrasive, rebellious seven-year-old wouldn't make much of a case. Verity thinks he held Sylvie responsible for Lily's leaving him, and for Lily's death."

"Well, Verity's the one who saw the son of a bitch in action," he said with a nod. "Which turned out to be damned lucky for Sylvie."

"Lily Costello had no luck ever," said Patience. "As a child, she was sexually abused by various men; and later her one good relationship, with her foster father, was destroyed by lies told by her jealous foster sister." Patience was silenced for a moment by a memory of the chilly room at Community and the sweating, ashen face of Sister Marsha Simms. A better person than herself would have pitied the woman.

"Her kid doesn't give off the signals of one who's been sexually abused," said Svoboda, who had seen many of the other kind.

"Lily herself was the classic case, growing up from a background of abuse to choose men who'd mistreat her. And the therapist says Costello probably would have been after Sylvie before long, particularly since she was growing fast and looked so much like her mother," Patience added with a grimace. "But somehow Lily broke the pattern and refused to let her daughter get caught in that same loop. Poor, brave, miserable woman." Patience lifted her glass in a kind of salute before taking a sip.

"What miserable woman are we talking about?" asked Verity, coming out from the kitchen. "If you mean either of those two bitches at Community, I hope both of them... Well, never mind. Here's crostini to hold you guys until the main event, which should be soon." She set down a plate bearing lengths of split toasted baguette topped with shreds of mozzarella, diced fresh tomato, and from the aroma, olive oil and fresh garlic.

The two of them watched her depart, and Hank raised his beer bottle in a salute of his own while lifting a section of baguette with his free hand. "Thank God Mike taught her to shoot. And somebody taught her to cook."

"Amen," said Patience, and she cocked her ears toward the kitchen, where pans clanged and voices murmured. She knew that Verity was feeling very fragile, not only because she'd shot a man but because she'd come to a painful empathy with Lily Costello.

"So what contribution did the two bitches, whoever they are, make to this mess?" Hank asked.

"Sisters Marsha and Catherine. Child abuse and abetting a criminal," she told him crisply. "In addition, their leader, a supposed Baptist minister with a shady past, is making an attempt to claim control of Sylvie and her inheritance. I mean to see him fail. Sylvie can't go back there."

"Um. Okay, I take your point." He handed her a piece of crostini and helped himself to another. "So then there's her actual daddy. Guy you told me about, teaches biology over in Susanville? You thought he was a—"

"Jerk. He hadn't seen her for five years, and didn't care to. He actually said he probably wouldn't recognize her. And suggested she should stay with the religious group where her mother had put her."

"Oops."

"Verity told me they did run into him at the hospital this afternoon, when he came to identify Costello. He went on his way after a brief exchange. Later, Sylvie told Verity that she wasn't going to be Sylvie Simonov anymore, she was Sylvie Medina. Lily's maiden name."

"Medina has a nice sound. So I guess you don't see this actual daddy as all set to make a good home for his daughter?"

"No, I don't."

"Where *do* you figure the poor little kid will wind up laying her head down?"

"I don't know. What I do know is, it's not your problem."

"That is one of my least favorite expressions in this world," he said. "Mostly because it's hardly ever true. How 'bout I get you another little nip of that weird stuff you drink, to sweeten your temper?"

In the kitchen, Johnny Hebert added a dollop of Dijon mustard and a slosh of balsamic vinegar to the salad dressing, then capped the jar and shook it vigorously. Freshly washed lettuce leaves filled a wooden bowl at the end of the counter.

"Smells great," he remarked to Verity, who stood at the stove moving a long-handled wooden spoon slowly through the contents of a big pot. "Want a little more wine?"

Verity shook her head. She'd been holding weirdness at bay by chopping, slicing, measuring, stirring. But the risotto was nearly done, and soon people would sit down at the table to eat and say nice things about the food while regarding her with loving concern.

"Maybe just half a glass," she said, and watched him pour. "Johnny, did you ever shoot anybody? Kill anybody? I'm sorry, you don't need to answer that," she added quickly.

"The answer is yes, just once." He wiped his hands on his apron, brushed damp black curls off his forehead, and picked up his own wineglass. "I answered a call and walked in on a guy, long known as

an abuser, who'd just blown his wife and two little kids away with a shotgun. He pointed the gun at me, and I shot him, and I can tell you it wasn't his body I saw in dreams later."

"I'm sorry. Thank you."

"You're welcome."

"I didn't have a choice, either," Verity told him. "Dev Costello spotted me and Harley's truck early on. He followed me to the Lost Coast, and then beat a poor old woman nearly to death to get directions to Community. When Catherine Ives drove the truck into Garberville, he followed *her* and picked her up and bought her a few drinks." Verity put a lid on the pot and turned off the heat under it.

"So Catherine cheerfully told him all about me *including* the fact that I was leaving the next day, and promised she'd try to see that I took Sylvie with me. Patience cornered her today and got her to admit that," she added grimly. "She insisted she didn't see him take the shells for my shotgun, but I don't believe her."

"This outfit calls itself a Christian community?"

Verity opened cupboard doors and reached for a stack of shallow bowls. "Some of them are good people." She turned and caught The Look again: worried questioning of her mental balance. "Stop that! They are."

"If you say so. Was she bribed, do you suppose?"

Verity sighed. "I'd guess only by a couple of beers and some male company. She says she wanted to get Sylvie back to her mother, and relieve her friend Marsha of a troublesome burden. I think she just couldn't resist the chance to make mischief."

Before Johnny could reply, the telephone at his elbow rang. He picked it up, said hello, and after a moment raised his eyebrows at Verity and put a hand over the mouthpiece. "Ted Blake. Wants to speak to his wife."

"Hang up!" she said, and then, "No, wait," and reached for the phone. "Ted… None of your business who he is!" she snapped. "No, I'm not hurt and yes, the man I shot has died. And no, I'm not charged with anything and Amos is fairly sure I won't be, but if it should happen he'll represent me." She paused to listen.

"No, you may not come here! You and I only diminish each other,

and I'm not going to play a part in that any longer. If you bother me again I will apply for a restraining order. Go make your own life, and leave me to mine." She turned the instrument off and handed it back to Johnny.

He laid it on the table and reached for her. "Verity?"

She pushed his arms away and shook her head. "Don't. Men and women just do such… I think men and women should probably get together only for breeding, like bears and elephants. And leave each other alone the rest of the time."

"Hey, what about wolves? And penguins?"

Verity groaned. "Oh, God, I don't… Penguins?"

"I understand the males are very good mates, even do hatching duty, and—"

"Never mind, I don't want to hear about it." With a giggle that had the edge of a sob, Verity raised her hands palms-out before her face in a warding-off gesture.

Waking to the sound of someone talking, but not the little girls, she'd kept very still and kept her eyes shut, waiting to know where she was and why. The warm ball of wiry fur suddenly moved away from her side, there was a thump and the *click-click* of toenails, and Sylvie remembered, and squeezed her eyes even tighter. When she was sure she wasn't going to cry, she sat up, slid off the bed, and went to open the bedroom door for Ralph.

In stocking feet she padded after the dog and toward the voices, one of them Verity's, down the short hall and across the living room to the open door of the kitchen.

She stepped into the doorway of the warm, bright room, blinked and caught her breath as she saw Verity there, hands raised to keep away the huge, black-bearded man who leaned toward her, reaching for her, backing her up against the counter.

"Oh, *do*-on't!" Sylvie wailed, and suddenly her knees wouldn't hold her and she hit the floor hard with her bottom.

"Sylvie!" Verity came in a rush, hand outstretched. The man came, too, and grabbed Sylvie's other hand before she could snatch it away, and they lifted her to her feet.

Sylvie kept a tight hold on Verity's hand, thin and strong; his was huge, like him, and she let it go quickly. "I thought...you were a pirate," she said.

"No ma'am, just kitchen help." He patted the front of the big white apron that was wrapped around his body, and smiled at her. "I'm Verity's friend, Johnny, and I'm happy to meet you, Sylvie."

This room, Sylvie found, was not full of that buzz she'd felt so many times but you couldn't really hear, that made your breath hurt and your skin prickle. Verity didn't look scared, and Johnny didn't have the stiff, clenched look that said meanness was coming.

She let go of Verity's hand and took a deep breath. Something smelled good, reminding her that she was really *really* hungry. "Okay. Can I help, too?"

They ate at the picnic table on the deck, because the early-evening air was mild and the kitchen hot. They had finished the meal and were variously sipping coffee, wine, and milk when a white truck drove into the yard. "Oh, I bet Harley's come to dismantle our booby trap," said Patience, getting up to collect plates.

"Sit down, let the servants do it," Svoboda told her. "What booby trap?"

She was telling him about their light and camera setup when there was a shout from the end of the driveway, and Harley came trotting back toward the house, camera in hand. "Hey! We got one!" he yelled.

"But it's really weird," he added as he ran up the deck stairs, several at a time. "Look at this."

Patience took the Polaroid print reluctantly, expecting to see Dev Costello/David Simonov. Instead she found herself looking at a small woman whose wrinkled face, fright-widened eyes, and gaping mouth were made foolish by a pair of stiff, ribboned pigtails.

"For heaven's sake. It's Germaine Jorgensen. I'll bet it wasn't us she was after, it was Ralph! And I'll bet, after the fright she obviously got, she won't bother us again."

Adults looked at each other in perplexity, while Sylvie, who'd been

smothering yawns, bounced from her seat at the table and hurried to the corner of the deck where the small dog was having his own dinner.

"My guess is she wanted her Toto back, for the Bed-and-Breakfast Faire," said Patience. "And I'd heard she was trying to quit smoking. Remember the peppermint, Verity?"

Peppermints and dognappers. As contrasting realities made her head spin, Verity felt that she might benefit from another glass of wine. "Maybe you could loan him."

"No!" said Sylvie.

"Don't be silly," said Patience. "She mistreated him, and he hates her. Given the chance, he'd try to chew her feet off at the ankles right in front of her guests."

"More coffee, anyone?" asked Johnny.

"Harley, would you like some supper?" asked Patience.

"Oh, no thanks. I have to go, I've got a date. Uh, Verity, could I ask you something?"

Oh Lord, I don't think so. But Harley looked troubled, so Verity got to her feet and followed him down the stairs and into the yard. "Harley, I'm really sorry about the damage to your truck, and I'll get it fixed tomorrow."

"No, that's okay. I know this guy works in a body shop, he says it's no problem. But I wanted to ask you, I don't know how you'll feel about it, but..."

"Harley, you're scaring me," she told him in a shaky voice.

"No, really it's just kind of dumb, but I found this next to the road and brought it back and cleaned it up but I don't know whether you'll want it, after everything."

Verity stared at the object on his outstretched palm: a bright and shiny-clean dart, its silvery flight glimmering in the lights from the deck. Probably it had saved her life, and Sylvie's. It was pretty, and useful, and bore no guilt.

"Harley, you're a love." She lifted it gently from his palm and then wrapped both arms around him for a hug that he returned heartily— just what she needed, a big, loving, brotherly hug. But wait a minute. Brotherly?

Verity stepped back and looked him over. Good old Harley. "Did you have a nice time with the Alfa?"

"Oh, yeah. Really great." His grin practically split his face.

"And you've got a date again tonight. Harley? Harley! You got laid!"

He turned bright scarlet. "Well, yeah, I... This woman, I knew her in high school, she was two years ahead of me and I was this short guy then, but I met her again at the university, and... But listen, we were really, really careful."

Verity gave a great whoop of laughter and turned as if to shout to the house. Harley grabbed her and put a hand over her mouth. "No! Verity, don't!"

"Okay. I won't." She hugged him again. "It'll be our secret."

Jerry Bauer

About the Author

Janet LaPierre came to northern California from the Midwest via
Arizona, and knew that she was home. After raising two daughters in
Berkeley, LaPierre and her husband began to explore the quiet places
north of the Bay Area: the Mendocino area, the Lost Coast, Trinity
County. Often working on a laptop computer in a twenty-five-foot
travel trailer in the company of a yellow Labrador named Emmitt
Smith, LaPierre has tried to give her award-nominated mystery
novels a strong sense of these far-from-the-city places. Her web site
can be seen at www.janetlapierre.com. She can be reached by e-mail
at janet@janetlapierre.com.

MORE MYSTERIES FROM PERSEVERANCE PRESS

Available now—

The Tumbleweed Murders, A Claire Sharples Botanical Mystery
by Rebecca Rothenberg, completed by Taffy Cannon
Microbiologist Sharples explores the musical, geological, and agricultural history of California's Central Valley, as she links a mysterious disappearance a generation earlier to a newly discovered skeleton and a recent death.

Blind Side, A Connor Westphal Mystery
by Penny Warner
The deaf journalist's new Gold Country case involves the celebrated Calaveras County Jumping Frog Jubilee. Connor and a blind friend must make their disabilities work for them to figure out why frogs—and people—are dying.

The Kidnapping of Rosie Dawn, A Joe Barley Mystery
by Eric Wright
Edgar and Ellis Award nominee, Best Paperback Original
A Toronto academic sleuth goes on an odd odyssey, to rescue student/exotic dancer Rosie Dawn, and find out who wants her out of the way. One part caper, one part satire, and one part love story compose this new series entry.

Guns and Roses, An Irish Eyes Travel Mystery
by Taffy Cannon
Agatha Award nominee, Best Novel
Ex-cop Roxanne Prescott turns to a more genteel occupation, leading a History and Gardens of Virginia tour. But by the time the group reaches Colonial Williamsburg, odd misadventures and annoying pranks have escalated into murder.

Royal Flush, A Jake Samson & Rosie Vicente Mystery
by Shelley Singer
Jake and Rosie infiltrate a dangerous far-right group, to save a good kid who's in over his head. The laid-back California private eyes will need a scorecard to tell the ringers in the gang from the real racist megalomaniacs.

Baby Mine, A Port Silva Mystery
by Janet LaPierre

The web of small-town relationships in the coastal California village is fraying, stressed by current economic and political forces. Police chief Vince Gutierrez and his schoolteacher wife, Meg Halloran, must help their town recover.

Forthcoming in 2002—

Open Season on Lawyers by Taffy Cannon

Somebody is killing the sleazy lawyers of Los Angeles. LAPD Robbery-Homicide Detective Joanna Davis matches wits with a killer who tailors each murder to a specific legal abuse.

Another Fine Mess by Lora Roberts

Bridget Montrose wrote a surprise bestseller, but now her publisher wants another one. A writers' retreat seems the perfect opportunity to work in the rarefied company of other authors…except one of them has a different ending in mind.

Critical Acclaim for
Janet LaPierre's *Baby Mine*

"The network of relationships...is the best thing in the book. LaPierre has a great touch for how people get along, and while the mystery is competently handled, it is the strength of the characters that gives this book its richness."

—Contra Costa Times

"LaPierre is so adept at creating a coastal atmosphere I could almost hear the surf and feel the sea air...also almost hear the neighbors whispering and speculating.... This mystery has it all: believable, likable characters, suspense, atmosphere, and good dialogue. For readers who want to leave the big city behind for a quieter, simpler locale, this is the series."

—Mystery News

"*Baby Mine* is an action-packed adventure from beginning to end. Without losing any of the pacing Janet LaPierre manages to paint some lovely word pictures of Port Silva and include some family conflict with the police reports.... HIGHLY RECOMMENDED."

—I Love a Mystery

"What good news! This wonderfully atmospheric series is back.... Trust us, each book can stand alone. All are rich in character as well as plot and atmosphere."

—The Purloined Letter

"LaPierre's densely packed, fully imagined mysteries transport readers to a small, close-knit California community whose idyllic surface often hides criminous secrets. In [*Baby Mine*] that peaceful facade is not just disturbed, it is shattered.... A lesser writer might lose control of a plot this busy, but LaPierre handles the reins quite nicely, and the tangles of the plot never turn into snarls or knots."

—BookBrowser.com